GHOST ORCHID

A story of lost connections
between mothers and daughters

B. W. Wrighthard

Hope you enjoy our book
Maryanne & Robin

Published by eBookIt.com.

ISBN-13: 978-1-4566-1622-9

Praise for *Ghost Orchid*

"Excellent storyline! I couldn't stop reading! Definitely ready for the sequel."

Regan Bough

"Reading your book now. It is wonderful. Cannot stop till I am done. Congratulations to you both."

Kathie C.

"I totally enjoyed reading this novel by two very talented women. I am looking forward to reading more of their novels and a sequel."

Sue Nesci

Maryanne:
For my children and their families—
Jeremy and Christine, Benjamin, and Kimberlyn,
who make it all worthwhile

Robin:
For Bob, Derek, and Alisha—
my life

Ghost Orchid

Those few weeks of summer
after the sphinx moth strokes you with its tongue,
your slender white petals float from thin stems,
drifting in air, no leaves for a partner,
while your dark roots, barely visible, cling
to cypress, pop ash, or pond apple trees,
never touching ground, never appearing
connected to the earth.

Robin Wright

Roots

The child emerges from a hidden origin unaware that her unseen roots have formed a tangled mass of invisible scars for everyone involved in the twisted journey—even while branching out to create new scars. Mysterious roots concealed until the inevitable day they appear to reclaim their rightful place in the restoration of the soul.

Maryanne Burkhard

Chapter 1

Spring 2005

Sara heard the screeching misery of seagulls as she stepped down from the cable car at the turnaround near Fisherman's Wharf. She watched their shadowy shapes disappear into the distance like a flock of ghostly creatures and felt an instant pang. Seagulls flew in flocks, like family, like she didn't have. All she'd ever had were foster families, and they equaled a strange bedroom in a strange home with strangers. How many times had life ground her down and flung her back into another home? Still, how could she have let her life spiral so badly out of control that the same fate was a real possibility for her own daughter? She pulled a pack of Marlboros from her pocket, cupping one hand around her cigarette to block the wind while lighting up with the other. A fellow passenger accidentally brushed her shoulder, but when he apologized saw her cigarette and frowned, waving away the smoke and huffing off as if she were a pariah. She knew she should quit, but she could deal with ridding herself of only one bad habit at a time. She shoved the pack and lighter back into her pocket and blew smoke rings that vanished. If only her addictions could disappear as easily. As easily as her daughter had been taken from her. She took a last drag, flung the cigarette to the ground, and mashed it to shreds. The cycle ends here. It ends now. It just has to.

* * *

Sara looked around the wharf. She could lose herself here among the tourists, think about her life, clear her head, plan her future. So many unresolved things needed attention. The choice to come here seemed easy compared to the one she'd faced that day she took a Muni to Golden Gate Bridge, intending to jump into the deep water below. That's where her daily dance with alcohol had led her. But just as the Muni screeched to a halt at the bus stop, images of her daughter Jamie had flashed in front of her. She shuddered as she recalled standing frozen while the remaining passengers emptied the van, and it sputtered away. Her whole body had trembled as she walked all the way to the Haight Ashbury free clinic. What she had begun at the clinic that day continued now as her day-to-day goal, sobriety. She could only dare to hope that success would bring a brighter future.

A group of passengers who had gotten off the cable car when she did headed toward Pier 39. Pier 39. A good place to go. Sara followed, glancing at flower vendors along the way. Just the act of making a determined decision about where to go had made her feel better. No more aimless wandering. Focus. She had to focus in order to get Jamie back. As she thought about how vital staying sober was to reach that goal, she shivered like the tourist in plaid shorts walking ahead of her. He had no doubt misjudged San Francisco weather and would surely make a shopping trip part of his vacation. Sara shook her head. If only her mistakes could be fixed so easily.

Like a pair of hands grabbing her, a voice called out, "How about a portrait?"

Sara turned toward the voice.

An artist with a goatee grinned. "Those strawberry blonde curls and green eyes would make a real neat contrast. All you need to add is a smile."

Smiles seemed like foreign objects these days but something in the artist's voice made her force a smile back.

"That's better!" The artist lifted his hand to the easel as if to begin sketching.

At the idea of having a portrait of herself, Sara's smile fell, and she looked at the ground as if she could find it, pick it up, and paste it back on her face. "Nobody would want a portrait of me."

"That can't be true. Not a beautiful lady like you." He motioned to a stool.

She slumped onto it. "You're right. That's not exactly true."

He slapped his knee. "I just knew there was a man who'd love to hang your picture on his wall."

"No man, but I have a daughter. Except she's in foster care." Sara couldn't believe she'd told him that. The artist nodded, set the pencil in his lap, and looked at her with such a penetrating gaze that she thought he was willing her to continue. "I had a problem, you know, went on a bender. When I got home three days later, my neighbor, my babysitter, had called the authorities—given my daughter to them." She felt as if she'd just vomited. The purging both cleansed and weakened her.

The artist raised Sara's chin with two fingers. "But you got that under control?"

How could she answer that question when each day was a new struggle to remain sober? She couldn't flip to the last page to see how the story ended. "I hope so."

"So hold up your head. Be proud and pride will find you."

She was afraid she'd choke if she said anything else. Pride. It would only find her through getting Jamie back. She rose and mumbled, "Sorry about the picture. Maybe another time."

"No problem. I'm here most days."

She started to walk away then turned around. "You know, I haven't even told my group about my daughter." It was true. But why him? Why now?

He leaned back so far only two chair legs touched the ground. "Sometimes it's easier to share with those you don't know than with those you do." He tipped his head and smiled then turned his attention to the next passerby.

Sara walked away and continued toward the pier as wind snapped the cruise line's blue and gold flags, and the bay's fishy odor whipped through the air in droplets. After spending thirty days in rehab and the last two months trying to get back on her feet with group sessions and AA meetings, Sara hadn't opened up as much as she had just now. The unburdening was a relief, and she believed more than ever that she would stay sober, and she would get Jamie back.

In rehab, a counselor had encouraged her to try all kinds of hobbies to aid recovery, and she learned she was good at painting watercolors. She'd always sketched, but no one had encouraged her, so she hadn't done much more than charcoals. She could blame any one of the so-called parents she'd lived with over the years for not nurturing her talent. Maybe if someone had, she would have picked up a paint brush instead of a bottle each time life ground her down. But the blame game never helped. She had to remember that.

After life with Leah and Jon, she lived in so many foster homes she lost count. Some good. Some not so good. But what she'd taken away from those years was that she had to count on herself. No matter what any of her so-called parents had said, no matter how kind some had been, no matter what they'd offered to do for her, in the end, it was Sara alone. Just Sara. Then it was Sara and Ramón. Then Sara, Ramón, and Jamie. Then Sara and Jamie. And finally, just Sara again. In group, they'd tried to pry the painful facts out of her, but she'd been a rock. She left without ever divulging her life's sordid truths, and so far, she'd resisted the AA confessional, too. Let them speculate. She'd done enough of that her whole goddamn life. But veering away from those thoughts was what she needed. She had her goals.

She looked at the booths that were increasing in number as she neared the pier. Stopping every now and then, Sara recalled her counselor's words, 'Face the past to fix the future,' or something like that. Even though she'd zoned out a lot during rehab, some thoughts stuck. At the pier's entrance, a booth showcasing handcrafted turquoise and silver jewelry caught her eye. She crossed the street. The jewelry reminded her of Jon and Leah. Before today, she hadn't thought of them in ages. Why should she? As far as she knew, they hadn't thought of her. But why would they? She was never really their responsibility. She walked over to the booth, remembering the jewelry they'd made when the three of them lived together. As a young child, she had been fascinated watching them and was thrilled when they let her hold the stones in her small hands, calling her their little helper.

Sara squinted against the sun. Was the sun playing tricks on her eyes, or were the memories playing tricks on her mind? She couldn't believe what she saw. She rubbed her eyes and looked again. Things like this just didn't happen. Or did they? The man with the thinning, gray ponytail looked like an older version of Jon. What she could recall anyway. She began to walk past the booth, believing such coincidences weren't possible, but when the man looked up, she was pretty sure it was Jon. He was crafting a bracelet. She stopped at the booth where he bent over the table, twisting a gem tool into the bracelet. The woman beside him looked at Sara, smiled, and said, "Hi. See something you like?" The man was now so absorbed in his work that he didn't glance up.

Sara opened her mouth but air was all that escaped. Finally, one word popped out. "Jon?"

The man raised his head, looked Sara over, and frowned. "Do I know you?"

"You're Jon, right?" Now she was sure. She'd remember that gruff voice anywhere.

He nodded, put down his tools, and searched Sara's face for recognition.

"Leah. You used to be with Leah."

He stood and leaned on the table. "Yes. Yes. Leah. But who are you?"

In his weathered face, she saw the same bright hazel eyes, but he didn't know her as Sara. And she wasn't prepared to speak the name her mother had given her. "I'm your, uh, little helper." When Jon squinted, cocked his head, and scratched it, Sara finally squeezed out the name she hadn't heard in years. "Orchid."

"Oh my God, Orchid! Little Orchid." Jon rushed around the table and embraced her in a bear hug then pulled back. "Not so little anymore." He measured with his hand. The top of her head reached nearly to his chin. He stared at her without blinking. "All grown up. Little Orchid has blossomed into a full-grown, lovely flower." He finally blinked but didn't take his eyes off her.

Sara felt tears form and struggled to keep them in check, but a few trickled down her cheeks. "You remember me."

"Of course I do, Orchid." Jon's lips curled into a tentative smile.

Sara could tell he didn't know what to say or how to act any more than she did. All she knew was that anger seemed to be gurgling up, swallowing her initial excitement. Why was that? Yes, Jon had disappeared from her life but so had everyone else. She willed her anger into a knot and begged it to stay lodged in her gut. "I'm Sara now, Jon." It took lots of strength not to add, but maybe I wouldn't have been if you'd stayed.

"Sara?"

"Sara Jenkins," she declared, emphasizing her last name.

"Well, Sara Jenkins it is then." He turned to the woman at the booth. "This is Melanie."

Sara nodded.

Jon kept staring, and she knew he was still uncomfortable. Finally, he spoke. "You had lunch?" Sara shook her head, but words eluded her. He turned to Melanie. "Can you cover things here for a while?"

"Sure." She reached into a canvas bag and pulled out a sprout-filled pita sandwich. "Brought my lunch, so you two go ahead and catch up."

The two walked side by side for several booths until Jon broke the silence. "Let's head down the pier to Sea Lion Bar & Grill. They've got the best view." He grinned but quickly looked away. She knew he was trying to set them both at ease, but it would take a lot more than small talk for that. They walked in silence as they passed the Italian handcrafted carousel. Music floated like a wispy cloud as children circled round and round, rising and dipping on their horses, chariots, tubs, and swings. She sighed when a smiling, dark-haired girl circled around in a rocking chariot. How she'd love to see Jamie smile like that. She looked away, stiffened, and walked on. She didn't want to see any more happy children.

* * *

On the way to their table, a busboy turned and ran right into Sara. The sound of breaking glass echoed through the room, and customers stopped eating long enough to stare. Sara looked at the floor until the tinkling sound of utensils against plates started again. The busboy ran to get a broom. A manager appeared, apologized, and led Sara and Jon to a table with the best view, offering them each a complimentary drink ticket. As they were seated against the panoramic wall of windows, Sara glanced out and saw Alcatraz in the distance then heard barking and saw a horde of sea lions on the rocks below the restaurant.

Jon pulled out her chair. "What'd I tell you about the view? Awesome, isn't it?"

"Yeah." Sara pulled her chair up to the table. Awesome was the right word but not the one she wanted to hear from Jon. Even 'I'm sorry' wouldn't make her feel better now.

A server approached the table. "Hi, I'm Lois and I'll be your server today. Will this be on one ticket?"

Jon nodded and tapped the table in front of him.

She handed them menus. "What can I get you to drink?"

Jon looked at Sara. "Need a minute?"

She shook her head. "Coke."

"That stuff'll kill you." He turned to Lois. "Corona for me."

Sara opened the menu. The words all ran together. All she could think about was the Corona Jon ordered. All she could see were pictures of cocktails. Focus. If she was going to get through this, she needed to remember what she'd learned in rehab. Count backwards. Start at one-hundred. Keep going. Don't stop . . .

Lois arrived with their drinks, ready to take their order.

Jon waited for Sara. She stopped counting at seventy-six and glanced at him. "Go ahead."

"I'll have fish and chips." He handed Lois his menu.

Sara closed hers. "Guess I'll have the same."

When Lois left, Jon picked up his Corona and Sara sipped her Coke. Why had she said yes to lunch? Seventy-five, seventy-four . . . What could they say to each other? Truth was she didn't know if she could ever say what she wanted to.

Jon set down his bottle. "So, tell me what's been going on."

Did he really want to know? Wouldn't she just love to see his expression when she filled him in on her lovely life? Lovely flower? Hah! What a joke. Silence hung over them like a wet sheet until she gathered her courage. "Where do I begin? I mean, it's been so many years."

"So, what are you now, twenty, aah . . ."

"Thirty-three." She couldn't believe it. He didn't even know how old she was.

He slapped the table. "Wow! Has it been that long?"

"Yes, it has."

"Boy, we really do need to catch up."

Sara shrugged. "Guess I could start when you left." She reached in her pocket and squeezed her lighter. "I didn't get to stay with Leah for long after you left. I got shuffled from one foster home to another. No one ever told me what happened back then." She folded her arms and slumped back.

"But why?" Jon looked puzzled as he leaned across the table. "Why couldn't you stay with Leah?"

"Not sure, but I started kindergarten not long after I went to live someplace else, so maybe it had to do with school and records." She picked up a napkin, flipped it over, and smoothed it out. "Just a guess. I was too young to figure it out back then."

Jon stared into space. "I didn't know."

She believed he was trying to find the words to say he was sorry, but what would that change?

He grabbed his beer. "Everything went to shit back then."

"Yeah, for me anyway."

Jon guzzled the rest of his Corona and signaled for another. She took a deep breath. "I ended up with no mom and no last name. I don't even know my real birthday." She stared at him.

Lois set their food on the table along with Jon's Corona, a bottle of ketchup, and a shaker of vinegar. "Can I get you anything else?"

Jon and Sara shook their heads.

"Enjoy your meal then." Lois scooted off.

Jon grabbed a hot fry and dropped it. He shook his hand then blew on it.

Sara sprinkled vinegar on her fish. "Well, can you fill in any blanks?" She speared a piece of fish and ate it. She'd waited a long time for answers and was sure he could provide some. He wasn't going to run off this time.

Jon looked at Sara and shrugged. "I don't know where to begin." He doused his fish with vinegar and the acrid odor made his eyes water. "You know the old saying, 'If you remember the sixties, you weren't there'?"

"I wasn't born in the sixties."

"No, but the sixties was a mindset." He wolfed down a piece of fish. "It ran well into the seventies, so that includes you."

Sara dipped a fry in ketchup. "Are you telling me you don't remember anything?"

"No. Just that details are fuzzy, so I don't know if I'll be much help."

"You can't tell me when the two of you met my mother?" Sara bit down hard on the fry. Un-freaking-believable.

"It's complicated." He shoved a few fries in his mouth.

"I think it's a pretty simple question." She drummed her fingers.

"You see, I sort of met your mom first, but not really."

What the hell was he saying?

"I was living on the streets here and there with other hippies. Then I stumbled into a commune where your mom was, and we kind of hung out."

"Hung out?"

He picked up his beer and glugged it down. "We just spent a few weeks together before I split."

Sara leaned forward. "But you must've met up again later?"

"Yeah, down the road, after I was with Leah. We wound up back at the commune that your mom was living at. I remember you crawling all over the place and getting into everything, but I don't remember your mom saying much about when you were born."

"If I was crawling, I must've been around six months. When would that have been?"

He squinted as if trying to pull out the lost memory. "Sorry. Can't remember."

"So, what, my mother never celebrated my birthday?" She jabbed a piece of fish and stuffed it in her mouth.

"Man, I really wish I could tell you more."

Sara shoved her plate aside. "I found out that a birthday was picked for me. My social worker let that slip, but I don't know the facts." Her voice cracked, but she was not going to cry, not, not, not. This twist in her day was really testing her one-day-at-a-time sobriety. Relief seemed one drink away. Don't do it. Count. One-hundred, ninety-nine, ninety-eight . . .

"I'm sure your mom celebrated your birthday, but Leah and me, we kind of came and went, so we weren't always around. I just can't recall being there for a party." Jon ate his last bite and pushed away his plate. "But Leah was the one who picked your birthday. Later that is. When you were with us. We, uh, just kind of guesstimated, you know?" He swigged his Corona. "Leah said you needed a special day, so we chose the first day of spring because it symbolized new beginnings. We'd settled in at the commune before your mom had to leave. I think maybe it was a couple of months?"

This was too much. "She didn't really know you but left me with you?"

"Remember, your mom and me had a history."

"History? Yeah, it's mine we're trying to figure out."

"I'm doing my best." He flipped his pony tail. "I do remember your mom leaving you with Leah when she went to work." He tipped his bottle toward her. "See, your mom actually worked at a regular job. I think it was some boutique in, uh, North Beach? Or was it the Haight?" He sat back. "Anyway, since you and Leah spent a lot of time together, you got real close."

"And that was good enough?" She thought about Mrs. Baxter and Jamie. How well had she really known Jamie's babysitter?

Sara wanted to run and hide someplace where she could sort through all she'd learned. "Is that all you know?"

He frowned. "You said you didn't know your mom's last name, right?"

She shook her head and held a steady gaze. "All I know is her first name, Fiona."

"I thought Leah knew all that stuff."

Sara didn't blink and could barely speak. "Didn't seem to. At least that's what I recall when the social worker came for me." She crumpled a napkin then looked up at him.

Jon shifted in his seat. "What did happen?"

"Really want to know?"

"Yeah, I do. I thought about you, you know, but when I did, I always saw you back with your mom or with Leah, for sure."

"Well, you were wrong. I pieced my history together from memory and bits of conversation I overheard through the years, and my imagination filled in the blanks." Sara twisted in her seat. "I had to have been about five years old. I remember a grumpy woman sitting at our kitchen table. Mrs. Parker, the social worker. But I didn't know who she was back then. That was in Daly City, where we moved after you left."

At that time Mrs. Parker had seemed like a monster looming over her. Sara either remembered or invented tugging Leah's bright paisley skirt and calling her Mommy. She wondered if even at that young age she knew that having a mommy should prevent anyone from whisking her away. But Leah had told Sara that she couldn't call her Mommy. She wasn't Sara's mother.

"When Mrs. Parker stood over me, I wanted to cover my face with Leah's long hair so no one could see me, take me, or make me leave." Sara knew it was an illusive memory. She couldn't have thought that at five, but Jon could decide for himself if the memory was real. "What I remember, or think I do, is clutching Leah's leg and crying through Leah's 'I'm sorrys' not to let the woman take me. That's when Leah gave me a Babar book that had belonged to my mother." She looked at Jon, but his expression remained unchanged. She told him her mother's first name was scrawled on the book's inside cover. No last name. Part of her history, unknown. All she had to cling to was her name—Orchid Sara—and Leah's final words, or what had evolved in her memory as Leah's final words.

"The last thing Leah said was, 'Remember when I said you could keep this flower from your mommy forever if we dried it and pressed it in the book? Well, keep this flower and you'll keep your mommy in your heart as I'm sure you're in hers.'" Sara leaned back and exhaled as if to expel her very spirit. "And then I was gone."

Jon shook his head. "I'm so sorry." He twisted his bottle. "I didn't know." He let go of the bottle. "Maybe I can help you a little. I do recall that your mom's last name was Irish and began with Don. Wish I could remember better." He smiled faintly. "The Don part stuck because my brother's name is Don."

He chugged his beer, and Sara's heart skipped a beat each time his Adam's apple pulsed. When he plunked the bottle on the table, she felt the air leave her lungs. Orchid Sara Don . . . Not complete, but more than she'd ever had before. But the name felt like an ill-fitting shoe.

He slumped in the seat and seemed to hesitate. "I remember we had a pay phone in the hall of the commune, and I answered it one day."

"So?"

"Someone asked for your mom. We didn't use last names much, but whoever called that day used her full name." Looking straight into Sara's eyes, Jon said, "When you were, maybe two, your mother left you with Leah and me to go back home to help with her dad. He'd gotten real sick."

"And just where would home be?" God, why couldn't he have told Leah all this stuff before he blew out of their lives?

"Not exactly sure. Some city in the Midwest. I recall her mentioning a river, in Indiana maybe? Sorry that I can't be sure."

As Lois breezed by and swept up the dirty plates, Sara told Jon she was going outside for a smoke.

When she returned, Jon said, "You know, the more I think about it, the more I do believe it was Indiana."

Indiana? Not a place she'd ever given a second thought. No matter where she'd lived in California, whenever Sara heard a mother call her child, she had turned toward the stranger's voice, expecting it to be her mother.

Jon looked down. "Her folks didn't know about you. She planned to tell them but didn't want the shock of taking you along and surprising them, what with her dad sick and all."

"What was the big damn deal? Was she ashamed of me?" Sara brushed back a tear. "I mean, why else would a mother leave her child?"

Jon shifted in his chair. "It was the seventies, and I guess back where she came from, there'd've been hell to pay carting home a baby without an old man . . . uh, husband."

"So she was ashamed of me."

"No. I didn't mean that." He paused as if to find the right words. "She just, you know, didn't want to rock the boat. She was afraid of upsetting them and, you know, the neighbors. Back then everyone worried about what their neighbors thought."

Sara's lungs tightened. "So, that's it then?" Her hands felt clammy and she rubbed them on her jeans. "Neighbors? It all boils down to neighbors? For that my mother abandoned me?" She struggled against the irony. She'd lost Jamie because of her neighbor. A neighbor who couldn't wait just one more day, and now her mother's abandonment comes down to neighbors. God, how she hated the word.

"Things are rarely all that simple, Orch, uh Sara."

"Seems simple to me."

Jon took a deep breath. "Right after your mom left you with us she'd call that pay phone and hope we'd be there so she could talk to you."

"Didn't you have her parents' phone number?"

"I'm getting to that."

Just then Lois stopped to ask if they wanted dessert. When they shook their heads, she thanked them and laid the check on the table. Jon slid it to the side. "I asked her a couple of times when she was going to tell her parents about you, but she said her dad was too sick and her mom was freaking out, and there hadn't been a good time to tell them yet."

"Did she ever tell them about me?"

He shrugged.

"So why didn't she come back for me?" Damn, she wanted a drink. Or at least another smoke.

"She might have. I don't know what happened after Leah and me split. See, one weekend we took you and went to visit Leah's folks, and when we got back to the commune, the landlord had evicted everyone—changed the locks. I told the S.O.B. I needed to get our stuff. Hell, I had your mom's folks' number in there too. He threatened to call the cops if we didn't get off his property. Said he'd found our stash and he'd have us arrested. But I think he just wanted to smoke it himself." Jon smirked. "Anyway, Leah and I took you and split for Grass Valley. We didn't know how to get a hold of your mom after that." The look in his eyes pleaded for understanding. "We did tell friends where we were going so she'd be able to find us. I don't know what happened."

Sara had no words. It sounded like maybe her mother had cared but shit just happened. God, how could such a stupid set of circumstances mess up her whole life?

"You okay?" Jon asked.

She could barely nod. It was all too surreal. She'd waited a lifetime to hear this story, and now that she had, it didn't make any sense. Sara had one more question. "You have any idea who my father is?"

Jon shook his head. "Man, what can I say, we all pretty much lived by the mantra, 'make love, not war,' back then." He grabbed a toothpick and stuck it in the corner of his mouth. "All that had to be tough to hear, but I'm sure your mom loves you and had a good reason for not showing up."

At least Sara had come back for Jamie. It was different. Jamie'd been taken from her. And she knew where Jamie was. Sara didn't even remember what her mother looked like. "What reason could ever be good enough to leave your child and not return?" Sara asked.

"Don't know. I just don't know."

Sara pulled out her pack of Marlboros and flipped it over again and again. "Do you have any pictures?" All she had was her memory of being with Jon and

Leah then just Leah. Then Mrs. Parker and all those others.

Jon cleared his throat. "We didn't own a camera, and like I said, we smoked a lot of dope, did heavier stuff quite a bit too, and well. . ." He hunched over the table.

"What?" Sara leaned toward Jon. He obviously had more to say.

"Well, things were, you know, a lot freer back then."

Sara clutched the edge of the table. What bomb was he going to drop now?

"It's just that your mom and me were, well, we had a thing back then." He didn't look at Sara. "Even after Leah and I were together. Leah didn't find out till after we'd moved with you to Grass Valley. She was furious and yelled 'we had a relationship, forget free love.' Then she kicked my ass out." Jon looked into Sara's eyes. "I lost track of you both after that and I'm so sorry."

Sara couldn't believe it. These were the adults in her life? What was wrong with them! No wonder she was so screwed up. They had treated a child worse than a pet. Taken care of her when it was convenient and tossed her away when it wasn't. She felt like the air had been sucked right out of her gut. Jon went to pay the bill, and she went outside to smoke.

He met her there, and they began the walk back to Jon's booth, listening to the sound of shoes scuffing across concrete. By the time the organ music from the carousel reached their ears, Jon had begun to tell Sara about some of the places he'd lived over the years.

Small talk. All they could manage now. Then Jon told her to keep in touch and wrote his phone number on a scrap of paper. Sara looked at it, thinking of the lost note with her mother's name and phone number then stuffed it deep into her pocket.

Chapter 2

Monday, Week Five

Fiona sat in Java Hut ready to get the meeting started. She tapped the decoupauged tabletop. Co-op members shuffled in, signaled by the clinking ceramic beads at the entrance. The only member not expected was Sara. But that was by design.

Fiona pushed a silver strand of hair behind her ear as Vic approached and said, "Hey, Babe. You about ready?"

"Sure am." She hoped the others were as fed up with Sara as she was. Better to have that troublemaker out of their lives.

When the outside door of the coffee shop slammed, she saw Stan tense up as he looked at the stained glass window he'd crafted for the transom. It was a replica of the original house right down to the yellow exterior and green shutters that was now Addicted to the Arts co-op. Fiona knew the transom and side windows were Stan's most valuable contribution, and he was always worried about them. He even had Vic make a sign, Please Don't Slam Door, in colors that matched the stained glass. When Stan had finished the windows for each side of the door, he framed them with bamboo, saying it wouldn't be a true hut without it.

"Wait!" Iris's loud voice caused everyone to look her way. The woman waddled into the room just before Vic locked the door. She made a dramatic gesture of pulling a frilly handkerchief from her pocket and dabbing her forehead. "Sorry," Iris panted between breaths. "Something came up."

Stan whispered to Fiona, "Doesn't it always?" but loudly said, "Oooh, aren't you the lucky lady." He raised his brows then winked as he walked over to her.

Iris blushed. "Oh Stan, you're so naughty." He flung his arm around her and, bumping her ample hips, guided her toward a table.

Monday was the only day Fiona could request this meeting because on Mondays the co-op closed all their businesses at five for cleaning, restocking, and any meetings Vic, the founder, deemed necessary.

The aroma of freshly brewed coffee wafted through the air. Fiona glanced at Stan and Rowdy Writer filling orders behind the ornate bar Vic had salvaged and restored from a demolished tavern. Stan nicknamed all the members based on their particular talent or quirk. Fiona had never heard him call her or Vic by a nickname, but Vic let it slip once that Stan had christened her Fiery Fiona and Vic, Buckin' Bronc. She assumed Vic's nickname was their little joke, but what could she say? Stan cowered to no one. And Vic, well, Vic got a good laugh out of it. Stan called himself Dandy-Stan-Your-Stained-Glass-Man, always making a sweeping gesture when he said the word *your*. Fiona told him he gave everyone nicknames because he couldn't remember their real ones. He always acted hurt, clutching his chest, as if she had stabbed him in the heart.

Fiona saw Rosie, Stan's Nosy Knitter, scanning the group, and when she locked onto Fiona's eyes, she snapped, "Where's Sara, the new girl? I think we need to discuss the scheduling problems, and she's part of that."

Perky Painter bobbed his head, looked at Fiona and said, "Yeah, that's right. We can't start till everyone's here."

Several others chimed in until Vic hushed the rumbling with a two-finger whistle. "Guys . . . and *gals*." Vic winked at Fiona. "We have to discuss something. Unfortunately, it involves Sara, and for now, we need to do it without her." He gestured to Fiona, and she stood.

Fiona adjusted her reading glasses and scanned her notes. "We all know that something's been going on here since," she squinted and looked at her notes again, "well, it's unclear exactly when, but most of you have reported items that have disappeared without receipts showing they were sold . . ."

Whispers floated amid the clanking of spoons until they rose to a loud chatter, and Vic once again whistled the noise to a halt.

"As I was saying," Fiona continued until Cautious Clem, the calligrapher, cut her off.

"Nothing of mine's gone missing." Clem looked at the others. Some nodded in agreement. "And," he added, "does Sara's absence mean she's a suspect? Perhaps the only suspect?"

Fiona wondered if he thought he was Hercule Poirot. Gasps followed as Clem stiffened and fingered the silver crucifix that always dangled from a chain around his neck. Fiona added, "If you let me finish, I'll answer your questions." She glanced at Vic, hoping to get a nod of support, but his face was unreadable. "As I said, we can't account for some items, such as two coffee mugs, a specialty ashtray, one vase, a set of embroidered placemats, and a garden elf." She scanned the members. "Quite a few items, don't you think?" Ooohs and aaahs rolled over the group like waves. That got them. Fiona was pleased. When the murmuring subsided, she asked, "Do you want me to continue reading from the list, or would you each rather cite your own losses?" She thought the impact would be stronger if the members named their own.

Some members nodded and others remained stone-faced, but Clem, once again in detective mode, spoke first. "I still don't see how this involves Sara." Heads stopped bobbing, and all faces swayed toward Fiona. "Are you about to accuse Sara of stealing?" Some members gasped while others sat back on padded chairs and crossed their arms. "If you are, you'd better have some solid evidence."

Before Fiona could respond, Stan joked, "Hey, Cautious Clem, you got the hots for Sara?" He laughed as Clem's face reddened. Stan raised his bushy eyebrows like Groucho Marx and grinned. "I mean, she ain't hard on the eyes, and we all know you two are buddies."

Ignoring Stan's comment, Clem said, "I just think we better be really careful before we accuse anyone of stealing." He looked around then rose and wagged his finger. "I can't believe any one of you is in a position to cast stones." As soon as the words were out, he sat and pulled his chair up to the table. His face reddened even more, and no one spoke until he broke the silence, shrugging as if to make amends for his uncharacteristic outburst. "And, anyway, as you implied, I probably know Sara better than any of you, and I don't see her as a thief." Then he glanced at Vic and said, "All I'm saying is where's the proof?"

Vic pushed against the table and stood, nearly knocking over a stand loaded with magazines. "Why don't we take a break? I know some of you need a smoke." He looked at his watch and suggested they all return in ten minutes.

While they eagerly scattered, Vic walked over to Fiona. Now it was her turn to be irritated. She didn't want to draw this damn thing out. But just as she started to lay into Vic, Clem stopped in front of them, ignoring her and speaking to Vic.

"I'm going to run out to the car and get some flyers. Don't start without me."

Fiona scowled. Who did Clem think he was? As he walked away, she turned her attention to Vic. "Why'd you do that? At this rate, we'll be here all night."

Vic slumped onto the chair next to her and covered her hand, trying to charm her into a good mood. "Babe, I just thought you needed a breather. Things were heating up, and I know you can lose your cool."

"Dammit, Vic!" She pulled her hand away. "You can't fix everything. When are you going to learn that?" Fiona stared at Vic. All these years and he still didn't have a clue about some things.

* * *

The group was reconvening. Fiona stood, wanting to focus on getting rid of Sara, as Clem raced in with a carton, and everyone looked at him. Fiona banged the table to get their attention. "All right. I don't think we need any further discussion." Clem started to speak, but Fiona glared at him. "We didn't have these problems until Sara arrived. What do we really know about her anyway? I'll tell you what, *nothing*. I say we take a vote on removing her from our ranks."

Murmuring filled the room, but one clear voice rang out. It came from the beaded entrance as Sara pushed her way into the room and stopped in front of Fiona.

"What's this all about, Fiona?"

Fiona's face heated up. She had no idea Sara was in the building. How in the hell had she gotten in? Clem! He'd gone out the back door for those damn flyers. Did he let her in? She gave him the fiercest look she could muster then turned to Sara, the little snot, standing there, taking it all in like a nosy eavesdropper.

"Seems you already know."

"What I *know*," Sara leaned her face in close to Fiona's.

Fiona resisted the urge to back up. She wasn't about to give the little witch the upper hand by thinking that she could be intimidated.

"What I *know*," Sara repeated as a splash of saliva hit Fiona's cheek, "is a lot more than *you* know." She stepped back and looked around the room. "And if you don't want everyone here to know what I know, you better end this stupid meeting right now."

Fiona swiped her hand across her cheek to remove the spit just as Sara turned toward her again.

"Because believe me, I won't hold anything back."

Fiona looked at Vic, and he shrugged. One by one, except for Vic, the members shuffled out. Clem was the last one out the door, and as it shut behind him, Sara unleashed her torrent.

As soon as I step out on the porch, the humidity sticks to my skin like flies to fly paper. I close the back door of my cottage before the muggy air slithers in. My window unit barely keeps up with the ever-present heat in this small community on the fringes of the Everglades. Already drenched with sweat, I lean on the rail and sip my coffee. Looking out from my stilted cottage, I'm eye-to-eye with the cypress trees that appear to rise from grassy islands in the swampland that begins just beyond my backyard. Despite the humidity, I love it here. It's peaceful and quiet, and if I mind my own business, I can keep it that way. I only have to ignore the mechanical sounds that often blend with nature in the dark of night. Ignoring things is something I'm good at. With ten-thousand small islands dotting the Gulf of Mexico near the State Preserve, anything can happen and often does. Wiping the sweat off my face, I finish my coffee. It's almost time to leave for work, but before I return to my home's artificial chill, I take a deep breath and inhale the dank, swamp air.

Chapter 3

Friday, Week One

Vic glanced at his watch as he walked to the desk, holding Stan's note. Almost time for the appointment Stan had scheduled. Much as he loved the co-op, interviewing new members was his least favorite job, but Stan had piqued Vic's curiosity when he called last night. That is, after Vic chewed him out for arranging the meeting without his consent. As he read Stan's note, he grinned:

Sara Jenkins, timid but firm,
here from San Francisco,
will sketch, watercolor, and earn
money, for us, I have no doubt.
Needed an interview,
and needed it now.
So . . .
I said you would see her
and see her now!

Stan's looped signature filled the bottom of the note. Vic shook his head. He and Stan had been friends long enough to know how far to push things and how to smooth things over. Stan had known how busy Vic would be today, so he'd repaired the table in Workshop B late last night, giving Vic more time for the interview. This Sara must be hot. Stan always had an eye for good-looking gals. Well, Vic had never known a red-blooded man who didn't, himself included, but he had Fiona to contend with.

What Vic couldn't imagine was why an artist would choose to move to Indiana from San Francisco. Not that anything was wrong with Indiana. It was his home and he loved it. He tossed Stan's note in the drawer, wondering if Sara had ties here. When he turned on the computer, he noticed a post-it in Fiona's handwriting on the keyboard. He pulled it off and read it. 'Hey Charlie, Chastity's lonely.' He grinned.

That Fiona. Ever since they'd met in high school, he hadn't been able to put her completely out of his mind, no matter who he was with. When they finally got back together this last time, she told him it had been the same for her. And now, here they were, working side by side every day and spending as many nights together as they wanted. However, she'd kill him if she knew he was interviewing this artist without her. Their opinions were yin and yang. But he had decided to rely on his own intuition this time. He'd probably regret it.

* * *

Vic went to Java Hut when Stan buzzed to say that Sara Jenkins had arrived. He greeted her and they sat at a table, chatting briefly before getting down to business. Vic scrutinized the watercolors that she pulled from her portfolio. He picked up a picture of seals sunning on the rocks near San Francisco's Cliff House. Purple flowers dotted a cliff on one side of the rocks, which sat amid a blue ocean. Swirls of white froth crashed the gray sand on the other. "I know this location." The colors ranged from vibrant to muted.

He wondered which color in the spectrum she'd begun with. Vic was impressed. As he flipped through her paintings, he noticed gray somewhere in each one. "And this one." He held up a picture of Aquatic Park with a lone flutist on gray bleachers alongside the stark white Maritime Museum, its bright American flag flying high in the far corner. "So, you're from San Francisco."

Squirming in her seat, Sara finally said, "From and lived around the city most of my life." Vic scanned her unpainted sketches. This is where Fiona would be helpful. She'd pry. He couldn't. Not his style. Well, he was sure Fiona would fire off questions later, after chewing him out. He hoped she'd find common ground with Sara because of San Francisco since he was leaning toward giving her a recommendation. She was younger than most of the members, but maybe youth was a spark they needed. Vic knew how hard it was to keep a place like this going. New members were usually enthusiastic at first, but some didn't have enough patience to get their work sold or to find students for workshops. Many would get a job outside the co-op and then say they didn't have time for co-op activities. Maybe a younger person would have the drive to handle both.

"I like your work, but there's a rule for accepting new members." Vic took a pencil from his ear and tapped it on the table at the same time he signaled Stan. He turned to Sara. "Would you like something to drink?"

Sara twirled a lock of hair and viewed the choices on the menu. She pushed the curly strands behind her ear. "Mocha Latte sounds good." She dropped her hands to her lap and looked shyly at Vic. "Is that okay?"

"Sure."

"Because I can just have regular coffee."

"No, it's no problem." Vic hollered their orders to Stan then began to explain how things worked at Addicted to the Arts. "First of all, we don't have employees per se. We have members. The rule regarding acceptance is that a majority of the current members have to approve your work." Glancing at the portfolio she was closing up, he continued, "From what I've seen, that shouldn't be a problem. I love the way your vibrant colors offset the gray."

"Thanks."

The sugary scent of Sara's latte sweetened the air as Stan delivered their coffee. "Drink 'em while they're hot," Stan joked.

"Thanks," the two said in unison.

Vic pushed an application across the table and picked up his mug.

Sara flipped the edge of the app. "But I'm not sure if I can even stay."

"Why?" Vic slid the pencil behind his ear. Why move here if there was a possibility she couldn't stay?

Sara picked up the stirrer and twirled it, mixing the whipped cream. "I don't have much money or any friends or family to stay with." She licked the stirrer clean then huddled over her latte.

"What brought you here, then?" Vic crossed his arms and leaned back. Maybe he *was* capable of a little prying. Fiona would be proud.

Sara looked at Vic and shrugged. "Seemed like a nice enough place, kind of quiet after living in a big city." She looked around the room. "And then I drove by this place, and well, here I am."

"Fair enough." He grinned. A new start. Not such a bad idea. Maybe that was the truth, maybe not, but he was done prying. "As it turns out, we have a vacant apartment upstairs." Vic figured he'd already be in hot water when Fiona found out about the interview, so what was one more thing. He knew she would give him hell if Sara turned up with a whopper of a story, but he was banking on Fiona being won over by her San Francisco pictures. Fiona had once told him he let attractive women talk him into things. She'd been furious, and they hadn't spoken for four days after that argument. Fiona only made up with him after the young woman in question left the co-op in tears. He'd been mad as hell at Fiona then, but she fought back telling Vic that whenever her voice rose an octave, he retreated like a turtle retracting into its shell. The truth was that Vic knew he couldn't stop her rants until she got it all out, so he'd learned if he couldn't shut her *up*, he could shut her *out* till she exhausted herself. Problem was she never let him forget his last retreat and used it against him later. He shrugged off his concerns. "Would you like to see the apartment?"

"That would be great." When Vic stood, she got up.

"We'll leave your stuff in the office." He grabbed her portfolio and led her through the beaded entrance to the main hallway. Before they reached the office, Vic pointed out the craft store, book swap, and workshop rooms in the back.

After dropping her portfolio in the office, they climbed the stairway to the apartment. Sara followed him into the living room.

"Sorry. It looks bare without furniture." He led her into the tiny kitchen and patted a stool at the end of the counter. "No room for a table, but you can eat here. Let me show you the rest of the place." They walked into a small hallway with two doors. He led her into a bedroom that would be swallowed by a queen-sized bed. He opened the closet. "It's not big, but if you don't have a lot of stuff, it should be okay." She smiled and looked around. He could only guess what she was thinking. Anyway, he wasn't trying to sell her on the apartment even though the rent would come in handy. "Let me show you the bathroom." He pushed open the other door, revealing a postage-stamp-sized bathroom. He stepped aside while she opened the doors to the medicine chest and the small linen cabinet over the toilet.

"Sorry, no tub. Only room for a shower stall when we remodeled."

Sara nodded. "That's fine. I prefer showers anyway."

He ushered her to the front door, and they stood on the landing while Vic locked the door. "So, what do you think?"

"Looks good to me." She paused. "Except I don't have any furniture."

"If everything pans out, I can bring over a bed, dresser, and couch if you'd like. I even have an old TV."

"That would be great."

He unlocked the office door and ushered her in. "I'll get you a rental app." He motioned to a chair and turned to the file cabinet, pulled out the form, and handed it to her. "You can bring this back with the co-op app." He sat down. "So, let me tell you how it works. We all have to work at the co-op. There's Handiwork House, Swapper's Fare, and the Java Hut, but you've already seen that. You basically man the shops the same as if you were an employee. The artists give me a list of what they want to sell at Handiwork House, and I input it into the computer. We record what's sold, so after the co-op's percentage, the artist gets paid. The book swap works a little differently since we take in books from anyone, but it's not complicated. Java Hut's a little different. You get a small salary, plus tips." He paused. "We make a good bit of our money there, and it can get busy at times. Especially on open-mic nights."

"I see."

"But Stan has first dibs on the Hut's hours." Vic clasped his hands together. "He helped me open this place. Fact is, we used to work construction and remodeled this old place together."

Sara nodded. "What about the workshops? You said something earlier about classes?"

"Yes. From what I've seen, you can teach watercolor or sketching, but you have to find your own students." He reached into a desk drawer and pulled out a flyer. "Clem does calligraphy and printed his own flyers for distribution. You can do the same. We can stack a handful on the display table in the front entrance."

She looked at the elegant black swirled letters announcing the desire to personalize invitations for weddings and other special events.

"That's just one way. I'm sure other members can give you more ideas."

She started to hand him back the flyer.

"Keep it. Clem won't mind."

She folded the flyer. "How do members decide what to charge? And how much do they keep?"

"Good questions." He looked at his watch. "We have pricing guidelines, and the co-op gets a percentage, but most of it goes back into the members' pockets." He twisted his watch and stood. "Sorry. I've got an appointment, but bring back the apps tomorrow. We can talk more then."

She stood and reached for her portfolio.

"Can you leave that with me?"

"Sure."

He walked around the desk, and she handed him the portfolio. "Oh, and by the way, most of our members work another job because it takes time to get things going here. You can't always count on enough money rolling in to pay the bills." He glanced at the calendar. "We hold meetings on Mondays. Three days from now, and that's when we'll vote."

"About the apartment, too?"

"No. Just get the app back tomorrow, and after I check references, I'll let you know ASAP."

Sara fidgeted. "Is it okay if I pay weekly?" She looked at him. "Just until I get a job and get a little ahead?"

"Weekly?" Boy, Fiona wouldn't like this. "Gee, I don't know." He stroked his chin.

"I saw a Help Wanted sign in a bar window not too far from here. I'm sure I can get a job there. I've tended bar before."

Sara reminded Vic of a helpless child. "I don't know." He could see the weekend with Fiona plummeting into the crapper if he gave in. But Sara seemed desperate. How could he turn down her request? Fiona was right. He was a sucker. "I don't know. I'm just . . ."

"I promise to pay regularly."

Ah hell. Be a man. Make a decision, but stand tough. "Okay, but just till you're settled in and making some money." There. That should satisfy Fiona.

"Thank you so much. You won't regret it." She grasped the flyer and applications.

As they stood at the door, he pointed to the main entrance. "That door'll take you outside." They shook hands and on her way out, Sara dropped a quarter in a donation jar for Jerry's Kids and pulled out a grape lollipop from the bowl next to it.

* * *

When Vic returned from his appointment with the new coffee vendor, he handed Stan their brochures then dialed Fiona as he headed for the office. He was still pondering how much to tell her when she answered, "Hello?" in a raspy question. He knew right away she'd been sleeping.

"Hey, Babe. How are you?"

"I *could* be better."

"How's that?"

"Well," after a hesitation, Fiona continued, "take a deep breath."

"What? What in the world for?" Vic walked into the office and closed the door.

"Vic, just *do* it," her breathy voice pleaded.

He sat down and inhaled so deeply that he leaned back in the chair, raised his head, and puffed out his chest. "Done."

"Did you get a whiff?"

Vic exhaled in a rush. "What are you talking about?" He turned on his computer while waiting for Fiona's explanation.

"Didn't the scent tickle your nose?"

"Fiona, what are you trying to say?"

"White Diamonds. You know, you gave it to me for my birthday. And inside the card, you wrote: 'Babe, this is the only kind of diamond you'll let me give you.'"

"And?"

"*And* I wear it on *special* occasions, which could be now if you'd hop in that Bronco of yours and head over here. Didn't you read my note?"

"Oh yeah, I read it." Vic laughed. "You are too much sometimes." Still chuckling, he dropped the papers on the desk and sat back. "Sure would love to join you, but I've got too much to do." That was what he loved most about Fiona, her ability to surprise even after all these years. She still came up with wacky ideas that startled and delighted him. Maybe it was what sustained their relationship. And no matter how much Vic enjoyed looking at other women, the curve of the breasts, the flare of the ass, he'd never felt as drawn to another woman as he was to Fiona. Certainly, the most unique compliment he'd gotten was from her. He remembered the night well. It was the first time they'd made love after she returned from San Francisco. They both drank a lot of wine at dinner and then opened another bottle when they got back to his house. They undressed each other quickly, kissing and laughing while grabbing buttons and zippers. Fiona pushed Vic onto the bed and danced wildly, watching his penis rise to her gyrations. Afterward, Fiona, a dot of sweat glistening between her breasts, had laughed and said, "Oh, Honey you really know how to blast me with that dynamite of yours." Vic thought of the contrast between Fiona and all the other women he'd slept with, even his ex-wife. They would say he was a good lover or use some lame adjective to stroke his ego. But not Fiona. On any subject, her mouth would fire words like a machine gun, and it was up to him whether to absorb the bullets or run. He'd done both over the years, but in the last few, he couldn't imagine being without her, despite how difficult she was sometimes.

"Well, can't say I didn't try."

"Hey, guess what?" Vic didn't wait for an answer. "I may have rented the apartment today."

"Really?"

"Well, I showed it and gave the woman an application. She's supposed to bring it back tomorrow, and she's applying to be a member, too. She's a good watercolor artist. Oh, and guess where she's from?"

"I give."

"San Francisco. Wait'll you see her work. It'll remind you of your old stomping grounds."

"You think?" Fiona didn't sound enthused. He was afraid of that. He knew it could only get worse and decided now wasn't the time to tell her about the weekly rental payments.

"By the way, Vic, how old is this potential member?" She laughed, but Vic could tell it was forced.

"Oh, I don't know, between twenty-five and your age."

"Probably closer to twenty-five, right?"

"Why? What does it matter? Her work is really good."

"And what does she look like, Vic? Not hard on the eyes, I'll bet."

There was that laugh again. The one she used when she wanted to sound like she was teasing but wasn't. Did she think he couldn't tell the difference? His instincts were right. The hurricane was brewing. "Fiona, go back to sleep. I'll talk to you later when you're awake." Vic hung up before Fiona could say anything else.

Vic had no sooner snapped his phone shut when there was a pounding on the door. He yelled, "C'mon in."

Rosie stormed in, waving a piece of paper and slamming the door behind her. "We need to talk." She set down her knitting bag, skeins of multicolored yarn bulging over the top. Two metal needles poked through the skeins, and a thread of yarn trailed down the side.

"What's up?" Vic took a deep breath and clasped his hands together. Rosie pulled up a chair as close to the desk as possible and shoved the schedule at him, knocking over her bag and spilling yarn. In one fluid motion, she righted the bag and stuffed the yarn inside then said, "Look at it, Vic."

Squinting, he scanned the co-op schedule. "What am I looking for, Rosie?"

She folded her arms and sat back so hard she tipped the chair on two legs. "Isn't it obvious?"

Shaking his head while holding the schedule, Vic said, "Afraid not," then set it down and added, "Why don't you save us both some time and just tell me what the problem is?"

Rosie grabbed the schedule and began pointing. "Look!" She tapped the paper several times. "Here, I was scheduled for a workshop." Vic bent over and squinted at the small printed name she pointed to.

"You're not scheduled for the C Workshop. It looks to me like . . ."

"Oh for God sakes, Vic, get some glasses." She shoved the schedule under his nose. "If you look close enough, you can see that the name has been whited out and changed. My name was there first." Her dark eyes blazed like a firestorm.

"You sure?" Vic began to regret not taking Fiona up on her offer. He'd much rather be in bed caressing her soft breasts than sitting here nursing Rosie's anger.

"Of course, I'm sure. I have a large class that night, and I specifically requested the largest workshop room." She grabbed the table's edge and leaned over the desk. "I can't possibly fit my group into either of the other rooms. Which, by the way, are not available now anyway." She pushed herself up and kicked the chair back. "Vic, I'm getting sick and tired of these cliquey members who stick together and disregard the rest of us. You need to deal with this problem." She leaned over and grabbed her knitting bag then started to leave but turned around before she reached the door. "That is, if you don't want a revolt on your hands. I know I'm not the only one who's been upset with things lately, so you'd better deal with it soon." She jerked open the door and slammed it shut behind her.

Vic walked to the small fridge, grabbed a bottle of water, and set it beside his cell phone. He looked at both. He started to twist the bottle's cap but stopped and picked up his phone instead.

"Hello?" Fiona answered too quickly to have gone back to sleep, and Vic hoped she hadn't been lying there mulling over the whole Sara Jenkins thing.

"Does your earlier offer still stand?"

"Honey, my bed is warm and waiting for you," she said, in that breathless seductive voice that aroused Vic, and he knew he'd made the right choice. He tossed the papers into the drawer and locked it.

"I'll be right there, keep those puppies warm," he said, feeling the swelling as he stood and walked toward the door.

* * *

Sara parked around the corner from Jerry's Place. It wasn't even noon yet, so she didn't know if the bar would be open. As she got to the door, a balding, middle-aged man was unlocking it.

"I'm just opening up."

Sara pointed to the sign in the window. "I saw your sign, and I've bartended before."

He motioned her in behind him. "Well, c'mon in. Might as well do it now."

There were a few tables in an alcove near the front door with a jukebox between the bar and closest table. Two-top tables lined the bar's opposite wall, and in the back were several booths.

"I'm Jerry." He pulled out a chair at a two-top and extended his hand. "This is my place." He laughed. Sara grinned as she shook his hand. He pointed to a door between two back booths. "We've got a couple of pool tables in there."

"That's great. Do you have a league?"

"We've got one starting up." He leaned back. "So, tell me about your experience."

Sara detailed her relevant work history, leaving out the bad parts. When she walked out twenty minutes later, she had a job. That is, if everything checked out okay. It's not a job she should have, not one that a recovering alcoholic dreams about, but with any luck, not one she'd need for very long.

* * *

Sara pulled into the parking lot of the motel. During the day you could read the sign, but at night when lights illuminated the place, the Sunny Days Motel sign became Su n D s Mot l. The two guys who'd stared at her earlier were hovering in the parking lot, smoking cigarettes and talking in hushed tones. She didn't like the way they looked at her and parked as close as possible to her room. As she turned the key in the lock, her hand brushed a scrap of peeling paint, and it tore loose, fluttering to the ground. She hurried inside and double-locked the door. Why did she always think the worst of people? She vowed to start thinking positive thoughts and willed away her concerns.

The applications would be her first priority. She grabbed the phone book and sat crossed-legged on the bed, filling out each bit of information in careful print. Vic's comments were encouraging, and it seemed a lucky break that there was an apartment available. Now, if the job at Jerry's Place came through, she'd be set. She finished the applications, folded them in half, and set them on the table then reached into her pocket for the sucker. She fell back on the bed and pulled up its covers while the air conditioner droned.

> "Would you like a lollipop?" Mrs. Parker held out a candy jar and Sara, clutching a rag doll, reached for a grape pop.
>
> "Thank you." Her words were barely audible. She held the sucker tightly but didn't pull off the wrapper.
>
> "You can eat it, Sara." Mrs. Parker flipped through her Rolodex then picked up the phone.
>
> Sara caught a few words here and there from Mrs. Parker's hushed conversation. "Yes, she's a

good child . . . quiet, most of the time . . . no trouble . . . yes, you'll be her third family . . ."

Sara's small fist clenched the sucker, and she held the rag doll against her chest. Why couldn't she stay with Mother Fisk? It wasn't so bad there. And the other kids were nice to her. Tears welled up and Sara rubbed her eyes.

A smile broke out on Mrs. Parker's face. "You will? Okay. We'll be there in an hour." She set the receiver down and wrote in an open folder then turned to Sara. "Well, dear, it looks like I've found you a new home."

Sara sat in the living room on an overstuffed chair and strained to hear what was being said about her at the kitchen table. She looked around. Drapes drooped from the tall window, and the shadows that stretched across the hardwood floor were like fingers reaching to grab her. She shuddered.

"So, her first name is Orchid, but you call her Sara?"

"That's right, and we use Jones for her last name."

"What do you mean you use Jones? Doesn't she have a last name?"

"We don't know it."

"How is that possible?"

"See, Sara's mother . . ." Why did Mrs. Parker have to lower her voice? Sara craned her neck to hear better. ". . . and then the couple who cared for her after . . . split up. Her mother's first name was in a book she left with Sara . . ."

"Is that why you haven't been able to locate her?"

Sara was beginning to dislike this woman. She asked too many questions. Sara covered her ears, scrunched her eyes, and screamed inside.

Sara opened her eyes when Mrs. Parker pulled her hands away from her ears. "Sara, dear, what on earth are you doing?"

"Nothing."

"Well then," she turned to the woman. "I'd like you to meet your new mother." Sara didn't hear another word.

Sara shivered in her lonely motel room as she bit off the last of the grape lollipop. She laid the stick on the nightstand then drew the cover back over her shoulders, crossing her arms tightly. Would tomorrow be the day she'd finally meet her mother?

Chapter 4

Saturday, Week One

Sara locked both car doors when the guys from yesterday walked out of their room and headed straight toward her Toyota. As they approached her front bumper on the driver's side, they split up, got in the car next to her, and drove off. Maybe she was paranoid, but who wouldn't be? In her thirty-three years, she'd seen more shit than a toilet in China had.

She tossed the co-op app on the passenger seat then looked over the rental app again. That was the one that required so much information and had given her trouble. Her background wasn't exactly spotless. Sara hoped Vic wouldn't delve too deeply into the references. She couldn't list Mrs. Baxter although at one time, she'd been Sara's biggest supporter. Not anymore. Sara leaned against the head rest.

> "Where have you been?" Mrs. Baxter slammed the door after Sara had stumbled inside.
>
> "I'm sorry." How could she tell her neighbor that she had left work with a handsome stranger three days ago for a night of whiskey-fueled lust but had awakened this morning with a hangover and no memory of how she got there? When she'd asked him for the time, he told her she'd be better off asking what day it was. Sara massaged her temples and muttered, "I'll just pick up Jamie now. She sleeping?" She started for Mrs. Baxter's spare bedroom.

"Hold up." Mrs. Baxter grabbed Sara's shoulder.

Sara shook off her grip. "Look, I know I owe you, and I've got cash." She shoved some bills at Mrs. Baxter. "I'll have more for you tonight." She turned toward the bedroom. "I'll just get Jamie now." Mrs. Baxter stepped in front of her. "What are you doing? I want to get my daughter."

"You should have thought about that three days ago." Mrs. Baxter picked up an official-looking letter. "Read this if you want to know where Jamie is."

"What did you do?" Sara screamed, waving the paper in front of her.

"Look here, you can't just leave your child with me and not return for three days." Mrs. Baxter folded her arms. "I couldn't reach you. And, it's not the first time you've been late."

"But you should've . . ."

Wagging her finger, Mrs. Baxter scolded, "Never mind what I should've done. I'm not Jamie's mother. You are." She plopped into a chair. "You need to get yourself together. Now, please leave and lock the door on your way out."

Sara dropped the rental app on the seat. She turned the key and her Toyota popped then sputtered. She pressed the gas pedal lightly, revving the engine, thankful that it started this time.

* * *

Sara squeezed into one of the few vacant spaces in the co-op's parking lot. She walked past the steps leading to the apartment, turned the corner, and entered Java Hut. Stan saw her and waved. She smiled and walked over to the counter. "Hi, Stan." She was glad she'd remembered his name. She knew how important names were.

"Hey. Sara, isn't it?" Stan leaned over the counter.

She nodded. "Is Vic here? I brought back the applications." She held them in front of her.

"He's in the office." Stan turned to a customer, "Be with you in a sec," before returning his attention to Sara. "You know where it is, right?"

"Through the beaded entrance, right?"

"You got it." The room was filling up with customers. "Just knock if the door's shut even if you see a Do Not Disturb sign."

"You sure?"

"Of course. Tell him Stan-the-Man told you it was okay." He grinned before bounding off.

Sara took a deep breath and turned toward the beaded doorway. She heard laughter as she neared the office and was glad to see that the door was open. Several members were gathered inside.

Vic looked past the people milling around his desk. "Oh, hi, Sara." Talking ceased and heads turned as he stood. Sara's face heated in a blush she couldn't will away.

"Hi, Vic." She barely spoke before Vic announced who she was to everyone. She was mortified and scanned the faces, looking for something familiar in one of them.

Vic scuffled through the crowded room till he reached Sara. "Hang on a minute. I have to tack next week's schedule on the bulletin board."

Sara nodded, relieved to see everyone follow him out the door. Some smiled at her on their way out, and she relaxed. She was antsy to get out there and look at the members' photos hanging along the top of the board. She'd been too nervous to do more than steal a glance yesterday, but today she hoped to finally see her mother's face.

Vic walked back in and pointed to a chair. "Have a seat." He sat down. "I guess you've filled out the apps?"

"Yes." She handed them to him.

Vic looked them over. "As soon as I check out the rental app, I'll let you know about the apartment."

Sara nodded, wondering what he'd find when he called her reference. She'd used a woman she met at the halfway house not long before they both left. She hadn't even called the woman to make sure the line was in service. All she knew was that after running into Jon, she had to find out where her mother was and wasted no time getting to the library. After an hour or so on the computer, she discovered that her mother's complete last name was Donnelly, and she had all the information she needed to be here now, so close . . . so close . . .

Vic broke her reverie when he stood. "Do you have any questions?"

His movement snapped her out of it. "Not that I can think of." How long had she been daydreaming? She stood.

Vic glanced at his watch. "Sorry, I don't mean to rush you, but I've got to give an estimate for some cabinets."

"It's okay." As they walked out, he locked the door behind them then turned to the members still there. "Maybe one of you guys can show Sara some of our Midwestern hospitality." He patted Sara's shoulder. "We'll be in touch soon."

"Bye."

A lanky man stepped away from the group. "Hi, Sara. I'm Clem. What's your craft?"

"Watercolors. And sketching."

"I do calligraphy." He turned toward the wall and pointed to the brief bio beneath his photo.

"Oh, Vic showed me your flyers. If I get accepted, will you make some for me?"

"Let's just assume you will be." Clem smiled. "I'll get some flyers printed up and placed in the lobby. That way, hopefully, you'll have some students ready to go when Vic gives you the good word."

"Great." She was already looking past him at the faces on the wall, squinting at the names.

Clem began to tell her how it was that he had gotten involved with the co-op.

She was hardly listening when she saw the face that belonged to the name that had led her here. She couldn't stop staring even though the photo must have been taken years earlier. Clem couldn't know that all she wanted was to snatch that picture and take it with her. But she couldn't tell him that. Instead, she pointed at the photos and said, "Tell me about them," then held her breath and waited till he got to the only person she was interested in.

". . . and then there's Fiona." He had her attention. "She and Vic are, well, a couple, I guess you could say."

"Really?" She encouraged him to continue.

"Yeah." He shook his head. "Stan's nickname for her is Fiery Fiona."

Sara pretended to listen while Clem chatted about the other members. When he finished, she thanked him and said she had to leave.

* * *

Jerry waved as Sara entered the bar. "Right on time." He finished drying a mug and offered her a soft drink.

"A Coke would be great. Thanks."

"We'll get started in a minute. I've got something to tend to first. Have a seat. Captain here'll keep you entertained while I'm gone." He pulled off his apron. "This is Sara. My new employee." Then he walked to the back of the bar and through a door.

"Hi Sara." Captain extended his calloused hand. "Welcome ta Jerry's." His gold tooth glinted when he smiled. He lifted his cane off the bar's edge and pulled it away from Sara's barstool. "Don't use it much, but ya never know when it'll come in handy." She scooted her stool closer to the bar and smiled but remained silent until Jerry poked his head out of the doorway and called to her.

* * *

Sara answered Jerry's questions as he filled out her new-hire paperwork in the small office. The room looked like it hadn't seen change or a coat of paint since before she was born. A yellowed pin-up calendar hung behind the desk, the days and dates of the past long gone. The woman with the bright teeth had tight flesh that was probably sagging by now, her children gone, her life a series of regrets and loneliness. Sara jumped when the phone rang. Jerry grabbed it quickly. "Sorry, I have to take this. Can you give me a sec?"

"Sure." As Sara got up she noticed the phone book on a table by the office door and grabbed it on her way out. Captain was gone. She sat at the end of the empty bar and flipped through pages till she found the D's. There it was. The address she was looking for. If her motel's phone book hadn't had missing pages, she'd have already had what she wanted. She grabbed a pen off the register and tore a page from the back of the book—expired coupons—and scrawled the address as quickly as possible. She slammed the book closed, replaced Jerry's pen, and sat back down, shaking. Knowing where her mother worked was one thing. Knowing where she lived was another. She shoved the paper in her pocket and waited.

Jerry called out. "I'm ready for you."

"Okay." She listened as he went over the bar's routine. When he was done, he asked if she had any questions. At first she said no because he'd covered enough, but then she remembered the address in her pocket and asked where Oakwood Way was. He gave her directions and she left.

* * *

Parked cars lined the streets Sara drove through. A rainbow of people walked the sidewalks, some carrying bags and scoopers for the dogs they were walking. Sara rolled down her window and smelled barbequed burgers. As she passed houses with boarded-up windows sandwiched between well-maintained homes, she wondered what her mother's house would look like. Would it hint at the life she'd lived all these years?

Finally, she turned onto a street that intersected Oakwood Way. She looked at the house number written on the scrap of paper and knew driving by wasn't going to be easy. Glancing down the street, she could see that Oakwood Way dead-ended, and it looked like her mother's house was in the last block. She noticed a woman walking a dog then saw her stop to chat with an odd-looking man wearing a ball cap. She couldn't pass the house now. Not with them outside. Who knows, that might even be her. Sara would have to turn around to get back out, and it'd be her luck that the car would stall. Sara turned and drove away.

* * *

When she closed the door to her motel room, she felt the walls closing in. She wanted to go somewhere, but cash was running low, and she wouldn't start work till Monday. She sat on the bed and thought about this latest turn of events. How had she let herself take a job at a bar? Was she that desperate to be here? God, she knew this wasn't something she should do. Sure, today it was easy enough to sip a Coke, but how easy would it be when, night after night, she served Heinekens, Screwdrivers, Long Island Iced Teas, or whatever? The adrenaline was pumping. She needed to talk to someone—now. She reached for her phone and punched in the number she'd memorized.

"Hello."

"Hello, Mrs. Robison, this is Sara Jenkins." A pause. Not good.

"Oh. Jamie's taking a nap right now. But she's doing just fine."

Sara swallowed the lump in her throat. "Well, I just wanted to tell her I love her. Would you tell her I called, please?"

"Yes."

"Do you think I could call back in an hour maybe?"

"I can't really say." Another pause and muffled voices before Mrs. Robison spoke again. "Actually, she has a party to attend this afternoon, so when she gets up, we'll be getting her ready for that. Perhaps you can try tomorrow."

"Thanks." Sara wanted to add 'for nothing.' There always seemed to be some reason Jamie couldn't come to the phone.

"Well, goodbye then."

Click. Sara sat on the bed with the deafening dial tone in her ear. She flipped her phone several times. Open. Closed. Open. Closed. Good. Bad. Coke. Bud Light. Bud Light. Jack Daniel's. Shit. She called her sponsor. After listening a lot and saying little, Sara hung up and tossed the phone on the bed. Even after her sponsor's encouraging words, she wondered what made her think she could do this—that she had the strength for this. Maybe she should just pack up and get back to San Francisco before Jamie forgot *her* mother.

Startled awake in my dark room by a whir that I know isn't my window unit's monotonous drone, I sit up in bed and listen to sounds that become louder by the minute. Crackling branches break the whooshing of saw grass being swept aside by the purr of an outboard motor. I lie back down and pull the pillow over my ears. I won't look . . . I won't look . . . My mantra is interrupted by a thud and sputter. Oh God, please don't let it crash here! I want to stay ignorant of whatever is taking place in the swamp below. Muffled curses float through the air and blend with feet tapping on wood. By the sounds, I know what's going on. One-two-three, pull, clunk-clunk. One-two-three, pull, clunk-clunk. I stare at the ceiling and will the engine to catch. One more attempt and I hear the motor rev. Thank you, thank you, thank you, I chant as the roar fades into a distant hum.

When silence reclaims my night, I slip out of bed, creep through the cabin, and peek out the kitchen window at the dark swamp below. Like me, it is now alone. I gaze at the vast darkness and see flickers of light like dancing fireflies. Other inhabitants of my world have heard the night's disturbance too, but as I stand here, I see the lights begin to vanish, like flames that have died on the wicks of candles. I turn back to my bedroom. Solitude is the swamp's friend, and I have made it mine.

Chapter 5

Monday, Week Two

When Jane Heffinger arrived home at dawn and yanked a shopping bag from her Jeep, she noticed a box wedged between her azaleas and the porch. It had to be from her mom. Who else left things behind the plants or under the garden hose?

"Damn it, Mom," she mumbled. She glanced down the street. Albert was already up, scraping chipped paint off his house, a job that he never seemed to finish. She was glad Mrs. Peabody wasn't standing inside her front door waiting for Jane to come home so she could chat. The agoraphobia that imprisoned Mrs. Peabody seemed to make her desperate for companionship.

Jane picked up the box and went inside. A Senseo coffeemaker, of all things. Of course, her mother would give her something useless. Either that or she'd forgotten Jane drank tea. She looked around the kitchen for a place to set the box and decided to leave it on the new tile floor. Cocoa meowed, hopped on the box, and stretched one paw over the edge, seemingly content with his new possession. Jane unlaced her tennis shoes and saw the blinking light on her answering machine. She pressed the play button.

"You have four new messages," the machine grumbled.

"Message one . . ."

"Jane. It's Mother. I tried your cell but it went straight to voicemail. Did you forget to turn it on again? Listen, it's 6:03 and I'm getting ready to stop by your house. I've got something for you, and I have thirty-seven minutes before I have to be at the club." Jane heard her mother's muffled voice tell her stepfather, Eddie, 'Have a good day, Dear,' before she lifted her hand off the mouthpiece to command, "Call me if you get this message in the next few minutes." Jane pressed delete then kept her finger poised over the button.

"Message two . . ."

"Jane. It's Mother again. It's 6:18. I'm sitting in your driveway. I thought you'd be home by now. I really want to leave this gift for you, but you know how this neighborhood is. It'll probably get stolen two seconds after I leave."

"Message three . . ."

"Jane. It's Mother. It's 6:25. I can't wait any longer. I know it takes six minutes to get from the bank to your house, so I can't imagine why you're not here yet."

"Message four . . ."

"Jane. It's Mother. I'm on the road. You know how I hate talking while driving, but I can't pull over. I should have been at the club three minutes ago. Did you get my gift? It's behind the azaleas. I hope no one steals it. Your hippie neighbor came out to walk that big, brown dog of hers while I was waiting. I don't trust her. Doesn't she know it's not the sixties anymore? She should dress her age and cut and color that gray hair. For the life of me, I don't know why you . . ."

Jane pressed delete before her mother's last rant ended. Who did she think she was anyway, giving fashion advice? Had she not figured out that, unlike her, not everyone liked to be a carbon copy of their friends?

She was reaching into the shopping bag and pulling out a jar of honey when the phone rang again. "Oh, for God sakes, can't she let it rest." Her answering machine clicked on and she heard her dad, "Janey, Hon, it's me. Can you give me a call when you get a chance? Love you." Jane lurched for the phone, almost tripping over Cocoa.

"Hello, Dad. I'm here," she panted, but her words fell into dead air. She hung up the receiver and was about to call him back when the doorbell rang. What? Was there a full moon last night? Jane groaned and walked to the door, opening it wide for her neighbor, Fiona.

"Hi Jane, is this a bad time?"

"Yes . . . but not for you." She held open the door as Fiona sashayed inside. "Where's Petrarch?" She expected her neighbor's chocolate Lab to be trotting alongside her.

"He's home. I already took him for a walk, and I didn't want to bother you because I knew you just got home, but while I was walking Pet I saw a lady, your mother I guess, leave something behind your azaleas. I wanted to be sure you got it."

"Yeah, Mom mentioned seeing you and that 'big, brown dog' in one of her zillion messages." Jane rolled her eyes and motioned for Fiona to sit on the couch.

"I'm surprised you've never given her a key."

"I really don't want her to have one, and it makes more sense for you to have my spare. Jane pointed to the Senseo box. "There's my gift. A coffeemaker. For a tea drinker."

Fiona smiled but said nothing.

"By the way, why are you up so early?"

"I've got to work at the co-op this morning. Vic had indigestion all night and didn't get much sleep. I was worried about his heart and convinced him to get checked out. I wanted to go with him but he insisted he needed me at the co-op. I'll be antsy until I hear from him."

"I'm sure he'll be fine." Jane couldn't imagine Fiona without Vic.

"He'd better be. I'm not ready to do without his sorry ass!" She lowered her voice. "And every other part of his body."

Jane laughed. "I'll bet. But don't you hate going in this early?"

Fiona perched her hands on her hips. "You know it. I detest mornings and everyone there is well aware of it." Cocoa rubbed Fiona's leg. She picked him up and leaned toward Jane. "But, there's this applicant I'd like to check out." Cocoa jumped down. "Hey," Fiona stood, raised her hands, and twirled slowly, "notice anything?"

"You've been shopping." She never knew what Fiona would be wearing. While Jane was most comfortable in jeans and a t-shirt, Fiona loved vintage sixties' clothes, like the orange peasant blouse she was modeling with her well-worn, bell-bottoms. With her waist length gray hair pulled into a French braid, she was definitely the antithesis of Jane's mother.

"Yes. There's a new second-hand store on Third St." She sat back down.

"A new second-hand store?"

"Gotta love those oxymorons." Fiona pulled a spongy ball from between the cushions and tossed it to Cocoa then looked toward the kitchen. "Say, I meant to tell you, I sure do like the new oak cabinets. They're a hundred times better than those old metal ones. By the way, is the bathroom finished?"

Jane nodded, motioning for Fiona to follow. She opened the door wide and made a sweeping motion. "Take a look."

Fiona stepped inside. "Oh . . . how wonderful. I wish my bathroom looked this good," Fiona cooed as she looked at the oak vanity with its marble sink. The vinyl floor tiles had been replaced with ceramic ones. The claw-foot tub had been reglazed and a shower with a wrap-around curtain added. "That shower head looks like it does all kinds of things," Fiona said, with a Cheshire grin. "Wouldn't Vic and I have fun with that nozzle."

Jane shook her head. When they first met, Fiona was always throwing Jane curveballs with unexpected comments. But now she knew Fiona well enough to know what to expect.

"Sure do envy you. What I wouldn't give for some major-ass remodeling in my house."

"Yeah, but you don't have to worry about your house getting sold out from under you. I'm not sure what my landlord has in mind, especially since he didn't raise my rent after the remodeling."

"Yeah, thank God I own my house. It would take ten trucks and twenty unemployed cabana boys to move me out." Fiona laughed.

A knock on the door made Jane roll her eyes. "I'd better see who that is."

"And I'd better see to Mother Nature." Fiona shut the bathroom door as Jane left to see who was knocking.

When Jane opened the door, her mom breezed past like a train whistling through a small-town railroad crossing.

"What are you doing here? I thought you were at your aerobics class?"

Her mom set her purse down on the couch. "I had to skip the class. Elizabeth called. She was up early. Couldn't sleep last night for worrying about wedding plans. She said she knew it was too early to call her mom and hoped she wasn't disturbing me." Winnie smiled. "Like I wouldn't be happy to talk to her about wedding plans no matter what time of day or night. And I told her I was sure that her sister wouldn't mind either."

"Stepsister. And, yes, I would mind. You know I work nights and sleep during the day." She wondered how many times she would have to remind her mom of this.

"Well, I've just never heard of such. Working nights at a bank. You'd think they'd be able to do all that computer stuff during the day." Winnie looked around. "Where's the Senseo I brought you? Did you get it? I didn't see it outside where I left it. Don't tell me that crazy lady took it."

Jane raised her finger to her lips. "Shhh."

The commode flushed and Jane whispered, "No, Mom. Fiona. That's her name. She's not crazy. *And*, she did *not* take it."

A moment later, Fiona stepped into the room and Winnie looked her up and down then focused on Jane. "You know how I hate it when you call me Mom. Call me Mother. That's what Elizabeth calls her mother." She turned to Fiona. "I'm Jane's mother. I guess the cat's got my daughter's tongue." Winifred looked at Jane and lowered her voice. "And her manners."

Jane turned red and looked at Fiona. "Sorry, Fee, this is Winnie, my mother. As she already mentioned." Then she looked at her mother. "And this is Fiona. My friend." Fiona reached to shake Winnie's hand. Jane relished her small victory at introducing her mom as Winnie instead of Winifred, the name she wanted in her new life with Edward.

Fiona left right after the uncomfortable introduction. Winnie showed no signs of leaving, and Jane feared how long she would stay when Winnie began twittering around the room, pulling dead leaves off Jane's ivy and spider plants. But before her mother reached the wandering Jew's dead purple leaves, her cell phone rang. Who else but Elizabeth? For once, Jane was glad to hear her stepsister's name, and as she shut the door behind her mother, Jane leaned back and sighed. Seeing her mom pick at the plant leaves reminded her how, at the age of twelve, Jane had seen the soft edges of her mom begin falling away, like the leaves on the philodendron her mom left behind when she divorced Jane's dad. Jane had tried to keep the plant alive, watering it on the weekends when she stayed with her dad, but the leaves wilted and the plant died anyway.

My clammy fingers can barely unbutton my work shirt. When the last button is undone, I toss the blouse on the floor and unzip my khaki shorts, dropping them too. I peel off my sweat-drenched bra and look down at the breasts I once was proud to flaunt. No longer firm, they are beginning to point downward, and a slight roll of flab hangs over my high-cut panties. I slide them down my muscled thighs, drop them in the pile, step into the tepid water of my claw-foot tub, and immerse my entire body, even ducking my head underwater. Droplets spill over the sides onto the cracked tiles and seep through to the wood underneath. Seconds later, my head springs up through the surface, wet hair plastered to my face. Straggling hairs cling to my shoulders. The cooling water chills my skin and goose bumps cover my exposed flesh. I squeeze a few drops of shampoo on my head and scrub my scalp into a mass of white froth. Closing my eyes tightly, I plunge under the water and vigorously rub the suds from my hair. When I emerge from my underwater haven, the water is dotted with islands of foam, and I lie back and look up through the skylight. The sky is robin's egg blue with floating, cottony clouds. Soon they will be hidden in the black night. I close my eyes and dream of a time when I was not alone. When I had a family. When I had friends who shared more than just a love of nature, like orchids and their mysterious lure. Of a time when . . .

Before long I am shivering in cold, oily water, and the sky above has turned a purplish black. The room is dark, but I find the tub's plug and pull it. As the water slowly drains, I lift my trembling body from the tub and grab the bath towel hanging on the bar. Tightly wrapped in the towel, I turn on the dim light and rub my body dry. My bumpy flesh smoothes out and I put on clean panties and an oversized T-shirt. My hair is frizzed from the humidity, which is once again seeping into my skin. I hurry from the bathroom and shut the door. My window unit will not cool the rest of the cottage if it has to take on the steamy bathroom air. I flip a light switch and illuminate the living room. I fall onto the couch and look at the refrigerator, remembering the tuna salad I prepared last night, but I'm too tired to get up again. Thoughts race through my mind and sleep eludes me. Tonight, solitude is not my friend.

Chapter 6

Monday, Week Two

Fiona rushed home from Jane's, so she wouldn't arrive late at the co-op. She was still reeling from how different Jane's parents were. Marv was down to earth and kind. And here Winifred was complaining about Jane's manners. Jane had always been a thoughtful neighbor and friend, so it irked Fiona to hear Winifred talk to Jane like that. She opened the door to let Pet out one last time. She had promised Vic she'd be at the co-op by 8:00, and now she had to hurry. She walked over to her hydrangeas and picked off a few dead blooms while Pet ran circles in search of the perfect spot.

Fiona slung her bag over her shoulder and headed out the back door. She unlocked and, with great effort, pushed up her garage door. Vic had offered to install an automatic door, but she'd resisted. Seemed like everything new was a big deal. When had resisting new things become the norm? She pumped the gas pedal, and the old VW bus sputtered to life.

* * *

Fiona sauntered into Java Hut. "Hey, Stan." She really needed coffee this morning. "Can a girl get a good strong drink around here?" She plunked her bag on the counter and sat down, noticing a vase of beautiful red roses on the end. "So, where'd the roses come from?"

Stan pointed across the room. "Rosie."

Rosie and Clem were huddled at a table in the corner, scouring a piece of paper. They looked up when they heard Rosie's name. Clem nodded in Fiona's direction, but Rosie turned her attention back to the paper.

When Fiona turned back to Stan, he was rattling off one of his famous spiels to another customer. She waved to get his attention then pointed to a mug.

Stan laughed and leaned in close. "But, of course, my dear. So, what'll it be?"

"Mocha latte—strong."

Stan wagged his finger. "Now that's a contradiction in terms."

Fiona furrowed her brow.

Stan stood in front of the latte machine. "Let's see." He flipped one hand. "Here's latte—con leche," he smirked, then flipped the other one, "and here's strong." He swayed side to side while 'balancing' the 'elements' in his hands.

Fiona nodded. "Point taken. Just get me a good, strong cup of java." She laughed and grabbed a couple of sugar packets. "Pronto."

"Yes'm. Stan saluted and turned to the coffee machine. Then, as if he had just realized how early it was, stopped and looked at his watch. "Just what are you doing here anyway? It's barely a butt hair past the crack of dawn."

"I'm covering for Vic." Fiona dumped the sugar into the mug of coffee Stan set in front of her. "He fought indigestion all night, and I insisted he get it checked out."

"Well, I hope he's okay, and I hope he gets some sleep. He's worse than a bitch-slapped bear when he hasn't had enough."

"Don't I know it." She wasn't going to let on even to Stan how concerned she was. Vic would be fine. He had to be. "But I'm going to call off tonight's meeting."

"I'll help you let everyone know."

* * *

"Fine." She really hoped to stick around long enough to grill Stan about the new girl, but the regulars were filing in. Stan's aptly named Stinky-Cigar-Smoker waved to her, and the man who wore blue flannel shirts regardless of the weather glanced her way. Well, she wasn't going to have time to get much out of Stan, but maybe a little. "Hey."

Stan turned toward Fiona.

"Have you met the girl Vic interviewed the other day?"

Stan slid a sleeve on a paper cup, filled it, and set it on the counter in front of Blue Shirt. "You mean Sara?"

"Yeah, I believe that was her name." Fiona fidgeted. She'd thought of little else since yesterday, but damned if she'd admit it. Something in Vic's voice had set off alarms.

Stan nodded at Stinky-Cigar-Smoker then went to the espresso machine to fill his usual order. When Stan returned, Fiona continued. "You didn't answer me."

"What was the question?" Stan watched as more customers arrived for their morning coffee.

Fiona cocked her head. "C'mon, Stan, you know. Sara. Have you met her?"

"Oh, yeah." He turned his attention to a new group sitting down then wiggled his eyebrows at Fiona. "And she's quite a looker." He grinned. "Gotta go." He left for the table before Fiona could say another word. She grabbed her coffee and headed for the office.

* * *

Before shutting the door behind her, she flipped the Do Not Disturb sign. It was early and emergencies were unlikely. Why not admit it, she wanted to snoop. It wasn't something she was proud of, but not being in control was difficult. She tossed her bag on an empty chair and set her cup down. Sipping her coffee, Fiona decided to check the desk for Sara's application.

Fiona shoved her key in the desk drawer and jerked it open. The application was on top. "Hmm. Sara Jenkins. Last address was in San Francisco," Fiona mumbled. She knew Guerrero Street was in the Mission District. Looking at the address, it seemed to be in the Mission Delores area. There was a phone number but no address for Sara's only reference. What? Did her reference camp out in Delores Park? Don't be catty, Fiona. Although, she did wonder how Sara had been able to live anywhere in San Francisco yet had to pay rent weekly here. She couldn't believe it when Vic told her he was going to let her do that. How like him to wait until she was pleasantly exhausted after sex to bring it up. Was he that afraid of her reaction? Well, maybe he should have been. She'd lectured him and he'd gone home, but when he called early this morning and complained about indigestion, she didn't resume the argument.

What she wished for now was to see what this girl looked like. Putting a face with the name would at least give Fiona a frame of reference. Why hadn't she insisted Vic take a picture with all applications? She couldn't resist picking up the phone and punching in Sara's reference number. She heard a recording saying the number was not in service. Fiona leaned back. She scanned the application and saw Sara's last job had been at a place called Amnesia, but there was no phone number. What kind of application was this? No decent references? Boy, would she give Vic the what-for, that is, if the doctor gave him a clean bill of health. A knock on the outside door startled her and she jerked forward, dripping coffee on the application. "Shit." She brushed the liquid away with her hand. Did she need a Do Not Disturb sign for that door too? She cracked it open.

* * *

Sara peered through the crack. Instead of Vic's brown eyes looking back, she saw a squinting pair of green eyes, much like her own.

"Hello," the woman said.

Sara knew who those eyes belonged to. She'd seen the younger version of that face on the wall outside the office. She cocked her head. Her body tingled and her palms began to sweat. Today was the day she'd meet her mother. Get a grip. Be cool. She recited the mantra she'd learned in rehab. Breathe in, breathe out. Count. One-hundred, ninety-nine . . .

The door swung open, and Fiona stood in the doorway with her hands on her hips. "Can I help you?"

Sara searched for a sign of recognition—any sign. Instead, Fiona's face was blank with indifference. How could she not know her own daughter? Had Sara been so easily forgotten? Replaced?

Grasping the door's edge and stepping back, her mother said, "I'm Fiona." She stretched her hand toward Sara.

A handshake? That's all? No hug? But after all Fiona didn't know who she was. Sara could barely find her voice yet finally managed to squeeze out, "I'm Sara." She lifted her trembling hand, but Fiona had already withdrawn hers. Sara dropped her hand to her side. "Is Vic here?"

"No. But if there's something you need, you can check with me."

Fiona's cold command made Sara want to cry. But she wouldn't. She would not. Not, not, not.

"Well, if you're Sara, you must be here about the apartment." Fiona gestured for Sara to enter. "So, what can I do for you?"

Sara sniffled and cleared her throat. "Vic said I could check on the apartment." She was relieved her voice didn't crack and her tears didn't spill.

Fiona exhaled a puff of air while a guttural hmm escaped through clenched lips. "I don't know about that. You'll have to check with Vic later."

Sara brushed away a tear she couldn't control. It shouldn't be this hard. She muttered, "Vic said . . ." but Fiona had turned toward the desk and was shuffling papers.

Fiona waved her hand. "Like I said, you'll have to talk to Vic about that."

Sara knew she was being dismissed. She swallowed so hard it felt like downing a pill dry. She wanted to run. But she couldn't yet. "When will he . . ."

Fiona cut her off. "Probably later today, but he has a lot to do." Fiona jutted her chin. "Anything else?"

Sara shook her head. Maybe she should go back to San Francisco. Coming here was a mistake. Sara hurried toward the door before Fiona could see her lips quivering or another tear falling. She wanted to tell Fiona to thank Vic, but no thanks. Just as she grabbed the door knob, Fiona said, "Okay, then."

It took all of Sara's strength to walk out the door and get to her car. She leaned her head on the steering wheel. What now? She felt like she'd been knocked down in a boxing match, and the ref was standing over her counting. She couldn't stay down. She had to get up. She lifted her head. She'd go to the riverfront. She'd sketch. That would calm her. It wasn't the Pacific Ocean, but at least it was water. Maybe she'd recognize the reflection staring back.

* * *

Arriving at the riverfront's small parking lot, Sara swerved into the only empty spot. She grabbed her sketch pad and charcoal pencil. What would she sketch? Would her hand stay steady enough to draw?

She had to try. Calling her sponsor wasn't the option she wanted now. Too much to explain. She wasn't sure how to put her feelings into words, so what could she say? That she'd just met her mother? No. This was a part of her past she'd kept private, and until she knew how it would go, she would avoid inviting pity.

As she got out of her car, two women with fat-cheeked babies in strollers nodded at her. A man with an Alaskan husky, who looked like he was being walked instead of the dog, zipped past her. The sun was just starting to spread its sizzling heat, and Sara looked for a shady spot. She saw joggers, bike riders, and walkers snaking the waterfront's narrow path farther down.

She left the asphalt path, walked down the sloping hill, and sat. No shade trees but she noticed two young boys fishing from a concrete piling at the water's edge and opened her sketch pad. First the boys. Ovals for their heads. Larger ovals for their trunks. Then elongated ones for the limbs. Murky water in front of them. Fishing lines cast and waiting. She felt calmer with each pencil stroke as she added details then smudged and shaded them into the picture.

When she finally stood to leave, she felt a slight, sticky breeze and realized the sun was no longer shining brightly. How long had she sat there? She closed her sketch pad, rubbed her fingers along the grass, and looked up at the sky. Dark clouds were rolling in.

Chapter 7

Tuesday, Week Two

Jane's Jeep bounced over the gravel road winding out of her dad's trailer park. Branches stretched high toward the middle, creating a canopy. When she'd left, her dad was heading for a nap. She'd tried to clean up his kitchen, scraping congealed soup from a pot on the stove and wiping dirty splotches from the floor. He'd left a cluttered pile of memorabilia, including a stack of Beatles' albums on the kitchen table, and she'd sorted it all into neat piles. It wasn't like him to leave such a mess. And taking a day off from his custodial job at the community college was rare. These things concerned her. Before his nap, he told her he'd come see her one day this week, so maybe then she'd find out what was going on.

As soon as she opened the Jeep's door, her cell phone beeped, signaling an SOS from her mom. Jane tossed the phone on the seat and steeled herself for a quick side trip. God, what was the urgency this time? With her mom, it could be anything from a hangnail to a heart attack, so she had to go, or she'd never hear the end of it. Besides, it'd be just like Elizabeth to show up and be her mom's hero.

* * *

When Jane parked at her mom's house, Mrs. Gentry was walking up her driveway and turned to look at Jane, shading her eyes with her mail. Jane waved as she jumped from the Jeep but got only a nod. According to Winnie, Mrs. Gentry was to be avoided because she liked to get in everyone's business.

Jane looked at Winnie and Eddie's house. Hostas and daylilies bloomed in a terraced border in front, and red geraniums in terra cotta pots lined the steps to the porch. Every time Jane came to Flagstone, the newest and priciest subdivision in the city, she was struck by the stark contrast to the trailer park she'd grown up in. When her mom married Eddie (Edward, as her mom insisted after Jane told her that she was not going to call him Father), Winnie made sure they built a house in Flagstone because anyone with any clout in the city—and Eddie had plenty—lived there. Her mom was determined to be somebody, and Jane was sure that ambition is what drove her mom from her dad. Jane hadn't been able to forgive her for that. It was such a shallow and ludicrous aspiration. To think that special bricks mortared into an expensive home in a prime location and a husband who worked seventy hours a week were the keys to being somebody was beyond Jane's comprehension.

She rang the doorbell, not knowing what to expect. She had a key for emergencies, but there had been no true ones yet. She saw the doorknob turn. Her mother stood in front of her, alive and very well.

"Hi, uh, Mother," Jane caught herself before she got The Look. She was in no mood for it today. "I got your message. What's wrong?" Her mom moved aside and Jane stepped in.

"Well, at least you didn't have the phone turned off. How come you didn't answer?"

"I was at Dad's and left it in the Jeep."

"What if I needed you right away?" Winnie huffed as she led Jane through the living room. "I wish you'd keep the phone with you all the time."

"Sorry." Jane wasn't about to argue. "So, obviously you're not dying."

"Whatever made you say something like that?" Winnie shook her head. "Sometimes I just can't fathom that wild imagination of yours."

"Sometimes?" Jane followed her mom toward the French doors leading to the inside patio. "More like never." She mumbled the last words. "What was so urgent?"

Winnie grabbed a large hardbound book and waved toward the French doors. "Let's sit out there." The outdoor patio was Winnie's pride and joy. She had the house built around it, and several rooms had French doors that opened into it. A rainbow of irises bloomed above the purple phlox that covered the garden, and red roses climbed a trellis in the center, releasing an intoxicating fragrance.

"Your flowers are in full bloom, I see." The one thing Jane had always loved about this house was the 'indoor' garden. Today, especially, she thought about the gloomy trailer she'd left her dad in and thought how unfair life was. Her dad deserved a home like this, too. It's not that she thought her mom and Eddie didn't, but they had so much. Winnie looked pleased that Jane had complimented her garden and started to explain how she'd planted the flowers. She didn't know that Jane was no longer listening.

Winnie set the book on the table, opened the sun umbrella, and they both sat down. "Here's why I called you."

Jane glanced at the book but stopped reading when she saw BRIDAL . . . She should've known. "To look at a bride's book? I don't know how to tell you this, Mother, but there's no wedding in my near future."

"It's not for you. It's for Elizabeth." She opened the book. "We need to look at bridesmaids' dresses. Elizabeth is getting opinions from her bridal party, and you need to make a choice, so she can make her decision."

"I told you, Elizabeth hasn't asked me to be in her wedding." She leaned back. "Don't you ever listen to me?"

"Well, she probably hasn't asked because she can never reach you."

Jane pulled out her cell phone and held it up. "Hello. Messages. They work." She stuffed it back in her pocket.

Winifred flicked her wrist. "Never mind. Let's just look at these dresses." She turned pages and pointed to styles Jane wouldn't wear to bed much less to a crowded church. Jane gave up. She'd just close her eyes and pick. Her mother was so absorbed in her mission that she'd probably never notice Jane's Pin-the-Tail-on-the-Donkey choice.

* * *

Marv pulled up to Jane's house but didn't see the Jeep. He looked at his watch. Well, he should've called first, but he thought he'd swing by after work today since he'd been feeling so poorly yesterday during Jane's visit. Just as he reached into his glove box to get a pad and leave a note, he heard rapping on his truck's window.

"Hi, Marv."

He turned to see Fiona's big smile and rolled down the window. Humid air, smelling of freshly cut grass, enveloped him while a nearby lawn mower buzzed and sputtered. "Hi, Fiona, how are you." He spoke loudly to drown out the noise.

"Doing fine. You just missed Jane." Pet jumped up on the door, his big paws clinging to the open window.

Marv reached over and patted his head. "Hey there, Pet, how you doing, boy?" Pet's tail wagged and he slobbered on Marv's hand.

"Sorry." Fiona tugged on the leash and said, "Down, Pet."

Marv smiled. "It's okay, but Rusty may not like it when I come home smelling like Pet." He laughed and rubbed his hands on his pants. "Any idea when she'll be back?"

"Afraid not. I had just come outside as she sped by."

"Well, I was going to leave her a note. Can you tell her I came by, and I'll try to call her later?"

Fiona tilted her head toward her house. "Why don't you wait inside? I can't imagine she'll be gone long. She usually leaves for work in about an hour. Probably just ran to the store or something."

"You don't mind?"

"Not at all. C'mon, I was just heading home."

"Okay then." Marv got out of the truck and walked alongside Fiona. He really needed to talk to Jane when his courage was up. If he waited another day, he might chicken out.

* * *

Jane ushered her dad into the living room. She put her milk in the fridge then stepped into the doorway while he sat in her recliner. "Hey, Dad, you want to try out this new coffee machine Mom got me instead of the instant stuff I keep for you? It can make one cup at a time."

"Sure, if you don't mind fixing it. That was nice of your mom."

As Jane turned toward the kitchen, she rolled her eyes. She didn't want her irritation to flare in front of her dad. "No problem for you, Dad." Now she had to read the directions. "Shit."

"Everything okay in there, Hon? You know, instant's fine."

Jane poked her head out. "You sure?"

"Yeah."

Jane felt guilty. She knew her dad would like brewed coffee better. "I just haven't had time to learn how to use the silly thing. You know Mom and her contraptions; she expected me to figure it out immediately." Jane tried to sound like she was joking and laughed half-heartedly as she set two cups of water in the microwave.

"Don't be so hard on your mom. She's just trying to help."

Jane scowled and crossed her arms as she leaned against the door frame. Did everyone think Winnie knew what was best for her?

* * *

In between sips of tea, Jane asked, "What was it you wanted to tell me?"

He set his mug on the end table and didn't speak for what seemed like forever. "Dad, did you hear me? Or did you change your mind? You know, if you don't tell me, I'm just going to pester you until you do because I can't stand not knowing something when there's something to know."

He chuckled. "Yeah, I sure do remember the many times you'd follow me, grabbing my pant leg and whining, "Come on Daddy, I want to know. With you, it was always wanting to know something. Where were we gonna go? What presents did we buy? What movie were we gonna see? Oh, I could fill a book with your, 'I wanna knows'!"

"So, do I have to say it again?" She knew he was only trying to lighten the mood, but she was running out of time before she had to leave for work.

He grinned then turned serious. "Well, Hon, remember two years ago when I had that . . . scare?"

She leaned toward him. "Of course, I remember. But they caught it in time, right? Didn't they?"

"Yeah, but I've been so tired lately." He reached for the mug and swilled the rest of his coffee. "Been working over quite a bit, so I figured that was why."

"So what'd your doctor say when you went for your physical?" She stared at Marv. "You *have* been getting annual physicals, haven't you?"

Marv shifted in the chair. "Well, uh, not exactly, I guess . . ."

"Dad!"

"Sorry, Hon." He leaned forward. "Guess I just let things go. Then I collapsed at work and they sent me to the doc." He covered her hand with his. "That's when I got news I didn't want to hear."

She looked into his brown eyes, eyes the color of the pine cones she gathered as a kid. The other families at the trailer park came and went, so sometimes she had no children to play with, but she could always depend on her dad. He would holler for her to close her eyes while she faced a tree and counted, his voice fading as he ran to his hiding place. She hadn't liked to close her eyes; she wanted to know where he was going.

He looked away. "You know my PSA count was . . ." He trailed off, seeming to want to avoid the word cancer. When he told her about the prostate cancer two years ago, Jane had thrown up.

She pulled her hand from under his and squeezed his arm. "They got your count down to zero after the hormone and radiation treatments, right?

He nodded. "They thought they'd gotten everything." He rubbed his hands on his pants. "Now they say my count is sixteen."

Jane knew that number was much higher than before his treatment. She felt like someone had grabbed her heart and wrenched it bloodless.

Jane bit her nails, something she rarely did these days. She'd started biting them a few months before she and her mom moved out of the trailer and into a small apartment on the other side of town, about the time the only kind words that passed between her parents were doled out like rare jewels.

She was vaguely aware that her dad was still talking—trying to minimize the gravity of the situation. She was already picturing him lying in a hospital bed, his face that ashen color that consumes the body just before death. She watched him pick up her mug.

"Here, Hon," he said, handing her the mug. "You look a little pale. Now, don't start all that worrying. My count's just gone up a little. Maybe the doc just wants to see me get the urge to wear high heels." It was the same joke he made two years ago when he found out taking female hormones was part of his treatment.

Jane forced a small laugh. They had joked about the possibility of his voice becoming high because of the hormones, but this time his joke sounded as tired as he looked. The treatment had worked fine before. He was back to good health wasn't he? How could the cancer return?

"What did the doctor say about treatment this time?"

He rubbed his hand across his chin. "The doc wants to remove my prostate gland." He opened his mouth to speak but stopped.

"So, that will take care of it? If there's no gland, then no cancer, right?"

"Yeah, should get the job done." He picked up his mug and shrugged. "Empty."

The young children, safely sandwiched between me and the chaperones, giggle as I lead the group over the bridge on the nature trail. I stop, and like a toppled row of dominoes, the tapping feet cease all the way back to the adults. Giggles turn to gasps when I point to an alligator straddling a floating log in the swamp below. Questions buzz through the air like bees.

"Oh, he's looking at me, isn't he?" one girl asks, jumping up and down, and pointing, "See his eyes? They're staring straight at me!"

A more pensive boy frowns and asks his classmate, "How do you know it's a boy?" and turns to me for the answer.

Before I can think of a response, a girl squeals, "Oh, look at his teeth. They're so sharp!" Just then the alligator slithers from the log into the murky swamp heading in the direction of the bridge, and all that can be seen is its scales floating like driftwood. "Can he climb up here?" she screams, and without waiting for an answer, runs back to her mother and shaking, clings to her leg.

Hysteria breaks out among the children, who begin running toward the pavilion. I blow the whistle I wear around my neck and all faces turn to me. "It's okay." I try to calm their fears. "The alligator will not climb up the bridge. It just wants to sun itself somewhere else. "Look," I point to a sun-drenched log on the other side of the bridge, "there it is now." The children ooh and aah as they watch the alligator wiggle onto the log, ignoring them. They turn around, and with the help of the chaperones, pair up, holding hands with a partner before we continue over the bridge onto the raised walkway to look at the egrets, pelicans, herons, and maybe even a wood stork or white ibis that take refuge in the tangled roots of the mangroves.

When the children have returned to their waiting school bus, and I walk to my old Cherokee, I reflect on the day: Children always remind me of the hollowness of my life.

* * *

Closing the door behind me, I flick on the light. I reach around the vase of eucalyptus leaves and grab the stack of yellowed newspaper clippings off the wicker shelf. Though I haven't looked at the photo in years, I know it's tucked between the brittle pages of faded words. The rubber band holding the stack together has dry-rotted and crumbles in my hand. Flipping through the aged articles, I find it. He's standing straight, red cowboy hat and black cowboy boots out of place on the riverbank. One hand rests on the stroller's handle, and the other holds a shiny toy gun. He squints into the sun and the camera's lens. I sit in the seat, my nearly bald head turned toward him, my hand outstretched, reaching for the gun, waiting for the "pow, pow" that he later said always made me laugh. I bundle up the clippings without a glance at the only other picture there—the one I can't yet bring myself to look at—stash the bundle back on the shelf then set my brother's picture against the vase, and walk away.

Children remind me of things left on the path not taken. Things left when the path got too narrow. Things forgotten, but not quite. Things . . .

Chapter 8

Monday–Tuesday, Week Three

Sara locked her apartment door and stood on the covered landing overlooking the co-op's parking lot. The only two cars there were her Toyota and Stan's beat-up faded blue Nova. She was here. Really here. When Vic had called to tell her she could move in, she panicked. After all, meeting Fiona hadn't gone the way she hoped it would. She also didn't believe Vic got a hold of her reference because when she tried, all she got was an out-of-service message. Maybe Vic had just given her a break. If so, she wasn't going to blow it.

Now that she'd been in the apartment several days, she knew things had to move along. The possibilities ahead were overwhelming. Since Vic had called a special meeting and the members had voted to accept her, she'd be able to use a workshop room to finish the picture she'd begun in San Francisco. She hoped it would miraculously move Fiona. She started down the stairs, her flip flops clapping against the steps.

Sara clutched the workshop key Vic had given her. He said she could use the room after she mentioned that the counter in the apartment was too small for her paints, brushes, and all the things she needed at hand to finish her picture.

She entered through the Hut where a few customers chatted while Stan was cleaning up to close for the night. "Hi." She walked over to him and waved the key. "I'll be in Workshop A tonight. Vic gave me the key and said I should see you about locking up when I leave."

Stan flung the dishtowel over his shoulder and looked up. "Oh. I guess he forgot to mention it." He set the mug he'd just finished drying under the counter. "How long do you think you'll be using the room?"

She shrugged. "Not sure. You know how it is. Sometimes you have to go with the flow." She smiled.

"Yes, you do." Stan twirled the towel then snapped it in her direction. When she jumped, he laughed. She wondered if he was ever serious for more than a few minutes.

"I'll come get you when I close up here," he reached for another mug to dry, "and show you how to leave without setting off the alarm."

"Okay." Sara headed to the hallway.

* * *

She flipped the light switch, illuminating the room with the fluorescent tubes above. An oblong table spanned nearly the entire length of the room. Folding chairs were stacked along the wall opposite a deep sink with locked cabinets above and alongside it. A few empty cabinets had no locks, and Vic said she'd have a cabinet in each room once she started conducting workshops.

She'd been anxious to paint this picture ever since the day she'd met up with Jon and had seen the little girl on the carousel. She'd sketched a rough draft that night while still inspired and had worked on it a little since. Now she hoped to finish it.

She set her case on the worktable and pulled out the MP3 player Ramón had bought her before he'd gone back to Nicaragua to care for his ailing mother. She'd first heard Enya in rehab and came to associate her music with healing. Enya's music calmed Sara and helped drown out voices in her head that told her she wasn't good enough, couldn't really create anything worthwhile, was an imposter. Her shrink wannabe and some in her group had suggested that Enya's lyrical, melancholic voice caused Sara to include gray in all her pictures, but she didn't care what anyone thought. She knew all about melancholy without the music. And now that Sara knew that, like Enya, she was Irish, she had even more appreciation for her music.

She reached into the case and gently lifted the sketch. She'd used hot-pressed paper instead of the rough-textured kind because she wanted bright colors for the carousel's chariot. The fine-grained paper would help keep colors bold and lines smooth when she added the finishing touches in pen and ink with her finest point nib.

Instead of drawing the smiling child who'd captured her imagination that day, she'd sketched Jamie from a photo, but hard as she tried, she couldn't give Jamie a genuine smile. She'd finally drawn windblown strands of dark, curly hair cascading around the corners of her mouth, so her button nose and haunting, sable eyes dominated, drawing in anyone who looked at them. She picked up her pencil and gum eraser to make a few changes. She'd placed Jamie in the center foreground and drawn the carousel in a slanting upward circle in a muted background. Jamie was the only child in focus. The rest were blurred in motion and unrecognizable. She hadn't even bothered with the details from the intricately designed carousel she'd remembered. She'd captured what was important to her—a child enjoying a carousel—Jamie, as she wanted to see her. And now she was painting the picture, hoping it would hang on a wall in Fiona's co-op. Maybe Jamie would be the bridge between Sara and her past.

She filled a few paper cups with water from the sink, set them on the table, laid down the palette, and squeezed globs of paint from her tubes. She used only primary colors, choosing the shades she liked best, cadmium red deep, cadmium yellow light, and cobalt blue, mixing them to create her own variations. Sara's painting process had become a ritual. It was often the only order in her life. She adjusted her ear buds and turned on the MP3 player then dipped her flat brush into a cup, squeezed out a bit of the red and the blue, swirling them into a misty gray. She uncapped the titanium white tube she used for lightening and squeezed a dollop into the gray mixture, dipping the brush into the water again, repeating the process until she created the shade she wanted. In wide, sweeping strokes, she covered the picture with a faint gray wash. Assembled nearby were her round and fine-point brushes, sea sponge, razor blade, and a roll of paper towels. She went from one to another while lost in Enya's melodies.

She swayed and painted, engrossed in her own world until she caught a flash of something out of the corner of her eye. She glanced up to see Stan jumping around to get her attention. She pulled out the ear buds and switched off the MP3 player. How long had he been standing there? "Sorry." She grinned and pointed to the table. "Kind of got lost in the moment. You been here long?"

"Not too." He smiled. "I've been known to zone out when I'm in the groove myself." He walked over to her painting. "Hey. Nice job."

Sara blocked his view. "I'm not done yet."

Stan backed up a step. "Keeping it to yourself till it's ready for unveiling, huh? When you're done, you might want to see Vic about a frame. He makes some really good ones." He looked at the wall clock. "Well, I've closed up shop, and I'm getting ready to head out." He walked to the door. "I need to show you what to do."

"Okay." She lagged behind until they reached the wide archway.

Stan turned to her. "You've got to exit through the main entrance. Any other door will trigger the alarm." When they got to the front door, he opened it and, as he stood in the open doorway, showed her the keypad on the side panel. "I'm going to punch in our security code. Sorry, you'll have to turn your head. Only the three top dogs are allowed the code. Woof, woof." His mouth curled in a crooked grin. "You know how it is." Sara managed a smile then looked away. A moment later, Stan said, "Okay, you can turn around now."

"You sure?" She couldn't hold back the sarcasm. She hated being the outsider in her own mother's co-op.

"Yeah, come on." As she turned toward the door, he pointed to a button on the side. "When you're ready to leave, press this button. You have five minutes to open the door without triggering the alarm. That's how Vic set it, so you have to haul ass." He grabbed the back of his pants like he was picking himself up by the butt and scooted forward to illustrate his point.

Sara wondered if he sat around thinking up these dumb gestures on his off time. Still, as corny as he was, he was amusing.

"And," he wagged his finger at her, "make sure you're really on your way out, 'cause it only works one time without the code being punched in again."

"Got it." Seemed simple enough.

"Good deal. Goodnight then, Sunny Sara."

Before the door shut, she managed a faint "Goodnight."

He tipped his head and half walked half danced to his car while she wondered how he'd seen her as sunny.

* * *

Sara stood at the office door and waited for Vic to hang up the phone. His back was to the doorway, and she couldn't help but eavesdrop. She was pretty sure he was talking to Fiona. Well, she was about to send Fiona's world rocking—she hoped. Vic swung around as he hung up the phone. He smiled when he saw her and waved her in.

"I wanted to bring you the key." She handed it to Vic. "And by the way. I'm teaching my first watercolor class tomorrow."

"Great." He reached over and hung the key on a hook near the file cabinet. "Did the room work out okay?"

"Really good, thanks again." She lifted her portfolio and opened it. "In fact, I have another request." She pulled out her finished picture.

"Let me see." Vic stood and leaned over the desk. "Hey. I like that."

"Thanks."

"Are you going to frame it?"

"Actually, Stan told me you make frames, and that was my other request."

Vic gently lifted the painting from the desk. "Let's see, it's what, an 11 by 14?"

"Yeah."

"I think I've got just the right frame for this picture. It's about the same color as the child's eyes." He smiled. "Yeah, I think it'll work just fine."

"Great." Now that she was this close, she had to take it a step further. "And I wondered if, uh, it could be hung somewhere?" There, she'd done it.

"Of course." He handed her the painting. "In fact, tonight's an open-mic night." He walked around the desk. "I'll have to get the frame from home, but I'll get it back here by say," he looked at his watch, "no later than 6:00, okay? I'll help you frame it and we'll hang it. We should get it done before things start hopping in the Hut." He threw his head back and laughed. "I mean, as much as things hop around here with only a caffeine buzz."

Sara didn't know how to respond. She was still thinking about tonight. About hanging the picture. About who'd be there. About what could happen. About, about, about . . .

Chapter 9

Tuesday, Week Three

Fiona swayed to the bluesy riffs drifting from the acoustic guitar. Stan had just whispered in her ear that her long hair shimmered like tinsel. She'd laughed, but he'd made her feel sexy, and that was just what she wanted to feel tonight. The guitarist, perched on a stool in the corner, seemed oblivious to anything but his music. Several customers sat at the Hut's small tables drinking coffee or tea, some talking, some listening to the music. Fiona looked around. There really was quite a crowd for a Tuesday night although she'd hoped the room would be packed. Maybe it was just about who was there and not how many. Jane had said she'd stop by before work, and Fiona expected her anytime. Of course, Vic would come when he got done with his office work. She had told them both that she was reading a new poem tonight, one written just for Vic. She knew he was going to like it. It centered on two of his favorite things. She smoothed her skirt and green blouse, the one that Vic said matched her eyes. Tonight was for Vic. God, she was glad that his chest pain turned out to be nothing more than a serious case of indigestion. When Fiona glanced up, Jane had arrived and was talking and laughing with Stan while he got her tea. Fiona motioned her over then leaned toward her. "So glad you came. I'm really excited about the reading."

"Glad I could make it. You've piqued my curiosity. I know you've been working hard on your poems."

"I can't wait to see Vic's face when I read this one." Fiona didn't want to tell Jane that some of the poems she'd written lately had taken such weird twists and turns that she thought they were shit. They didn't seem to have anything to do with anything she cared about. It was really strange. She'd dabbled in poetry for years, but sometimes she'd go through phases where the spark of an idea would turn into some crazy line like, *low moan crying through night's shaded room.* What was that about? She liked writing mildly erotic poetry. Poems Vic enjoyed hearing as much as she enjoyed writing. When this current poem landed on the page, she felt a tug of relief. She'd begun wondering if any decent poems were ever going to emerge from her again, and if her muse had deserted her for good.

As if on cue, the beads clattered and Vic appeared. Fiona noticed how nice he looked in the new khaki pants and navy shirt she'd bought him. Hopefully, he was wearing the Polo cologne she gave him for his birthday. She was getting heated up, and she hadn't even read his poem yet. Then Vic turned, pushed aside the beads, and took a framed picture from Sara. Sara. The girl who wanted rules changed to suit her. And Vic was perfectly willing to do just that. Fiona rose and looked at Jane. "Be back in a sec."

"Sure." Jane turned to Clem, who sat at a nearby table with Rosie, her needles clacking with each knit and purl.

As Fiona left, she smiled at Clem and said to the woman sitting at the table, "Welcome to our Open Mic night. I'm Fiona."

The woman smiled and said, "I'm Charly," then nodded toward Rosie, "Rosie invited me. We're neighbors."

"Well, Charly, we're glad to have you," then she turned to Rosie. "You know, not everybody wants to hear your clicking needles. People are here to enjoy themselves, and I'm sure you want Charly to hear the music and readings."

"Humph." Rosie rested the needles on her lap. "I don't seem to be bothering anyone but you." She picked them up again and resumed knitting.

"We'll see about that." Fiona smiled at Clem and Charly, but turned off the smile as soon as she walked away from the table.

As Fiona turned and headed toward Vic, she heard Rosie say, "Can you believe the nerve of her?"

Well, nobody was going to disturb her reading, that's for sure. Fiona caught up with Vic as he looked for a place to hang the painting. He had installed hooks in the studs around the Hut and even in the hallway, so the artists could display their work.

Ignoring Sara, standing alongside Vic, Fiona said, "There's an empty hook over there," and pointed to a spot in the far corner. She hooked her arm in Vic's and glanced at the picture of the young girl with caramel-colored skin, dark curly hair and even darker eyes, sitting in a carousel's chariot. "This yours?" she asked Sara.

Sara nodded, and Fiona turned her attention back to Vic, who seemed to be sizing up angles.

* * *

"I think the light might be better here." He stood near the counter and looked at a location reserved for the best displays. Then he smiled at Sara. "I like this picture." He turned to Fiona. "Don't you?"

She shrugged.

"You don't recognize the location?"

"Should I?"

He turned back toward Sara. "Tell her."

Sara cleared her throat and murmured, "Pier 39. San Francisco."

"Well." Fiona looked directly at Sara. "Not a place I spent much time." She untethered her arm from Vic's and waited while he hung the painting. She didn't like the front-row billing Sara's picture would get in this prime location, but she could see Vic wasn't going to be deterred. No problem. After her poem, she had a feeling she'd have more sway. She could be patient, despite rumors to the contrary.

"Perfect." Vic nodded at Sara.

Yeah, just perfect, Fiona thought, as she folded her arms. "The reading is going to start soon. Jane's here. I got you a table front and center." She ignored Sara, hoping the girl would be on her way now that she'd gotten what she wanted out of Vic.

Vic smiled at her. "Great."

Now that was more like it. She sidled up close to Vic and began walking him toward the table.

He stopped abruptly and turned to Sara. "You're going to stay, aren't you? Fiona's reading a new poem."

Sara looked at Vic and Fiona then shrugged. "Sure."

Fiona fumed as she led them to the table and introduced Jane to Sara. Tonight she didn't want Vic distracted. She knew how Vic was. It wasn't that she didn't trust him. He'd always been flirtatious. Or as he would say, helpful and considerate. But he didn't cheat on her. That she was pretty sure of. So why was she so bothered? Let it go. Focus on the reading. Fiona was determined not to let this turn of events bother her. Vic's poem. Yes, he was going to enjoy it. He always liked her poems. He said so. Over and over. In the Hut, in the car, in the bedroom . . .

* * *

As the musician was playing his last song, Fiona moved toward him, nudging Rosie, reminding her to keep the needles quiet.

Fiona waited near Sara's newly hung picture, which she ignored along with the twisting in her gut. As the song ended, she grabbed the mike. "Good Evening." She stepped back as it trilled. She smiled and tried again, this time not quite as close. "Glad you enjoyed Devon Richter. We hope to have him back again soon." She clapped and the audience followed suit. While they were clapping, the musician bowed then pulled coins and bills from his guitar case and gently set his guitar in it. Fiona stepped to the corner where they stored the wooden podium Vic had made and began pushing it toward the mike. She grunted and looked at Vic for help, but there he was laughing it up with Sara, well, and Jane. She sucked in her breath and shoved the podium next to the mike. Her plan was to introduce the other writers and read her own poem last.

Everyone quieted down and listened while she announced the first reader. Between readers, she sat in a chair off to the side of the mike. She would have liked being able to see Vic, Jane, and Sara. Well, really just Vic and Sara, but they were sitting to her left and glancing at them would be a noticeable movement.

When she stood at the podium after the last reader, Fiona said, "Thanks to all our talented writers. I'd like to close with a poem I wrote for someone very special." She flashed a grin at Vic. "The poem is titled 'Sex and Margaritas'." When she looked up, Vic and Sara were whispering. Fiona cleared her throat, and they looked at her.

She had memorized the poem and didn't expect to have to look at her note card, but the distraction left her a bit flustered. How was she going to see Vic's reaction if she had to focus on the words in front of her? She'd just have to check out his reaction when she finished. She smiled and, with as much enthusiasm and flourish as she could muster, read:

"The air an aroma of sizzling steak
and peppers, the sun a bikini of light. Hunger springs
like a tiger from the gut of the jungle. You plunge
ice into tumblers, splash
Cuervo into the mix. The cubes dance
like stars somersaulting from their night sky portrait.
We stretch out on the porch like fat
gold cats. Waiting
for more."

Fiona looked up and was glad to see just about everyone looking back. Everyone but Vic. He was leaning over the table toward Sara. Fiona gritted her teeth. "This concludes our reading. Thanks for joining us."

Everyone clapped. Fiona looked at Vic, who had turned around when the clapping began. When he caught her eye, he clapped and smiled. Damn him. He hadn't paid a bit of attention. What had he been doing? Oh, she knew what. Fiona looked at Jane. She was nodding and smiling. Fiona managed a half smile in return. When she looked back at Vic, he was talking to Sara and pointing at the painting.

Fiona marched over to the table and looked only at Vic.

"So, what'd you think?"

"Oh, Babe, very nice, very nice."

"Nice? What was the poem about?"

"Well, sex and margaritas." He reached for her hand, but she pulled it away. He wasn't getting off that easily. "Babe, you know those are two of my favorite things." He winked.

As far as she was concerned, the way she felt at this moment, he could just do without both for a long time. Vic pulled out a chair for her and she sat down. She glanced at Jane and Sara. Jane was looking at Sara and nodded her head in Stan's direction. The two women got up and walked toward him.

"Seems to me your two favorite things are Sara and her picture of some brat." Out of the corner of her eye, Fiona saw Sara stop. She didn't turn around, but Fiona knew she must have heard. Well, too bad. She was Vic's accomplice.

"What is it with you tonight?" Vic stared at her. "Don't tell me you're jealous."

"No. I'm not jealous." Seemed like she always had to explain everything to him. Was the day never going to come when he would get it? "I wrote this poem." She pointed her finger at him. "For you. I wanted you to enjoy it."

"I did enjoy it."

"You were distracted."

Vic pushed a strand of Fiona's hair back from her face. "Read it to me tonight. It'll be just the two of us. No distractions."

Fiona knew it was as close to an apology as she was going to get. Vic's behavior disappointed her, but there wasn't a damn thing she could do about it.

"Okay. Tonight. My house. Bring gifts and your best groveling voice."

"I'll be there as soon as I finish up here."

"Fine. I need to talk to Jane." Fiona saw Jane talking to Stan, but Sara was nowhere around. Jane saw Fiona and nodded bye to Stan.

"Sorry about the scene with Vic."

"No problem. Did surprise me, though. I thought you guys were the perfect couple."

"Perfection's overrated." Fiona was surprised herself. She didn't realize Jane thought that about Vic and her.

Jane smiled. "Well, I've got to get going, but I really enjoyed the reading. Thanks for inviting me."

"Thanks for coming."

Jane turned to leave but looked back at Fiona. "Hey, tell Sara bye for me, okay?" She looked at Sara's painting. "She's good. I really like this painting, and I'm not a kid-person." She smiled then walked toward the door.

Sara this. Sara that. Fiona looked at the picture again. Though the little girl was riding on the carousel, she didn't look happy. What was it in those dark eyes? Fear? Boredom? Why should Fiona care what it was? She turned away. It was Sara's painting and it had taken Vic's attention. Attention he should have showered on her, but she couldn't help looking at the child again. The little girl's lips were partially covered. You couldn't see if she was smiling, and the look in her eyes pierced you. It was like her body was a shell and beneath that shell lurked something intense. Some kind of . . . hunger. That's the only word Fiona could think of. Hunger was what looked back at her from that painting.

She turned and there was Vic talking to Sara. That girl could appear out of nowhere. Well, Fiona wasn't going to talk to her again tonight. She turned to see Stan loading a tray for the dishwasher he used when the place was busy. "Hey, Stan. Need a hand?"

"Oh, I'd be careful with that kind of language." He raised his eyebrows and grinned. "You know I can always use a hand." He looked toward Vic. "But, Fiona, my darlin', while I appreciate your offer, I humbly decline as I cherish my life more than my need." He cracked up while Fiona's face reddened.

"You're too much, Stan."

"That's what all the ladies say." He carted the tray through the swinging door into the small kitchen, grinning all the way.

Fiona sat there for a moment, waiting for Sara to leave or for Vic to come find her, but she gave up and huffed her way to them.

She leaned into him and wrapped an arm over his shoulder. "Darling, don't you think it's time for us to close up and go home?" He looked at her. "My bed's warm." She winked, ignoring Sara. That ought to show her.

"I can hardly refuse that offer." Vic grinned at Fiona then turned back to Sara. "Guess I'd better move things along here. Glad you stayed."

Sara looked uncomfortable. "Yeah, uh, me too." She backed away from the table. "I liked your poem, Fiona."

Fiona forced a smile.

As Sara began to leave, Clem caught up with her, and the two of them left together.

"Ah, alone at last." Fiona cooed in Vic's ear. Now she had what she wanted.

Walking to the jukebox, I pass a handsome blond at the bar. I tuck my hand in the pocket of my khaki shorts and clutch a handful of change. I pass this corner tavern every day on my way home from work and haven't stopped even one time, but seeing the young boy in a cowboy hat pushing his little sister's stroller outside the pavilion today, made a thirst rise. Three drinks later and I'm grabbing four quarters, so I don't have to listen to any more sorrowful country songs. I look at the jukebox selections while I feel the handsome man's eyes on me. My skin is warm from the gin and my head feels like it's stuffed with cotton. Carly Simon's "You're So Vain" woos me. I smile, knowing that he's still watching. I turn the knob that flips the cards and stop at Van Halen's remake of "Pretty Woman." Seems like a good choice. I select it. Then there's the Bee Gees' "Night Fever." Risky message, but I press the number anyway. I can't pass up "Something" by the Beatles. My big brother loved the Beatles. He played their albums all the time and the music drifted through the wall separating our bedrooms. Thanks to him I grew to love their music too. I can still picture my brother's exaggerated imitation of Ed Sullivan announcing them on his show. I laugh and decide chance is mine tonight. I turn and tell my admirer that I have one more selection. He slides off his barstool and stands next to me. His thigh grazes mine as he reaches around me. He chooses "Light My Fire," and I think he's every bit as sexy as Jim Morrison was.

He holds out his right hand. "Dance?" I smile and nod as he wraps his arms around me. He tucks my hair behind my ear then whispers, "I'm Bruce." My lips brush his cheek as I tell him, "That's a nice name." I think I must be acting as giddy as the gin is making me feel, but I don't care. It feels good to be holding a man who is holding me and not to worry about what else is happening on a planet that, like my head, is spinning through space. I lean into Bruce's shoulder. He pulls me closer, and I whisper my name in his ear.

Chapter 10

Wednesday, Week Three

It was well past noon when Sara woke up. Her watercolor class would begin in less than two hours. Even though she expected only a small group, she was nervous and stood under the shower extra long to let the warm water calm her.

After last night's reading, Sara and Clem had strolled along the riverfront. Clem said the path was one stretch of the Greenway Belt the city was constructing for hikers and bikers. He'd laughed at his rhyme and told her he'd been around Stan too long. Under the lampposts' light, Clem had turned and pointed out where the USS LST ship was moored. On their long walk to the casino's pavilion, Sara squinted through the dim light at a pagoda-shaped museum and a War Memorial encircled by plaques. They came to a one-way road that dipped down to the river, and Sara couldn't see anything except shimmering water and shadowy outlines.

"So what's down there?" Sara had asked Clem.

"That's the newly remodeled plaza where people can launch their boats. Can you make out the bleachers from here?"

"Not too well. I'll have to come back during the daytime."

"Maybe we can come for the Fourth of July fireworks," Clem had said, "but we'd have to come early because the bleachers will be packed."

"Fireworks, huh?"

* * *

Sara turned off the water and grabbed a towel. As she dried off, she remembered what she hadn't told Clem. Fireworks could be in her future, but they may not have anything to do with the Fourth of July.

Clem couldn't know what his company had meant to her last night, especially after Fiona's attitude at the reading. Clem even told her how good he thought her painting was. Sara appreciated his compliment but didn't want to go into detail about the girl in the picture being her daughter, and Clem hadn't asked. She was somewhat surprised when he invited her to church. She'd politely declined but didn't share her tainted religious views. Clem may not get her to church, but he may just give her pause about long-held grievances. He'd been kinder to her than anyone else she'd met in this town.

In fact, when Clem mentioned church, it reminded Sara about her sponsor's message. A local church, St. John's, located downtown, held regular AA meetings. She should return his call, but then she'd have to either go to a meeting or admit she hadn't. Besides, without some money to pay the phone bill, she wouldn't be able to call anyone, and another week's rent was due first anyway. She'd get to a meeting soon enough. She got dressed, grabbed her wallet, and left for her class.

When Sara approached Vic's office, she heard Fiona and Vic talking. The last person she wanted to see right now was Fiona. She stood outside the open door for a moment, trying to gain courage. Ninety-nine . . . ninety . . . eighty-three . . . Finally, she had no choice. She could leave and return after the class, but Vic may not be around then, so she stepped into the doorway and knocked.

Vic was sitting at his desk and looked up. "Come on in, Sara." Fiona stood behind him.

"Sorry to bother you," she forced a faint smile, "but I wanted to bring you next week's rent."

Sara counted the bills into Vic's hand, and he stuffed them in a bank bag. He turned to Fiona. "Babe, would you put this in the safe while I record Sara's payment?"

Fiona pursed her lips and grabbed the bag, looking at Sara. "When do you think you'll be able to pay monthly? We're not a motel, you know."

"Fiona," Vic chastised.

Sara gulped. "I know. But, I thought . . ."

Vic interrupted. "It's okay."

Sara wondered if he was talking to her or to Fiona, who stood by the desk clutching the bank bag. Then he smiled at Sara. "I know it's only temporary. By the way, how's the other job going?"

"Fine. Not as many hours as I'd like, but maybe things'll pick up here after today."

"That's right. You've got a class this afternoon. Good luck."

"Thanks."

Vic smiled as he tapped away at the keyboard. Fiona still hadn't moved toward the safe.

Sara could tell Fiona wanted her out of there, and she couldn't think of any place she'd rather *not* be. She turned toward the door.

"Close it on your way out." Fiona's sharp words stung as Sara stepped out of the office. She wanted to slam the door. Deep breaths.

* * *

Sara stood at the head of the oblong table, three smiling women surrounding her. "And so, now that we've sort of gotten acquainted, I have a suggestion about today's session. How about a trek to the riverfront to sketch?"

Myrtle, a plump middle-aged woman in a nylon jogging suit, spoke up first. "Well, I don't know. It's kind of hot today."

"Oh, Myrtle," her younger, thinner friend, Thelma, poked her arm, "we can use the exercise. It's not a long walk. Leave your jacket here and roll up those sleeves."

The youngest woman, Kim, who looked to be around Sara's age, pushed back her chair and stood. "Let's go."

Sara handed each woman a sketchpad and grabbed a box of sharpened pencils. "I saw a train at the riverfront. It's an old L & N with several cars, including a steam switch engine and a 1900 caboose. I think it'd be a good place to start."

* * *

The women sat on the grass sketching and chatting. Sara didn't add much to the conversation but listened intently. Myrtle dominated with her concerns about her eight-year-old granddaughter's grades slipping since her son and his wife had separated. Myrtle elaborated on the situation and how worried they all were about the girl. She directed her comments at Thelma but looked at Sara and Kim for nods of agreement. Sara couldn't help but think about Jamie and their situation.

"Sara Jenkins." The Social Services clerk clutched a file and looked at the bevy of people in the waiting room. Sara stood and walked toward the door. "This way." The clerk led Sara through a maze of cubicles to a tiny area cordoned off by vinyl folding curtains.

Sara slumped into a metal chair and waited for the social worker. Deep breaths. She'd never accept not getting Jamie back, no matter what.

After losing Jamie to the system, she'd ended up in jail for public intoxication and then fired from her job. She'd finished court-ordered rehab two days ago and was living in a halfway house on Guerrero Street.

"Sara Jenkins?" A familiar voice interrupted Sara's thoughts. "I'm Mrs. Parker." She frowned and looked at the file. "Have you been here before?"

Mrs. Parker. Of course. Sara said, "No, but you know me from San Mateo County. Sara Jones."

A sign of recognition flashed across Mrs. Parker's face. "I remember you. How long has it been?"

Sara took a deep breath. "More than a dozen years."

"I won't lie to you, Sara. I'm terribly disappointed to see you here."

"I know," Sara mumbled. "But, here I am. Send me to another social worker if you want."

"Do you have a problem working with me?"

"No."

"Okay then." Mrs. Parker thumbed through Jamie's file. "I see your daughter's in foster care. Why don't you tell me what happened."

"I was tending bar, but then, well, I got fired."

Mrs. Parker squinted as she read through the file. "It says here you left your four-year-old daughter with a neighbor. She called after three days." Mrs. Parker sat back. "So, do you want to start over?"

Start over. That's exactly what she wanted to do. Sara filled in the details and hoped Mrs. Parker would have some sympathy.

"What about the baby's father?"

"He's out of the picture."

"I'm sure you want your daughter back." She opened the file. "Let's see what we can do."

Recalling that day as if she were still sitting next to Mrs. Parker, Sara nodded at Myrtle, having no idea what she'd agreed with.

"See, Sara agrees. I told you ladies."

Thelma said, "Myrtle, you always think you're right."

Sara leaned toward Myrtle and glanced over her shoulder. "That's a good sketch. You really captured the caboose. It'll make a great painting."

Myrtle smiled and held it up. "You think so?"

"Definitely. You've got talent." Sara stood and went to the other two, praising their work as she stooped to observe what they'd drawn. "Looks like you've all done a good job. Think we can begin painting them in our next class?"

In a chorus, they chimed, "Yes," closed their sketchpads, and stood, wiping off the dirt and grass. Myrtle held out her arms for Thelma's help, and Sara half expected Myrtle to tumble over her. She could picture them rolling down the embankment, arms entangled as Myrtle's weight propelled them.

* * *

Jane climbed into her Jeep and turned the ignition after meeting with her boss about schedule changes. The engine responded with a low whine. She tried again. Click, click. She punched the steering wheel. Why hadn't she taken her dad's advice and bought the rechargeable Jumpstarter? She hadn't even bought cables after she turned down his offer to buy her some. She pulled out the key. No sense flooding the engine. She headed back inside. A loan officer told her he had cables in his car, but he had a customer who was completing an application, so she'd have to wait till he was done. She flipped open her phone and dialed the Hut. Someone would be there, most likely Stan. It rang twice before she heard Stan's familiar voice.

"Hi there, you've reached Addicted to the Arts. If your addiction runs along different lines, you've got a wrong number, but . . ."

"Stan?"

"Yes, this is Dandy Stan-Your-Stained-Glass-Man . . . hang on a minute."

Jane heard muffled voices and figured Stan was waiting on a customer judging by the whoosh of the latte machine and clinking of cups before he came back on the line.

"Still there?"

"I'm here, Stan. It's Jane."

"Hey, Jane-not-so-plain, what's up?"

"I'm at the bank and my battery's dead. Anyone there with jumper cables?"

Jane could tell Stan was busy by the background noise and chatter, and it took a few seconds for his response. "I'm sure there's someone here who can help, but I'm swamped at the moment. Can you hang tight for a few?"

"I'm just down the street. I'll walk over there."

"Okay. Ciao."

* * *

Jane cut across the co-op's parking lot and didn't see Fiona's VW bus or Vic's Bronco. She walked down the alley, stopping to toss a couple of fast-food wrappers in a trash can.

The aroma of fresh coffee filled the Hut, and Jane looked toward the counter expecting to see Stan, but instead saw Sara filling an order. Jane got in line behind the last customer.

"Hey, Jane, what's your poison?" Sara asked.

"Oh, I don't want anything to drink. I was looking for Stan. He said someone here might have jumper cables."

"Oh, well, he had to run to the office, so I'm covering for him." Sara turned to Iris sipping her tea. "Hey, Iris, can you keep an eye on things for a few minutes?"

"Sure, Dear."

"Come on, Jane, I'll take you back there."

* * *

Before they entered the office, Sara pulled the schedule from the bulletin board and looked at Jane. "Got a couple of changes to make." She cracked open the door. "Stan, someone here to see you."

"Well, then, fair lady, I bid you enter." Jane followed Sara in. "Jane-not-so-plain. I see you made it here in record speed."

"Sure did."

"Haven't had a chance to ask around about cables."

Sara spoke up. "I have cables. My car is out back if you can wait a few minutes. I'm almost done making changes." She looked at Stan. "That is, if you're done here. Iris is in the Hut. Don't know how long she can stay."

"Yep. Just about."

Jane sat down and asked Sara, "Are you sure you don't mind?"

Sara shook her head. "Not at all."

"I really appreciate it." Jane kicked off a tennis shoe. "Fee isn't working today?" She looked for the wastebasket.

"Fee?"

"Sorry. Fiona. I call her Fee." She shook her tennis shoe, and a pebble dropped into the wastebasket.

"I see." Sara drew in a deep breath. "She was here when I stopped at the office earlier." Sara coiled a lock of hair until it was tight against her scalp. "When I left, she was mad as a hatter." Sara let go of her hair. "About like she was at the poetry reading."

Jane raised her eyebrows but didn't say anything. She wondered what the deal was with Fiona. "Oh." She slid her foot into her tennis shoe.

Sara snatched the schedule from the desk. "There, all done." Sara and Jane said goodbye to Stan. Outside the office, Sara tacked the revised schedule back on the bulletin board.

* * *

Sara got in her Toyota and scooped up some empty bottles, fast-food sacks, and torn envelopes from the front seat then reached over and unlocked the passenger door for Jane. She turned the key and the car sputtered a few times before the engine caught. "Guess Ol' Bessie here isn't in too great a shape."

"Sure it's okay to jump my Jeep? Because I can always call my dad."

"Nah, it'll be fine. Might be a problem with the starter. The battery's new." She revved the engine and drove off. When they came to a red light, Sara turned to Jane. "So, how long have you known Fiona?"

"As long as we've been neighbors. A few years."

Sara nodded and stepped on the gas as the light turned green.

Jane asked, "How long have you lived here?"

"Long enough to know that there's not much to do." Sara laughed. "You have any ideas?"

"Not really."

"Why not?"

"I work nights, so I'm kind of upside down. Although that may change, according to my boss."

"I guess that'd make it hard to go with the flow." She screeched to a halt at a stop sign. "Unless, that is, you're going upriver."

Jane laughed and nodded. "Turn right here." They drove half a block then Jane pointed to a parking lot. "Here we are. My Jeep's over there."

Sara swung the wheel so sharply that Jane slid and only stopped short of banging heads with Sara because she grabbed the seat belt loop.

"Sorry! Forgot to mention I'm not much of a driver. Haven't driven much the last several years."

Jane looked at Sara and grinned. "I can believe that."

"Only got my license again when my boyfriend, well, ex-boyfriend, gave me his car." She hit the brake and put the car in park.

As they got out of the car, Jane said, "That's the kind of ex-boyfriend I want," and laughed.

"Trust me. He owed it to me." Sara popped the hood then got the jumper cables from the trunk while Jane went to her Jeep and unlatched the hood.

Jane walked to where Sara was uncoiling the cables. "Do you know how to do this?"

"Sure do. My ex, Ramón, made quite a production out of showing me how to use them." Sara snapped the cables into place on her battery. "Again and again,

I might add." Shaking her head, she looked at Jane. "As if I didn't have it down after the first try." She walked over to the Jeep and attached the cables, showing Jane where they went. "Okay, now start her up."

Jane stepped into her Jeep and turned the key. The motor turned over. "The proverbial kitten," she said.

"Meow," Sara answered and they both laughed.

Sara tossed the cables back in her trunk.

"You should let me buy you a beer for this." Jane slammed the hood while the battery charged.

"Not necessary." Sara wanted to add, really not necessary, and please don't offer again. Guess it's a good time to cop to not drinking. "I don't drink." There, now she'd committed herself to sobriety. Her AA group would be proud, especially her sponsor. "But I could have a Coke."

"Okay, but you made me realize that I don't even know a good place to go."

"I work at Jerry's over near the co-op. You want to meet there one night?"

"Sure, that makes it easy. I get off around 1:00 a.m. Will that work?"

"Should be fine. Things are usually slow by then, so Jerry will probably let me quit a little early."

"When do you work next?" Jane asked.

"Tomorrow."

"Want to meet then?"

"Sounds good."

"Great! Thanks for all your help. Now, it's off to Pep Boys." She waved as she drove off.

* * *

Sara turned the key in the ignition. After a few sputters, it started, and she reached for the Marlboros in the glove box, pulled out the lighter, and lit up. Meeting Jane again like this was quite a development. She knew Jane and Fiona were friends, but she hadn't realized how comfortable their relationship was until she heard Jane call her Fee. She flicked ashes out the window. Jealousy surfaced, and she struggled against the thought that she'd been so easily replaced. No mother had ever replaced Fiona. Instead, Sara had searched for comfort with friends. She leaned back and took a deep drag. Her face paled as the ghost of thoughts past hovered overhead like the seagulls she remembered from Pacifica.

> The three teenage girls huddled on the fishing pier at Sharp Park. The smoke from their cigarettes blended with the morning fog rolling in. "So where'd you go to school before?" the brunette asked Sara.
>
> "Colma." Sara blew smoke. "Just for a short time." She took another drag. "Before that, Daly City."
>
> The freckled redhead lit another cigarette. "Why'd you move?" She handed the pack to the brunette, who had pilfered it from her mother's carton.
>
> Sara sucked in hard and didn't answer. Just then, a bald man carrying a pole and a sloshing, bucketful of fish approached them, glaring. Sara pulled the cigarette out of her mouth. "What are you staring at? Mind your own business." He

frowned at Sara's outburst. "Go on. Leave us alone before I tell someone there's a perv on the pier."

The man began walking away then turned. "You'll be lucky if I don't report you three delinquents."

"Get outta here." Sara shouted at his back.

The brunette stood. "We'd better leave." She darted a quick look at the redhead, who nodded.

"Why? What can they do to us for skipping a day of friggin' school?" Sara held out the cigarette and waved it in the air. "And for smoking? At least it's not mary-ju-wanna."

The two rebellious girls who'd befriended Sara got up. "We really gotta go. Our parents'll kill us if they find out."

Sara waved them off. "Go on then. I'm not going anywhere."

"Will you be at school tomorrow?" the redhead asked.

"Not if I can help it." Sara threw her butt over the rail then craned her head toward the girls. "Hey, can I bum another cigarette?"

Throwing the pack to Sara, the brunette said, "Sure, you can have the rest. If Mom or Dad catches me with cigarettes, I'll be grounded for life." The redhead nodded and the two waved goodbye to Sara.

Lighting up another smoke, Sara figured the most she had to lose was her current home. She was used to that. She'd actually liked living with the Pfingstons. She felt like she was in a real family for the first time since Leah and Jon. Then Pop

P. got hit by a drunk driver and Mom P. had to spend so much time taking care of him that they couldn't keep her.

Sara tapped the cigarette on the railing and watched the ashes fall into the ocean. The drone of the waves blended with the haunted screeching of seagulls. She looked up at the flock. Flying shadows.

Flying shadows. A ghost traipsing past. A memory of fleeting comfort. Sara took one last drag then flicked the butt out the window. She watched it twist through the air before landing on the pavement intact. The fine tobacco leaves were securely stuffed in the paper. A desperate smoker could still manage a toke or two. Despite being tossed, the butt could still serve its intended purpose. Funny how some things of worth were so easily discarded.

Shafts of fading sunlight sparkle like diamonds on the brackish waters that border the restaurant. I sit at the bar alone, shoring up my nerve with gin and tonic. I'm early; he's not late. Glancing at the clock behind the bar, I know I have time for one more. I nod at the bartender and chug the rest of my drink as he ambles toward me. Giving me time to finish, he wipes the counter while he walks. I slide my glass to him. He picks up gin in one hand and tonic in the other and pours them together into a clean glass. I push a ten across the counter and when he pulls change from the register, I wave my hand and shake my head. Nodding thanks, he pockets the tip before turning to a customer hailing him from the end of the bar. A musky-smelling stranger climbs onto the stool beside me. "Hello," he says, but my eyes say don't bother. *"Can I buy you another drink?" he asks. "I'm meeting someone," is my dismissive answer before I swerve away from him. Why did I come so early? I'm not good at this anymore. I ignore his grumbling as he moves away. I wonder why I agreed to this dinner. It's not something I usually do. In fact, I haven't done it in more years than I want to remember. Years I want to forget.*

* * *

I down the rest of my gin and tonic and step off the stool to escape. When I turn toward the door, I see him. His chocolate eyes melt my resolve to go. Or is it the gin? We walk toward each other, he with a broad smile and I with a pasted one. I can still leave. Make some excuse. A headache. An upset stomach. My hands sweat, and I rub them on my jeans. "Hello," he says, and I can't move. "Have you been here long?" he asks, but my mouth is sewn shut in a Raggedy Ann smile.

Chapter 11

Wednesday, Week Three

Jane checked the clock on the dash after the new battery was installed. She had enough time to go to her mom's and confirm her bridesmaid's dress. Might as well get it over with. Elizabeth had caught her off guard the other day when Jane answered the phone without checking caller ID. Now it was official. She was included in what her mom no doubt considered the Wedding-of-the-Century. It probably hadn't been Elizabeth's idea. Jane had a feeling Eddie was tired of Winnie's harping and pressured Elizabeth to include her. Just great. Now she'd have to wear some ugly dress and march down the aisle of some pompous church with a pasted-on smile.

Today had already been a bust, so she had a good excuse to cut the visit short. Jane didn't want to spend any more time than necessary on this wedding. Especially now when she was worried about her dad. She wondered if her mom knew that his cancer had returned. They had a funny after-divorce relationship. After his first cancer scare, Jane's mom asked about him all the time but would then act irritated and say that he never did take care of himself, that getting him to go to the doctor regularly would take an act of God. But if you peeled back the anger, it was superficial, like a scab protecting a wound until it could heal, except hers never did. Sometimes Jane couldn't help but think that her mom felt guilty about the divorce.

Her dad hadn't wanted it, but he didn't fight her. Just let her go. Jane would never understand that—never.

* * *

Jane parked in her mom's driveway. When she saw the closed living room drapes, she knew she should've called first. She got out and rang the doorbell then waited a few minutes before pulling out her cell phone. Before she punched in her mom's number, there was Mrs. Gentry, right on cue, as if she could sniff out anything different in the neighborhood.

Jane waved. "Hi, Mrs. Gentry. How are you today?"

Mrs. Gentry approached the driveway. "Are you the lady from Goodwill? You've gone to the wrong house." She pointed across the street. "I've got two bags of clothes ready to go."

"No, Mrs. Gentry. It's me, Jane."

Mrs. Gentry stared at her.

"Winifred's daughter."

"Jane, yes . . . well . . . Jane. You're the one getting married?"

"No, that's Elizabeth."

"Yes, I remember. You're the other one."

Jane shook her head. "Always nice talking to you, Mrs. Gentry." She wondered if the sarcasm was lost on the nosy neighbor.

Mrs. Gentry looked Jane up and down, appraising her t-shirt and jeans. "Well, you know you're welcome to these clothes if you want them. Those people from Goodwill said they'd be here at 3:00 and it's 3:05 now. You'd think they'd be more responsible." She hobbled back across the street.

Jane punched in her mom's number, but before the phone rang, the front door opened. "Jane?" Winifred said, moving her hand so Mrs. Gentry couldn't see the half-filled glass she was holding.

From across the street, Mrs. Gentry shouted, "A little early for cocktails isn't it, Winifred?"

Winifred raised her glass. "I'm just having a little Hawaiian tea."

"Yeah, and she only puts a little white wine in it. Never too early for a wine spritzer, is it Mrs. Gentry?" Jane suppressed a laugh as her mom shot her a dirty look. The day was no longer a total bust.

Mrs. Gentry mumbled something about manners then turned her back to them.

"Why did you do that?" Winifred asked as she and Jane walked inside.

"What?"

"She's old and set in her ways. Now she'll be leaving information about AA on the door and lecturing me on the merits of a twelve-step program!"

"Just tell her to mind her own business."

"I can't do that. She's my neighbor for heaven's sake, and she has powerful friends."

Jane rolled her eyes as she followed her mom into the kitchen. "Yeah, you've told me that about a hundred times, but the real reason you don't want to make her mad is that her two sons do business with Eddie, and you don't want to take any chance on them pulling their accounts. Might mean a few less spritzers."

"You mean Edward, and I can't believe you're talking to me like this."

"Oh, Mom, lighten up."

"Mother." Winifred corrected and poured more wine into her glass. "Elizabeth would never talk to me like that."

As Jane opened the refrigerator to grab a bottle of water, she mimicked her mom's words. But when she shut the door, she faced her mom and faked a smile.

"Speaking of Elizabeth, her wedding plans are going great. She's narrowed down the bridesmaids' dresses to three styles and wants everyone's opinion before she makes the final decision. For the color, she chose aquamarine, which will really accentuate her eyes."

"Aquamarine? Get real. Anyone can have aquamarine eyes if they pop in the right contacts. Anyway, she's not wearing the dresses. Is she including lenses for us so we'll all match?"

"For heaven's sake, can't you be nice? You never try to get along with her. She's the one who always puts forth the effort, trying to make this a family, trying to be thoughtful." They headed into the living room. Winifred walked over to the mantelpiece and picked up a Hummel figurine of a little girl holding a flower basket and a doll. "See what she and Laurance gave us for our anniversary?" She cupped it in her hands and carried it to Jane.

Winifred shoved the Hummel at Jane. She read the inscription: Forget Me Not, "You've got to be kidding me." God, her mother was dense. "On *your* anniversary, she gives you a Forget-*Me*-Not Hummel, and you think she's being thoughtful?"

Winifred grabbed the Hummel. "I wish you were more like her." She carefully placed it back on the mantle then breezed past Jane. She snatched her wine glass and gulped down the rest of her spritzer. "Sometimes I just wonder." She shook her head. "I wonder where I went wrong. I must have. I surely must have for you to have turned out so spiteful and inconsiderate."

"Really? You're the pot calling the kettle black!"

Winifred glared at Jane. "That's no way for a daughter to talk to her mother." Winifred clenched her wine glass. "Elizabeth's been more of a daughter to me than you've ever been." She slammed her wineglass on the table and it shattered. "See what you've made me do? You're nothing but your father's daughter. Why do I even bother with you?" She stormed out of the room, leaving Jane alone.

Jane was stunned. They'd had arguments before, but her mom had never been cruel. She wanted to run from the room, but her legs seemed rooted to the floor. Was her mom really disowning her own flesh and blood? She was at the door before realizing she'd even moved. She slammed the door shut behind her. When she got outside, she stood for a moment then turned and looked at the house. No Winifred to stop her.

* * *

Jane screeched to a halt in her driveway, but before she made it to the front door, a high-pitched, "Oh Jane . . . Dear . . ." whistled from across the street. She could pretend she didn't hear. After all, she'd had enough for one day. Jane didn't want to have to deal with Mrs. Peabody too. But then a louder trill burst through the screen door, "Yoo hoo . . . Dearie . . . hello-o." She'd better go see what Mrs. Peabody wanted or her phone would be ringing the minute she stepped through the door. Once Mrs. Peabody wanted someone's attention, her focus was like a bloodhound on a rabbit. Jane crossed the street and forced a smile.

Mrs. Peabody stood, puffing her salt-and-pepper hair. "Hello, Dear. How are you today?" She pushed open the screen door. "Can you come inside for a few minutes?" She stepped back, squashing her ample bottom against the front door.

"Sorry, I don't have time now because I have to get ready for work."

"Well, could you just come in for a second?" Mrs. Peabody pleaded.

Jane went up to Mrs. Peabody's porch and peeked inside as her neighbor pointed to her living room. Stacks of clipped coupons were spread out on the coffee table. A pair of scissors lay next to a coupon holder. "I want you to look through these coupons and tell me what you can use."

Jane stepped back. "I really can't." She looked at her watch. She couldn't waste time explaining her day to Mrs. Peabody.

"Okay, then, Dear." Mrs. Peabody closed the screen door but stood behind it.

Jane ignored Mrs. Peabody's sad expression and turned to leave. As she got to the bottom step, her conscience got the better of her and she turned around. "I'll come back tomorrow, I promise." Jane pulled the keys from her pocket and jangled them in her hand as she headed for home.

"Okay, Dear, I'll leave the coupons out for you. And I'll have some special treat." Jane turned to smile at Mrs. Peabody just as her neighbor shut the door.

Jane had never seen Mrs. Peabody venture outside the house, but she wasn't a gossip. In fact, she often said, 'I don't cotton to hearing any,' whenever someone tried to fill her in on the neighborhood news. Likewise, she never shared much about herself. Maybe that's why no one knew if she had any children or what had become of Mr. Peabody. Except maybe Albert. They'd been neighbors longer than anyone else on the block and seemed to be friends. He mowed her lawn in the summer, shoveled her walkway in the winter, and was her all-around handyman.

Oh well, Jane thought, as she closed her front door and hurried to get ready for work, tomorrow she'd make good on her promise.

Chapter 12

Thursday, Week Three

Sara had swapped shifts so she could sort the new batch of books with Fiona. She was going to face Fiona with the truth. No more stalling. Time to sink or swim. She picked up a copy of *The Great Gatsby* and flipped to the end. ". . . borne back ceaselessly into the past." It was like Fitzgerald had transcended time and space and written that line just for her. She closed the book and stared at the front cover, a deep blue face with gold eyes and a painted red mouth, hovering above an explosion of light. She set the book aside to start an F pile.

A cardboard box full of children's books looked like the next project to tackle. She picked up one about a cat named Pumpkin. Jamie had this book and loved when Sara read it to her. Sara was flipping the pages as Fiona walked in.

"Good read?"

Sara held up the book for Fiona to see.

"Aren't you a little old for that?" Fiona stood with her hands on her hips.

"My daughter has this book. She loves it." Before she realized it, she'd let Fiona know she had a daughter. Oh well, this was the time. She'd promised herself. "She's with, uh, friends." Okay, okay. Getting there. Getting there. And hitting so close to home. Surely Fiona couldn't let this coincidence pass her by. She waited for a response, but Fiona reached into the box and pulled out more books then pointed to a row of empty shelves. "Let's start over there."

"Do you have any kids?" Why did she say that? Now how could she expose the truth without looking like a complete idiot? Well, it was time, one way or the other. Surely Fiona wouldn't deny the truth when asked.

Fiona stopped. She didn't look up for several long seconds.

"That doesn't concern you." Fiona turned her back and slapped books into pile after pile.

Sara slipped out of the room. How dare she. Not concern her? Before she could enjoy a false comfort that at least Fiona's answer wasn't a flat no, she was at the office door. It was unlocked. Vic wasn't there. No one was. She needed to talk to Jamie. Right now.

* * *

"Okay, I love you, Jamie." Sara sucked in her breath, pulled out the picture she carried in her pocket and traced one of the hearts that bordered it. Jamie had colored it for her before she was taken away. Just then the office door creaked. Sara looked up to see Vic standing in the doorway.

Vic's left eyebrow arched, and he didn't move.

Sara knew he expected an explanation. She shoved Jamie's picture into her back pocket. "Sorry, Vic. My cell phone's screwed up, and I needed to make a call." She couldn't tell him she'd practically camped out last night at the nearest Sprint store to pay the bill first thing this morning. She'd gotten an evil look as the clerk counted out the ones and then seemed pleased to tell her it had already been shut off, but they'd have it back on sometime tomorrow for sure.

"Well," Vic stepped into the room and closed the door, "I'd appreciate it if you'd ask first." He brushed past Sara and dropped the schedule on his desk. Sara was aware of all the red marks and strike-throughs on the current schedule since she'd probably marked it up more than anyone else. She couldn't help it if her job at Jerry's had to come first right now. She needed it to pay the bills. Sara had to cancel several shifts at the co-op because Jerry's other employee was having babysitter problems. She planned to tell Vic she'd make up her time the week after. Hopefully, things would be better then. She didn't want to hang around long enough for Vic to realize most of the changes were hers, so she hurried toward the door. Just yesterday, when she returned from helping Jane, several members were huddled around the bulletin board, grumbling about the schedule but had hushed when she walked by. Vic frowned as he looked over the schedule. It seemed he'd forgotten she was there. As she edged closer to the door, he looked up at her.

Sara smiled but lowered her eyes. This was no time to get on Vic's bad side. "I really am sorry, Vic, but you weren't around, and I didn't think you'd mind since the office door was unlocked." Sara knew if the door was unlocked, Vic was somewhere in the building, but she had expected to get the brush-off from Jamie's foster parents again. It figured that the one time she shouldn't have called, would be the one time they'd let Jamie talk.

Vic wagged his finger. "Just make sure it doesn't happen again." Then he smiled. "So have you met some guy who can't live without you?"

"What?"

"It's just that you seem distracted, and I couldn't help but hear the tail end of your conversation."

"Oh." Sara's face turned red, and she wound a lock of hair up to her scalp.

"Sorry. It's none of my business."

So, he thought she was talking to a boyfriend. She began rubbing one hand over the other. "Oh, no, nothing like that. It's . . . nothing like that." She crossed her arms and hoped he wouldn't press her for more information.

"You don't have to explain. I was just teasing." He stood then stuffed papers into a zipped folder. Sara was glad he had an appointment.

Just then Fiona stormed in. "Vic," Fiona looked at Sara, "Sara needs to get back to the bookstore. I'm taking a break."

Vic looked at his watch. "You're taking a break? We just got back from lunch a little bit ago."

"So?" Fiona swung around and headed for the door but stopped before opening it and looked at Sara. "When you agree to fill in for someone's shift, you're expected to be there for the full shift, no excuses."

"I was just heading back."

"You'd better hurry. Here's the key. I'll get it back from you later." With that said, Fiona was gone.

Sara clutched the key and hurried out of the office as she heard Vic's computer shutting down. She wished everything in her life could be handled as simply as walking away. Close a door, poof, problem solved.

Chapter 13

Thursday, Week Three

Marv sat up in bed and rubbed his face, as if he could erase the tiredness, then nudged Rusty. "Come on old boy. We need to get going." Rusty jumped down and wagged his tail while Marv followed him out the door. "Go on, boy." Marv held the gate open for Rusty then went back inside and headed for the bathroom to inspect his face. Lately, he hadn't worried about shaving every day. A little stubble made him feel right at home with the students, but today he wanted to look presentable. He'd taken a personal day for his doctor's visit this morning, but he had other plans, too. After turning it over and over again in his mind, he'd decided he would stop by the co-op for a chat with Fiona. He thought she might be able to help him find his sister. If not, she surely wouldn't be upset that he'd asked. He remembered her saying that she was usually at the co-op selling crafts or books if she wasn't leading a workshop. He hoped she'd have a few minutes to spare. In the past he would have worried about bothering her, but his way of thinking was changing.

People always said you never knew what could happen, and wasn't it true? Though he'd been surprised the first time he got cancer, this time it was a shock. And what about other things in his life? He never thought when he married Winnie that they'd end up divorced. Weren't there always things that came out of left field? He sure hadn't expected his baby sister to leave and then quit calling, or to just plain disappear, but that's exactly what she'd done. He always thought she'd come back. When she was ready, that is. But it wasn't looking likely.

Now, he worried about how Jane would react if he were to die. He shivered, but not from the cold shaving cream on his face. He was thinking about things needing to be taken care of. Things he knew he had to do.

* * *

After leaving his doctor's office, Marv decided to take the scenic route down River Drive to see Fiona. The city had really revamped the riverfront. Now he could drive down into the plaza and park by the water. Marv thought that one day soon he would bring Rusty down here, maybe take a sack lunch, relax, enjoy the view, and let his old dog go for a swim. But his reason for coming downtown quickly overshadowed everything. He wanted to see his sister, and he needed help finding her.

He parked his old pickup on the street in front of the co-op. A rainbow-colored sign, Addicted to the Arts, hung above the door. Marv walked into a foyer that opened into a wide hallway with clusters of cushioned chairs. He looked through the archway and saw several doors and had no idea where to go. A table nearby was covered with bright orange and green flyers, announcing the co-op's hours, events, and what specialty items were available this month. Marv grabbed one. Steam from a mug captioned an invitation to try *the best coffee or tea in town* at the Java Hut. An easel stood in the corner with a picture of a sax player and a date he was set to play at Java Hut. Marv walked through the hall where two women sat on oversized chairs. He saw a sign: Swapper's Fare, glanced at the flyer and read that this was where the book swaps were held. He peeked through the open door and didn't see Fiona. Java Hut's beaded entrance was across the hall. He'd try that last. Handiwork House was next, and as he walked by, he saw hand-crafted items but no Fiona. In the back were rooms with the letters A, B, and C above their doors. The C door was open and he looked inside. On top of two oblong tables were stacks of palettes, canvasses, tubes of paint, and coffee cans filled with brushes. Blue padded foldout chairs skirted the tables, making the room look ready for an eager group. Since no one was there, Marv headed to Java Hut. As he zigzagged his way across the Hut, he looked for Fiona. He didn't see her and approached the man behind the counter. "Is Fiona working today?"

"Yeah, she should be here after lunch." He turned to a man hunched over a newspaper. "Isn't that right, Vic?" The man looked up and nodded.

"Thanks," Marv said.

The man named Vic folded the paper and got up. "You want me to give her a message? I'm meeting her for lunch."

"No, I'll just come back. Thanks again."

* * *

Fiona pulled on Pet's leash as he ran toward Albert. "Hi, Albert," Fiona said, as Pet tried to jump on him.

Albert's baseball cap hid his downcast eyes and covered his balding head. His scrawny arms were stretched to accommodate stacks of flattened cardboard boxes he was taking to his backyard. He shifted from foot to foot, swaying as if unable to stand still. "H-h-hello." No one on the block knew much about Albert, except that he was an avid recycler. Fiona and other neighbors had found him sifting through their garbage cans for recyclables and were now used to his nocturnal scavenging. He stacked everything in piles in his backyard and when he had enough of one type of material, he loaded it pile by pile into the rusted bed of his Ford pickup and presumably hauled it off. Until then, they sat like giant ant hills in his compact yard. Since Albert never invited neighbors into his home, Fiona sometimes wondered if his house had as many stacks as his yard and garage. He didn't have a job that anyone knew about, and his age was indefinable. No doubt he was over fifty, but he could even be in his sixties. Fiona suspected that he received a disability check. Beyond that she was mystified as to how he survived. Sometimes she and other neighbors would bring him a plate of food, with some excuse so he wouldn't be embarrassed. They often told him it was a thanks for something or other he'd done. For instance, on garbage days, they never had to worry about the wind scattering their empty cans because Albert always returned them to their rightful spots.

"Say, Albert, I've got a few boxes you can have if you don't mind coming over." Fiona had a kiln and pottery wheel in her shed and was always ordering materials, so it didn't take long for the boxes to build up.

"O-o-okay." He set down his stack on his front lawn and turned like a robot toward her house.

Fiona looked at her watch. She would have enough time to send Albert on his way with the boxes before leaving to meet Vic for lunch at Los Lobos del Rio, their favorite Mexican restaurant.

* * *

Fiona had already downed one margarita and was enjoying the brightly painted murals of women in colorful skirts and white peasant tops and bullfighters standing ready in front of charging bulls when Vic arrived.

"Sorry I'm late." Vic motioned to the server, pointed at Fiona's empty drink, and raised two fingers before he slid into the booth.

"Well, what took you so long?" She licked the remainder of salt off the rim and reached for her water.

"Had to deal with a scheduling mix-up." He dipped a chip into the hot salsa.

"I can just guess who the mix-up involved." Fiona crunched a chip. "Rosie's not only nosy she's also a royal pain in the ass."

Vic shook his head. "Now, Babe, put your claws back in." He laughed. "She's not so bad." He dipped another chip. "Some of her complaints may have merit." He wiped the salsa that dripped on the table then reached for her hand. "Anyway, we're not here to discuss business. Let's just enjoy lunch, okay?" He lifted her hand and kissed it.

* * *

Fiona was straightening books when Marv walked in.

"Hi, Fiona."

"Marv?" A book slid from Fiona's hand. "Hi, how are you?"

He caught the book and handed it to her. "All right for an old geezer." He stepped back and grinned.

"Oh, Marv, you can't be an old geezer because if you are, what does that make me?" Fiona smiled. "What brings you down here anyway?

"Actually, I was wondering if I could talk to you for a few minutes. Maybe when you get your coffee break?"

"The only coffee break I get is when I decide this old behind needs a rest and that would be about now. Just let me get someone in here to cover for me."

"I don't want to be any trouble."

Fiona flicked her wrist. "No trouble. Why don't you head on over to Java Hut, and I'll meet you there in a couple of minutes. Do you know where it is?"

"Sure do. I'll get us a table. Are you drinking coffee or tea today?"

"Don't worry about that. I'll take care of it when I get there."

* * *

Fiona fumed. Sara was supposed to be helping her shelve books but had disappeared not long after Fiona got there. Fiona locked the door and went to the office. There was Sara talking with Vic. The nerve of that girl. Fiona felt her face heat up.

"Vic," Fiona looked at Sara, "Sara needs to get back to the bookstore. I'm taking a break."

Vic looked at his watch. "You're taking a break? We just got back from lunch a little bit ago."

"So?" Fiona swung around and headed for the door but stopped before opening it and looked at Sara. "When you agree to fill in for someone's shift, you're expected to be there for the full shift, no excuses."

"I was just heading back."

"You'd better hurry. Here's the key. I'll get it back from you later."

* * *

Fiona backhanded the beads to the Hut, leaving them crackling behind her.

"Everything okay?" Marv asked.

"Yeah, everything's fine. You know how it is. Always some problem to deal with in a place like this."

"Well, I sure don't want to bother you."

"No bother." Fiona patted his hand. "Let me get us some coffee. Anything special?"

"Just black and strong."

* * *

Fiona returned with their drinks. "So, Marv, what's on your mind?"

Marv held the mug close to his face and blew at the steam. "I need to find someone." He stared at his mug. "My kid sister. I haven't seen her in years. I was hoping you could help me find her through the internet."

"Well, Jane is better at that sort of thing than I am."

Marv hesitated. "Well, truth be told, she doesn't know I have a sister."

Fiona choked on her coffee, and Marv reached over and patted her back. She snatched a napkin and wiped the drops that dribbled down her chin. "I see." Marv leaned back in his chair. Fiona twisted her napkin before answering. "I'm not too great with computers but how about we get on Vic's and check it out."

When they got to the office, Vic was gone. Fiona knew his appointment would take a while, so she was confident she'd have the office long enough to help Marv. She flipped the Do Not Disturb sign and ushered Marv inside then pointed to a chair. "Have a seat."

Marv shifted in his chair while Fiona booted up the computer. "My sister's been gone a long time. For years I thought she would come back, you know, when she was ready." He looked down.

"You don't have to explain. Let's just type in her name and see what happens."

"Her name's Glenda Louise. I don't know if she ever got married, so I guess go with Heffinger."

Fiona focused on the keyboard. "Did she have a nickname?"

"Boy, did she ever." When Fiona stopped typing to look at him, he continued. "She hated her name because the kids called her 'Glenda the *Not* Good Witch,' but my personal nickname was Glenny. Guess I've always liked adding *y* to names." He grinned.

"Did she use 'Glenny' at all? Because I'm not getting anything for Glenda." Fiona looked at Marv for guidance.

Marv shrugged.

"I think there's a way. . ." Fiona leaned back and stared at the ceiling trying to recall something she'd read or heard about searches. "Oh, let's try Glen with an asterisk." She fingered the keyboard. "It's like a 'wild card' in case of incorrect spelling or a typo."

"Whatever you think'll work."

After a few minutes of pecking away, Fiona frowned. "Sorry, still nothing." She paused. "Do you know any Glen Heffingers?"

"No. We've got relations spread out here and there, but we never had those family reunions, so could be relatives, but I don't know, and I can't imagine Glenda would go by Glen. No, no, Glenny would never go by a boy's name. She may've been somewhat of a tomboy, climbing trees in the woods near our house, but she loved playing with her baby dolls best. And helping Mom in the kitchen. When she asked me to play with her, she never agreed to play cowboys and Indians with me—ever."

Fiona decided against mentioning the possibility of his sister using the name Glen for safety purposes. Marv didn't seem prepared to think too far outside the proverbial box. She began typing again. "I'm getting some possible different last name spellings, but unless they're typos, I don't know what to say." She turned to Marv and asked, "And you don't know if she got married?"

"Never got an invite to a wedding." He seemed deflated when he spoke. Fiona guessed he'd expected to see the day when he'd sit in a church full of fragrant flowers and smiling faces.

Fiona leaned back in her chair. She was trying to decide which question to ask first but didn't want to be nosy. Oh, who was she kidding? She'd never been shy before. "You're such a nice guy, Marv, how'd you end up estranged from your sister?" There, she'd done it, and with a little kissing-up. Wouldn't Vic be proud? Marv twisted in the seat. Fiona began to feel guilty. Maybe she hadn't been so diplomatic after all. "Never mind. It's really none of my business."

Marv stopped squirming. "No. It's okay." He looked down at his shoes. "I think I really do want to talk about it." He straightened up. "She was quite a bit younger than me. Fact is Mom lost a baby in between us two, a girl, born dead. I think she never quite recovered from that. I was too young to remember much before the baby, but I know life was a lot more fun then. Mom started going to church soon after." Marv furrowed his brows and looked up at Fiona. "You grew up here, right?"

Fiona nodded.

"Then maybe you heard of the church. The House of *Divine* Deliverance." Marv exaggerated in mock adoration, rolling his eyes.

Loud laughter from the hallway drifted in, and Fiona was glad she'd locked the door and put up the sign. "You mean that storefront church that used to be downtown?" Marv nodded. Fiona measured her words carefully because she remembered the church well. She and her friends made fun of it when she was growing up. She took a deep breath. "I never personally knew anybody who'd actually belonged to it. I was in the group that smoked pot and listened to Dylan."

Marv shook his head. "That place kept me away from any church ever since."

"So you had to go, too?"

"Oh yeah. When Mom got religion, she didn't keep it private. Even poor ol' Dad had to go, 'cept when he could weasel out of it."

"So, by the time Glenda was born, your mom was a full-fledged member?"

"Sure was." Marv looked down again. "But it was more than that with Glenda. It was like she could never be good enough, or do enough to please Mom. I kind of think Mom always looked at Glenda and saw the baby girl she'd lost. Leastwise, I think that's where the problems began."

"Makes sense. Your mother could fantasize the baby who died into perfection. Poor Glenda didn't stand a chance."

Marv nodded. "And attending church didn't change that. See, when it came to church, I got off easier than Glenny did. I had Dad to fall back on. We found ways around getting too involved, sometimes a friend who needed help. Mom would balk, but Dad would remind her 'bout charity. 'Course sometimes that friend was just a fishing pole needing to be baited and thrown into a lake." Marv smiled but it quickly faded. "But, and I guess both Dad and I have to share the blame, Mom forced her religion on Glenny, and as long as she did that, Dad and I were off the hook, so we just left things alone, you know?" He cleared his throat several times.

Fiona got up, thinking about how many times she had just left things alone rather than take action. She opened the fridge, pulled out a bottle of water, and handed it to Marv.

"Thanks." He twisted the cap and took a drink.

"Sorry, I should've offered it to you earlier." Fiona sat back down. "Did the church have something to do with Glenda leaving? That is if you don't mind me asking?"

"No, no, it's fine. The church probably had more to do with it than I care to admit. But there were other things too. Life has that way of piling up hurt and bad circumstance and a person just can't always seem to find a way to grab onto the good that's there." Marv sighed. "See, Dad died, and then I moved out. And as Glenny got older, she got wilder, sneaking out at night. Then staying out all night. But, if all that wasn't enough, she took to staying away for days, coming home all mussed up because she'd been God-only-knows where. Well, I probably don't have to tell you they fought like the dickens until Glenny found a guy to move in with, which really drove Mom nuts, and then they hardly talked to each other." Marv took a sip of water. "By that time I was married and busy with my own life. I guess I didn't realize how bad things were with Glenny or didn't want to know." Marv shook his head. "I only saw her one time before Mom got real sick. She was out of it on something. I was furious at her. That wasn't no way to. . ." Marv coughed and took another sip of water. "Anyway, I was busy with Mom, and I didn't check up on Glenny. Didn't see anything of her for months. By the time Mom passed away and I went to Glenny's apartment, she was, well in a state I can't talk about." Marv's words floated like a raft drifting toward shore and his face went slack.

"You okay?"

Marv nodded and took a deep breath. "Then, not long after that, she was gone. Disappeared. I found that fella she took up with, but he was no help. I haven't seen her since. 'Course, she called a few times years ago and talked to Winnie, but Winnie never could make heads or tails out of what she was saying. After that—nothing."

"That's sad."

Marv nodded. "She drank quite a bit when she was still living at home, so who knows what she got to doing down the road. I recall her stumbling in late sometimes when I was visiting over to the house. Mom would just scowl. Not sure what happened after I'd leave. Until Glenny moved out of Mom's house, she was stuck going to that church, and coming up through school she got teased constantly for the way she dressed." Marv finished his water. "One thing I remember, and this might help us find her 'cause maybe she's into it in some way, she really liked plants." He set the bottle on the desk and leaned back. "We had gone to Florida one year, the only real vacation I remember, and Dad, ever the family gardener, got Mom to let him take us to an orchid show."

Fiona flinched.

"Is something wrong?"

"No." She averted his eyes and twisted in her chair. Some words could still cut deeply. "You were saying something about your sister's love of, uh, orchids." She reached for her water.

Marv was silent till Fiona set the bottle down. "After that, Glenny was obsessed with orchids, but Mom wouldn't let her grow any plants. Mom always threw

Jesus and working for Him at her. I guess Glenny had to rebel."

"What a story."

"Yeah, and how do you tell your daughter that she has family she never heard of, you know?" Fiona was silent and Marv continued. "But Janey is so much like her." Marv's face got a pained look. "That's why I want to find her too. For Janey. I should have tried years ago." Marv stood to leave. "I'd better go. Thanks again." He gave Fiona a quick hug.

She squeezed his shoulder. "I'll keep trying, Marv. Maybe we'll get lucky." She wanted to comfort him with soothing words, but she'd never been great at that kind of thing, so they walked in silence to the front door.

"Scotch on the rocks," I tell the bartender.

He smiles and says, "No gin and tonic tonight?"

I shake my head and watch his heavy hand pour the scotch, filling the tumbler higher than he should. "Thanks," I say, shoving a ten across the counter. He winks and nods before I swivel around and scan the tavern. He knows to keep the change. I tip well when I drink, and I began drinking as soon as I left work today. I lift the glass and think of the half-empty bottle of J & B hidden under my passenger seat. Gin and tonic is where the cycle starts. Scotch comes later. A swig or two a day, just to unwind. It's one of the things that landed me in this small town so long ago after six months of sharing a shelter with cockroaches and thieves. Finally, I was dried up and working again.

When my eyes adjust to the darkened tavern, I see his blond head in the crowd. I take another sip. Should I go over and say hello? I begin to step down, but then he bends slightly and twists, and I see a mass of auburn curls pressed to his chest. They begin swaying as one to the music, and before I can turn around, he faces me and catches my eye. I raise my glass in a mock salute and he nods with a grin. I swing back to the counter and finish my scotch then set the tumbler down in front of where the bartender is mixing a drink. "Another?" he asks. I nod and reach in my pocket, but a hand covers mine. I look up and Bruce is standing there smiling. He throws money on the counter and sits down while I pick up my glass.

"So, how've you been?"

I glare at him. I need courage, and it's here, sloshing against the ice cubes. I take another sip before responding. "Where's your curly-haired friend?"

Instead of an answer, Bruce disarms me with a crooked grin and unexpected kiss that ends too soon. I raise the glass to my lips, throw my head back, and imagine it's not the tumbler touching my lips while I hear Bruce say, "I'll call you," as I watch him walk away.

Chapter 14

Thursday, Week Three

After Sara finished sorting and shelving the new cartons of books, she returned to her apartment and turned on the TV, flipping through channel after channel. The somersaulting of images and sounds made her dizzy. Flashbacks. Like scenes of her life. But where were the missing pieces? Today should have been the day. If not today, then when? When would she be able to claim what was rightfully hers? Her mother. She turned off the TV and paced. She couldn't start the day over. And even if she could, would it end differently? The apartment was folding in on her. Escape was what she needed. But if she went to Jerry's now, a bottle would be her escape. She'd have to find some other escape until her shift began.

She walked aimlessly. She'd expected that finding her mother would be her panacea, connecting then and now, before and after. That she would be transformed into the person she was meant to be and would finally belong somewhere. But after today, she wondered what made her think that. When she heard a truck's horn and looked up, she realized she'd arrived at a busy intersection near the river. She stepped back to the curb until the light changed then crossed the street and climbed the embankment. The wind was strong and blew her hair into a wild, tangled mass of curls. Brushing hair out of her eyes as she lumbered along the winding path, she glanced at the river and saw choppy whitecaps slamming against each other.

* * *

Only a few customers remained at the bar when Sara carried her last empty pitcher back up front. She was counting her tips, surprised at how much money she'd made, when she saw Jane walk in. "Hey, Jane." Sara looked at the clock and saw that it was past 1:00. A new day. And off to a better start.

"Hi, Sara, will you be off soon?"

Sara looked at Jerry. He nodded. She turned to Jane. "Just give me a sec."

Jane pulled out her money as Sara finished up. "You said you drink Coke, right? And I'll have a Heineken." Jane laid some bills on the bar.

As Sara got the drinks, she said, "Why don't you grab a booth, and I'll be right there."

"Will do." Jane took the drinks to the back.

* * *

While Jane nursed her Heineken, Sara sipped her Coke. Sitting with a drinker was definitely harder than serving one. Good thing she hadn't come to Jerry's earlier when she needed an escape. Coke wouldn't have satisfied then. She reached for her Marlboros.

"I thought I smelled cigarette smoke in your car."

"You don't smoke?" Sara asked, waving a cigarette. Jane wrinkled her nose. "Will it bother you if I do?"

Jane shrugged. "It's not like you're the only smoker in the bar."

Sara grinned. "You got that right. Don't worry. I won't blow the smoke in your direction." She swiveled and lit up, taking a drag and holding the cigarette away from the booth.

As they sipped their drinks, a couple of giggling girls in short shorts along with their James-Dean-wannabes walked in and headed to the poolroom. The plunk of pool balls interrupted the girls' drunken banter. Sara and Jane laughed when they heard someone holler, "Oh baby," followed by, "Yes mama."

When Jerry walked by, Sara said, "Need any help?"

"Nah, I've got it." Jerry went into the poolroom.

Sara stubbed out her cigarette. "Are you ready for another beer?

"Sure."

As Jerry came out of the poolroom, Sara said, "Would you mind bringing Jane another Heineken on your way back?"

"Okay. You ready for another Coke?"

"No, thanks, I'm good."

Jane pulled out her money and set it on the table.

Sara wanted another cigarette, but she didn't want Jane to think she was a chain smoker, so she picked up her Coke and twirled the straw. "You should've seen Stan the other day."

"What'd he do this time?"

"Well, for a change, the joke was on him."

"This I've got to hear." She sat back with her Heineken. "So, tell me about Stan-the-man."

"He was busy working and laughing like always. Then his latest lady showed up, and boy was she pissed." Sara took a sip then set down her Coke. "She was yelling and waving a red-laced teddy she'd discovered under his bed." Jane furrowed her brows, and Sara leaned in close. "Not hers, of course!" She sat back and spread her palms on the table. "She made that quite clear to anyone within a mile's earshot." Sara fiddled with her pack of Marlboros. "His face was as red as the teddy when he begged me to cover the Hut then followed her out the door like a whipped pup." Sara laughed and swung her legs out of the booth, pulling out a cigarette. "When he returned, he wasn't happy."

Jane grinned and shook her head. "I'd like to feel sorry for him, but he brings it on himself."

"Yeah, guess he won't be getting any tonight." Sara lit up. Chatting with Jane reminded her of Pacifica, the only time she remembered having girlfriends.

They were giggling when Jane's smile froze, and she set down her bottle. Sara spun around to see what had caused the change and saw a tall guy in well-pressed khakis and an oxford shirt, nod. Sara turned to Jane. "Who's that?"

He was walking to their booth right behind Jerry. "You'll soon find out." Jerry handed Jane her Heineken, and she handed him a five. Jerry turned, swerving to miss running smack into Laurance.

"Jane?" Laurance asked. "So surprised to see you here this late." He had a slight British accent.

"Laurance." Jane said his name like a declaration. "I might say the same about you." Laurance looked at Sara. "By the way, this is Sara. She's an artist at Addicted to the Arts co-op." Laurance nodded. "Sara works here, and we decided to meet for a drink when I got off work." Jane looked around. "What brings you downtown? Where's Elizabeth?"

"So, are you your sister's keeper now?"

"You mean stepsister." Jane corrected. "And not by any means am I her keeper."

"Jolly good." He laughed. "Yes, stepsister." He turned to Sara. "And my, umm, my fiancé."

"Sounded like you had a little trouble getting that last word out," Jane said. "Pre-wedding jitters?"

His face flushed and he threw up his hands. "Mind if I join you?"

Jane scooted over so he could sit down. "I see you like Heineken, too," Jane said as he lifted his bottle. "Somehow I didn't take you for a beer drinker."

"Ah, Jane, me lass, ye never knew me," he teased in a faux Irish lilt. "I'm a chap of many tastes."

"That so?" She raised her eyebrows and bobbed her head. "But you still haven't answered my question."

"Question?" He looked at Sara and winked. "To be or not to be, that is the question, is it not, Sara?"

"To be *what* or *not* to be what, is more like it." She joined in the fun.

He turned to Jane. "Ah, you see, me lass, *she* gets it." They all laughed together until Laurance piped, "So glad I popped in for a nightcap."

"Nightcap?" Sara couldn't help but think this guy was cute with his funny speech.

"Well, we Brits, you know, are a breed apart." He smiled.

Jane jumped in, "Don't you mean a sea apart?" then laughed before Sara and Laurance caught on.

"You know, Jane, you're nothing like I thought. Certainly nothing like Elizabeth . . ." He stopped and looked down.

"Go ahead. Finish your sentence." Jane stared at Laurance and he blushed. "Never mind. I know what you were about to say." Jane shook her head.

Sara shared Laurance's discomfort as Jane said, "How about another round?"

Laurance slid out of the booth. "Yes, jolly good idea. My treat." Laurance pointed to Sara's glass.

She covered it. "I'm fine. Thanks anyway."

Laurance turned and headed to the bar.

Sara whispered to Jane, "He seems really nice." Jane nodded, shrugging. "I mean, he's different, but different's not so bad. Too bad he's taken. You two tight?"

"No. This is probably the most we've ever spoken to each other." Jane looked down and quietly added, "I guess you got the message that Elizabeth and I aren't exactly bosom buddies?"

"Yeah, I kind of got that."

Laurance returned with the Heinekens and a bowl of unshelled peanuts. "I come bearing gifts."

"Thanks." Jane held up her bottle for a toast. "Three beers and a buzz. This has got to be it for me, that's for sure."

"I thought we were just getting started." Laurance lifted his bottle. "Bottoms up." He took a drink. "Thank you, God, for small favors and good beer."

"Aahh, there's the rub." Sara put out her cigarette.

"A Shakespeare fan?" Laurance questioned at the same time Jane said, "The rub?"

"Whoa, one at a time, please." Sara leaned back and pointed at Laurance. "First, you." "Yes, I like Shakespeare. Took a Brit Lit class my one semester at

City College." Then she looked at Jane. "And to your point, the rub—God, isn't *He* the rub?" They both looked at her questioningly. "I mean, growing up I was told to pray to God for anything I wanted or needed. But then I was told the answer could be no, so how could I know that God was listening?"

Laurance nodded. "I know what you mean. I was told somewhat the same thing, from my mum, not my dad. He was a bit of a skeptic." He tapped the booth. "But one time, I guess I was about ten or so, I had asked God for a bike, a shiny, new, red bike. Oh, I had my request down to a detail, that's for sure." He paused, and it looked as if he might not finish the story.

"Well? Did you get what you asked for?" Jane asked.

Sara chimed in, "You know what they say, be careful what you ask for."

Laurance looked at Sara and grinned, "Spot on." He nodded then turned to Jane. "Yes, indeed, I got the bike. But a week later, a car swerved into me while I was riding, and I spent the next six weeks in a leg cast."

Sara slapped the table. "See? What'd I tell you?"

"But that's not the question, really, now is it?" Laurance intoned, and the two women waited for his answer. He sat back and explained. "I mean, it's not just the bike, but other things over the years that I've gotten after praying. I look around and see people in wheelchairs, hear about children starving or killed by a stray bullet . . ." He shook his head. "Oh, I could go on, but you get the picture. There's so much sorrow in the world, and I can't help but wonder, even as God seems to answer a prayer of mine, who He might be neglecting in order to fulfill my request." He looked up at the women. "That's the eternal conundrum, is it not?"

Sara shook her head. "Never thought about it that way." She looked at her pack of Marlboros. "Something new to think about, I guess. But I doubt it'll be tonight. Tonight I'm so tired I'll probably sleep like the dead."

Jane jumped in. "While you guys ponder God's neglect, I'll ponder God *Her*self—I mean, *if* She exists." Her eyes twinkled. Jane feminizing God didn't escape Sara's notice, and when she looked at Laurance, they both shook their heads and smiled.

* * *

Jane left first. When Laurance got ready to leave, he offered Sara a ride, but she declined, preferring to walk home. She shivered. The day's heat had turned into an unseasonably cool night. When she thought about how the day had begun with Fiona—there was always Fiona—she cringed. She wanted so badly to get this whole thing over with. Out in the open. Decided. One way or the other. But could she handle the consequences? Surely Fiona couldn't turn her away once she knew the truth. Could she? She stuffed her hands in her jeans and hunched her shoulders as she strode along, her words to Laurance ringing in her ears, *Be careful what you ask for. . .*

Chapter 15

Thursday, Week Three

Vic nuzzled his face in Fiona's hair, breathing in the familiar scent of Patchouli Rose shampoo. She lay facing the ceiling on a damp, twisted sheet in the crook of his arm while he caressed the inner thigh of the leg she'd flung over his hips.

"Okay, Vic."

"*Okay*, Vic?" He grinned and probed farther. "How about, 'Better, ah, much better, Vic'?"

He laughed when Fiona crooned, "Yes, ahh . . ."

He continued stroking her until she came again. When her sighs subsided, and she rolled her leg off of him, he said, "Wish it was like the old days when ol' Charlie here," he touched his limp penis, "stayed hard long enough for Chastity," he reached over and lightly pinched her moist clitoris, "to enjoy a repeat performance."

Fiona turned toward him. "Such a long time we've known each other, Darling, that I know when something's on your mind. Which, by the way," she fondled his penis, "may affect old Charlie's performance—not that I'm complaining about the lack of a full-fledged encore!" She grinned then grew quiet. "But seriously, Vic, what's wrong? Did something happen when you met with the contractor?"

Vic sighed. "No." He pulled his arm out from beneath her and sat up. He knew if Fiona called him Darling when she wasn't being sarcastic, she wanted something. She wanted him to admit that she knew him better than anyone else did. He'd learned that on some level long-term relationships often came down to that. "Babe, sometimes I think you know me better than I know myself."

"So, if not the meeting, then what?"

He put his arms behind his head and rested on the headboard. "Mike."

Fiona wrapped the sheet around her and scooted next to him. "Oh." She touched his chin and turned his head toward her. "Tell me what's going on."

Vic thought for a moment. He knew more prodding would follow until he opened up, as she called it, so he might as well begin. "Not really sure, but he left me a couple of urgent messages." He looked down and shook his head. "Wouldn't you know, the one day I went off and forgot my cell phone, he called twice, and when I tried to call him back, all I got was his voicemail." He picked up the crumpled bedspread and twisted it.

Fiona grasped his hand, and he stopped. "You know kids have a flare for drama where their parents are concerned."

"But he never calls me. I'm always on him about it, but it doesn't change anything. So I know something's up."

"It can't be that dire, or he'd certainly have called you again." Fiona flipped the hair off her forehead. "Mike knows you're there for him whenever he really needs you."

Vic stared at the ceiling. "I've tried to be there. But you know Mike, if I don't ask 'how high' the minute he says 'jump,' he'll retreat to his corner and pout."

Fiona touched Vic's arm. "He just tests you because of those first years after the divorce."

"You'd think he'd be over that by now. After all, we had all those years when he came to live with me."

"Surely he hasn't forgotten all you did for him."

"You'd be surprised what kids forget." He took a deep breath. "Seems they forget a lot when they have kids of their own." He pointed to himself. "*You* become the bad guy again. You know, your mistakes are all they remember." He shook his head. "Not right away, but later, when their kids start growing up. Then they seem to forget all the good you did. They're so damn determined not to make your mistakes. That's all they see."

Fiona stroked his arm. "Well, you're close now, right?"

"Define close." As soon as the words slipped from his mouth, he regretted them. Rule number one: never ask Fiona to define anything you don't really want an answer for. He heard her voice, but he really wasn't listening.

". . . and that's what I think your problem is."

Fiona's face was right up to his as she spoke, but what the hell did she say the problem was?

"Don't you agree?"

Now she was stroking his cheek. If he wasn't careful, in a minute she'd be on to him, and he'd be up the damn creek without a paddle again. Wing it. "Well, I think the problem was that he was a teenager when he came to live with me. Fourteen, hell of an age. Sometimes I think he doesn't want to let go of the anger. Maybe he wants to carry it around like a trophy."

There. That ought to satisfy her. Couldn't get much deeper than that, right?

"Hmmm."

Uh oh, maybe he'd been way off the mark. Time for a distraction. Vic craned his neck to see what time it was, but the clock was facing the window. "What good does my clock do if you turn it away from us?"

"Don't care about the time when I'm in your bed. Especially when we're having such a good time." She batted her eyelashes.

Vic couldn't help but grin. "You're just too much, Babe."

"Watch it, buster. Them's fightin' words."

He pinched the extra flesh on her hips and kissed her forehead. "I love every inch of you." He reached around her and grabbed the clock. "And the more inches each year adds, the more I can love." She slapped his arm as he turned the clock's face. "Ouch!" He laughed.

Fiona grabbed the clock and moved it out of his reach. "Ha, ha, now you have it, now you don't."

Vic lay back down. Clearly, Fiona was determined to tease him into a better mood. It was working. How he loved her like this. Much better than the Hurricane Fiona that had almost been unleashed today at the office. Her anger used to turn him on, but these days her fury sometimes worked like a cold shower. As Fiona would say, 'It's a bitch getting old!' But getting old with her was going to be a blast. He just wasn't sure if it would explode or implode.

"Hey, Vic." She knocked on his forehead. "Anyone home?"

Vic rubbed his forehead, pretending to ease the pain.

"Lost in your thoughts?" Fiona nudged closer. "Six bucks for them."

"Oh, really? That much?" Vic held out his hand to collect his fee.

"Ha, ha."

"Ha, ha yourself. Gotta make a buck any way I can."

"Okay then." Fiona pointed to her crotch.

Vic waved his finger and laughed. "Damn, woman, I'll be happy to do that for free." He threw off the covers and swung his arm and leg over her naked body.

* * *

Vic awoke to sunlight streaming in through the flimsy curtain. He sat up and reached across Fiona to see the time, tenderly kissing her breasts before covering them.

Fiona opened her eyes. "What? What time . . . ?" She yawned.

"After 8:00. I told Stan I'd be in this morning to meet with some vendors."

"Oh, okay." She rolled over.

Vic headed for the shower. When he returned, Fiona was rubbing her eyes. "What are you doing trying to wake up at this early hour?" He kissed her forehead.

"Just remembered. I promised Mrs. Peabody I'd come over this morning. She asked if I could pick up a few things. I put her off yesterday, but she seemed so sad." She sat up and stretched.

Vic walked over, leaned down, and kissed her before he turned to get dressed. After last night, whatever was going on with Mike seemed less troublesome.

Chapter 16

Thursday, Week Three

The flashing lights of an ambulance greeted Jane when she turned onto her street after leaving Jerry's. When she stepped out of her Jeep, she saw paramedics hurry to Mrs. Peabody's door. Jane's beer buzz was instantly gone. She stood transfixed for what seemed like a long time until the paramedics emerged pushing a covered gurney. As they loaded it into the ambulance, she heard one of them state the time Mrs. Peabody expired as the other wrote on a clipboard. Expired—as if she were a credit card—that couldn't be renewed. Jane shook her head and walked over to Albert, who stood hunched against the railing.

After trying to console Albert and suffering through several minutes of his tortured explanation, Jane headed home. The relief she felt yesterday when she'd avoided Mrs. Peabody's coupon clipping was now replaced by guilt. Did Mrs. Peabody have any family to notify? Maybe Albert would know. But she hadn't asked him tonight. He was too upset. She'd never seen him sad before, but tonight he looked broken, and she wondered how deep their friendship had been. She hadn't seen any lights on at Fiona's and figured she was spending the night with Vic. Maybe later they'd talk to Albert together.

After watching the ambulance lights fade in the distance, Jane went inside and flipped on the light. She rehashed the information from Albert as she leaned against the door. Turns out he had seen Mrs.

Peabody late in the afternoon and didn't think she looked well. He'd gone home but had paced most of the evening then returned around 1:30 this morning when he saw a light on inside. She didn't answer his knock, so he went to the back door. He'd been reluctant to reveal that Mrs. Peabody kept the door unlocked. Jane shook her head as she kicked off her sandals. Who'd have ever imagined that homebound Mrs. P would leave her back door unlocked? Jane headed to the kitchen. She was also surprised that the 9-1-1 operator had been able to understand Albert. It seemed Mrs. Peabody was still alive when Albert arrived. At least he could feel good about that. He'd been a good friend.

As Jane opened the fridge, Cocoa trotted over, meowing and rubbing her leg until she shut the door and picked him up. She cradled him and stroked his head, nuzzling her face into his fur. Before she could lift her head, he squirmed and jumped down. Her buzz had definitely been replaced by a foul mood. So much for Laurance's pleasant nightcap. Jane knew she wouldn't be able to sleep, so she went into her spare room, which was filled with Earth Day literature and posters, one imploring people to help free Lori Berenson from her Peruvian jail cell, another to *Think Green*. She booted up the computer. Her old high school boyfriend, Greg, had contacted her recently and they'd been exchanging e-mails. She wasn't sure she wanted to see him even though he'd been pushing her to get together, but maybe reading his e-mails would help get her mind off everything else. His messages induced memories she hadn't thought about in years, and tonight was a good time to escape.

She clicked on the first one and read:

> **Hi Janey, my Jewel,**
> **Just wanted to tell you again how glad I am to be back in touch with you.**
> **Hope you're wanting to reconnect as much as I am.**
> **Love, Gee**

Greg, or Gee, her pet name for him, was the only person besides her dad who ever called her Janey or got away with it. My Jewel was his pet name for her in the past—what he had started calling her on those summer nights they made out in his car. They'd sit in the parking lot of the Eastside Baseball Field after a movie or some lame party, and he would grope her. But his foreplay was a challenge for glory. He'd cup her breast like it was the first fly ball he'd caught in Little League then preen like he had after scoring the home run that won the high school its first-place trophy.

Their dates slowly turned into evenings in the guest house on his parents' property while they were away. First Greg just touched her on top of her clothes—her breasts, between her legs—and would move her hand over his jeans. The night he unbuttoned her blouse, pushed her bra up and cradled her bare breasts, his heavy breathing and hardness excited her, but before he could pull her jeans down, she gently pushed his hands and sweating body away, saying, 'Not yet, Gee. I'm just not ready,' then zipped her jeans and buttoned her blouse while he headed for the bathroom. Jane had tried not to think about the release he found there when she heard his moans.

The last time she'd seen him she thought she was ready and had helped him tug her jeans off while he whispered, 'I love you,' over and over. But before he could slide her panties down and slip inside her, she said, 'No.' She didn't try to explain because she couldn't. He must have thought she was joking because he laughed and pulled down her panties. Once again she refused and rolled away from him. 'For chrissakes Jane, why not?' He had actually waited for an answer. She curled into a ball, wondering why she couldn't go through with it. She didn't know when the voice in her head start telling her good girls don't . . . He asked if she would touch him, but when she rolled over and looked at him, she froze. His angry look had frightened her, but for only a minute. Then he zipped his pants and barked, 'Let's go.' She watched his back as he walked out the door, not even holding it open for her. He hadn't said another word, even when he pulled up to her mom's house and she said, 'I love you,' instead of goodbye. Until the recent e-mails, they hadn't talked since that night.

Now, so many years later, she wondered why she had thought love and sex were intertwined like a vine through a fence. She guessed she had been too naïve to realize that the fence could be torn down and the vine still live or the vine cut away and the fence remain sturdy and firm. She hoped Greg looked back on their past with some humor, that he didn't hold her youthful naivety against her. Jane was now pretty sure the voice had come from her mother, but that voice had been stilled over the years. If only she could still her mother's voice now. Since their argument, she had let her mother's phone calls go to voicemail.

But she didn't want to think about her mother. Since Greg had contacted her, she'd begun fantasizing. Even the thought of him simply brushing her hair back from her face made her warm. She read his next e-mail:

> **Missing ya.**
> **L, G**

His third message directed her to a website where she retrieved a card with an animated heart that opened and said:

> **You're always here!**

Each one had short, simple messages or some cheesy line that he knew Jane would find funny. She chuckled when she read,

> **Me Tarzan, you Jane.**
> **The jungle is lonely without you.**

Who else could send her something that corny and still make her laugh. She hit reply and began typing, but when she hit the send key, she was knocked offline. Too tired to try again, she decided to write him in the morning. She sat back and stretched her arms, yawning so loudly that Cocoa trotted in and rubbed against her legs. "Okay, Coke, I give, time for bed, huh?" She knew he'd hop on her bed and curl up in the curve of her knees. For now, her cat's affection would have to do even though it was a sorry substitute.

I reach behind my head and turn the clock to see the time illuminated in red: 12:13. I roll over. I've tossed and turned so much that the sheet is twisted, and I try to unwind the billows of cotton from my restless legs. Finally, I stumble out of bed. Feeling my way through the bedroom, I stub my toe on an antique, cast iron doorstop and curse. The black terrier stop is heavy as a barbell, but I've taken it everywhere I've lived because it belonged to my father. Hobbling down the hallway, I mumble, "I'm sorry," and accept the throbbing pain in my toe as penance for my sins. My eyes adjust to the moonlight filtering through the blind's broken slats on the living room window in back of the cabin, so I don't have to turn on a light. Without thought, I open the refrigerator and see a half-eaten carton of blueberry yogurt with a spoon lodged in it and the lid thrown loosely on top. I take a few bites and close the door. I pace the length of my small living room until my toe stops throbbing, and my leg muscles no longer twitch. Now I want something more, and I search the cabinets. I know what I'm looking for, and I know it's not there. I scavenge the garbage can and see the empty bottles of Tanqueray and J & B. I yank them out, grab a glass, and tip them upside down, shaking out any possible drop. I can't stop even though I know I should. It's a need I recognize. A need I despise.

* * *

Frenzied, I return to the bedroom and grab the bra I left on the chair, almost ripping my nightshirt when I pull it off. I yank my jeans and a t-shirt from the closet and slip into them before slipping into the night. I'm Alice sliding down the rabbit hole.

Chapter 17

Friday–Saturday, Week Three

By the time Vic left the meeting with the building contractor, Mike still hadn't returned his call. At that point, Vic wasn't sure if he was more annoyed than worried. Just as he reached for his phone to dial Mike again, it rang. "Hello, Mike?"

"No, Vic, it's me." Fiona sounded subdued. Quite a change from her frisky mood the night before.

"Hey Babe, what's up? Did you finally make it to the co-op?" She hadn't yet arrived when he left for his meeting, so he figured she had gone back to bed after she went home.

"Yeah, I'm in the office now, but I'm heading for a class in a few minutes." She paused. "You won't believe this, but Mrs. Peabody, you know, the neighbor I was supposed to shop for today?"

"Yeah."

"She died last night."

"Sorry to hear that. You okay?"

"I'm fine. Just a little shocked. I feel kind of guilty, though, for putting her off yesterday, but that's life I guess." Vic heard Fiona sigh before she continued. "So, have you talked to Mike yet?"

"Not yet, and I'm starting to get pissed."

"I'm sure there's a good reason." He heard shuffling before she spoke again. "You coming back to the co-op later for Devon's encore performance?"

"I plan to, but right now I'm heading to the house." Vic was hot and tired and wasn't looking forward to tonight, but he wouldn't admit that to Fiona.

"Want me to come over? I can get away for a little while."

"No, I've got a few things to take care of." In truth, he just wanted some time to himself. He loved having Fiona stay over from time to time, but now he wanted to grab a nap.

Fiona's words cut into his thoughts. "Okay, but if you want to talk, you know where to find me. In the meantime, I'll cover things here."

"Thanks. Love you."

"And you."

Vic hung up before he heard her phone click. He loved Fiona but he didn't want to listen to her speculations right now. What he wanted was for Mike to clue him in. He hadn't phoned Mike's apartment in case his wife wasn't aware of Mike's distress call. She already had her hands full with their twin daughters, and Vic didn't want to add to her worries.

* * *

Vic sat in his recliner and flipped through the mail but stopped when he came across a letter from Mrs. Nathan Greenfield. Valerie. Mike's mom. Vic hadn't talked to her since Mike's wedding a few years back. He massaged his forehead as if preparing for the headache reading the letter would bring. He assumed Val's reason for writing him had something to do with Mike.

Vic leaned back in the recliner, lifted the leg rest, and ripped open the envelope. When he pulled out the stationary, a lavender scent floated in the air. Just like Val. Unfolding the letter, his mind drifted back. He shook off memories that hadn't crossed his mind for quite some time, and read:

> **Dear Vic,**
>
> **I know you must be shocked at receiving this letter. I'm equally shocked to be writing it. But since I've gone this far, let me tell you why I'm writing.**
>
> **Nate and I are separating, and he's staying in our home. Seems backwards, doesn't it? But it really was the only way. I haven't held a job since our first daughter was born, and I couldn't afford the big house.**
>
> **I know things went really sour with you and me, but I've been thinking a lot about us lately. About Mikey, Mike, as he insists now. I think about his responsibilities: wife, daughters, job, National Guard.**
>
> **I know I failed him years ago, but I want to make it up to him, so I'm moving to St. Louis. It's only an hour from here. I think if I live near Mike and his family, I can get closer to him, maybe help out some. And I think I can get a job in St. Louis. Nate will support me for a while anyway, and one of our daughters lives there now, too.**
>
> **I just thought you should know. I haven't even told Mike yet. Remember when we were The Three Musketeers? I've been thinking a lot about those days. What happened to us, Vic? Where did we go wrong? I'll get in touch soon. It'll probably be a week or so before I can move out and get a place.**
>
> **Always,**
> **Val**

Vic looked at the closing lines again. Always . . . Always, Val. He sat up. Always something. First, Mike's messages and now Val's letter. And, 'get in touch soon'? What more does she have to say? Guess he'd have to wait to find out. No other choice, it seemed. Vic glanced at the clock. So much for the nap he thought he'd get. He wasn't so tired anymore anyway. Might as well go to the co-op. Crap. Fiona. He better not let it slip that he'd heard from Val. He knew the fury Val's letter would unleash. It wouldn't be Hurricane Fiona. It'd be Fiona-the-Volcano, and the eruption would spew flames that would blister and burn for a long time. Fiona had always been jealous of Val being Mike's mother even though Fiona was anything but maternal and wouldn't marry him even if he begged her. But there was no figuring Fiona, that's for sure. Maybe he could slip into the office unnoticed and pick up the schedule to look over. Leaving the rest of the day's mail unopened, Vic headed out the door for the co-op.

* * *

Vic grabbed the schedule from the bulletin board, entered the office, and locked the door. He'd been keeping the schedule on the computer as well as the bulletin board since Clem had taught him how to use Excel, so he turned on his computer and opened the file. As he looked closely at the hard copy, he saw handwritten names on top of correction tape in five places. Comparing it to the computer file, he saw it was Sara's name that had been replaced. What was going on? He shoved the schedule aside and leaned back. He didn't need one more thing to worry about. No doubt Fiona would have something to say about this when she saw it. He decided he didn't want to sit there any more than he had wanted to stay home. A walk would do him good. He turned off the computer and locked the office door. Outside, sunshine danced on windshields, spinning glare into Vic's eyes. The day's humidity clung even as evening approached, and Vic inhaled the warm, moist air. As he began to turn off Fifth onto Riverview, he saw Sara at the door to Jerry's Place, a bar he'd never been to. She was holding the door open as an elderly man hobbled out and stepped into a waiting taxi. Vic changed direction and crossed Riverview to Jerry's. One beer sounded good, and maybe he'd find out why Sara had missed so many shifts.

A weathered man sat at the bar. Vic squinted in the darkened room and saw Sara walking to a back booth.

"Hey there, set a spell." A gnarled hand patted an empty stool next to him.

"Don't mind if I do." Vic sat down as Sara was returning. As soon as she noticed Vic, she smiled.

"Hi." Sara went behind the bar to fill her order. "What are you doing here?" She reached behind her for three mugs, set them down, and pulled the lever on the tap.

"Having a beer. At least I will be when you take my order." Vic grinned.

"You want draft?" She set three full mugs on a tray, spilling a little of the froth.

"You have MGD on tap?"

"Sure do."

"Good, that's what I'll have." Vic nodded toward the tray. "But go ahead and take care of your other customers. I can wait."

She set the tray on the bar. "I'd better get it now," she nodded at a table in the back, "or it could be a while." Vic turned and saw that they were signaling her. When he looked back at Sara, she had already filled a mug. Vic slapped a few bills on the bar as Sara rang up the beer, and he held up his hand against the change she started to give him. "Thanks." She shoved the tip in her apron pocket. "See you in a bit." Vic watched her carry the tray in the air like a pro and wondered whether this job was the reason Sara had to change so many of her shifts at the co-op. The weathered man's gruff voice interrupted his thoughts.

"I'm Cap'n. Ha'n't seen you here b'fore." He slurped his beer. "You from these here parts?"

"I am." He reached over to shake Captain's rough hand. "I'm Vic. You know Addicted to the Arts a few blocks down? That's my place."

Captain nodded. "Not that I ken say I been 'er b'fore." He smiled and a gold tooth glimmered. "Passed by't on my way here once er twice. Heard some good blues comin' outta that place."

"Sometimes we have musicians at the Java Hut. It's part of the co-op. We've got artists of all kinds who teach classes there." Vic picked up his mug. "That place is my pride and joy." He took a drink.

"Sounds innerestin'." Captain's smile broadened. "Jest ain't shure the likes 'a me would fit'n 'at place."

Vic smiled back. "Everyone's welcome." Vic pulled out his cell phone.

"'Spectin' a call?"

Vic laid the phone on the bar. "Yeah, my son left me a couple of messages, and I tried calling him back, but so far he hasn't answered."

Captain nodded.

"First I was worried, but now I'm getting annoyed." Vic threw back half of his beer.

Captain took a drink then wiped his mouth with the back of his hand. "I may not look so good on the outside here," he pointed to himself, "but two parts 'a my body are still alive 'n kickin'."

"Oh?" Vic wasn't sure what to make of this old man.

Pointing to an ear and then a shoulder, Captain said, "My ears work jest fine, and these here shoulder's're still broad 'n strong."

Vic reared back his head and laughed. "Well, Captain, if there're two things your kids make you need sometimes, they're it."

"I hear ya, son." Captain raised his mug to Vic, and their glasses clinked. "Ain't got none a ma own, but I sure helped raise a boatload of 'em over the years!"

Both took another swig of beer before Captain asked, "So what kinda hell's yur kid been raisin'?"

* * *

When Vic finished his story, he took his last sip of beer. "So, that's how it is. Mike and now his mother." He looked up to see Sara filling another order behind the bar and turned his attention to her for a moment. "Hey Sara, can you come see me in the office one day this week?" The place was filling up, and Vic knew they'd never have a chance to talk now.

"Sure." Sara quickly resumed mixing drinks. Before she stepped away with her full tray, she looked at Vic and Captain and pointed to the tap.

Vic covered his mug and shook his head while Captain shoved his toward Sara.

After Sara walked away, Captain asked, "So, is Sara part 'a that there arts place you tole me about?"

"Yeah, and she seems like a good kid. It's just a little tough with her and Fiona, my, uh, damn, I don't know what I'd call her."

"Paramour?" Captain's crinkly eyes twinkled in jest. Vic arched an eyebrow and the old man continued. "Thou hast kept the secret of thy paramour." Grinning, Captain looked at Vic. "I read *The Scarlet Letter*." He grabbed his mug. "Long time ago."

The old man had piqued Vic's curiosity.

Captain chuckled. It seemed he knew what Vic was thinking. "See, son, I lived in N'awlins years ago. Captained a tug and lived in the French Quarter with a lusty Creole barmaid. She shore did love her books." He took a swig. "Had to pick one up m'self a time or two. Some stuck right here." Captain tapped his forehead then guzzled more beer. "So, is 'at what she is? Your paramour?"

Vic laughed. This old man was chockfull of surprises. "Yeah, but don't let *her* hear you call her that." He shook his head. "She and Sara there," Vic nodded in Sara's direction, "seem to be having trouble getting along. Both a bit stubborn, I think. So that's another problem." Vic had done more talking tonight than a politician campaigning for office.

Captain nodded.

Vic looked at his watch and knew he had to get going. His phone would be ringing any time now if he didn't show up at the co-op, and Fiery Fiona was not the Fiona he wanted to be explaining anything to right now. He stood and patted Captain's shoulder. "Nice meeting you." Vic pushed the stool under the bar. "And thanks for having broad ones."

"No pro'lem."

"Stop by the co-op sometime and have a cup of java on me."

Captain tipped his head. "I jess may do 'at, son."

* * *

The next morning, Vic woke up later than usual. He ran his hand through his tousled hair and rubbed his unshaven chin. He had already gulped two cups of strong coffee and was pacing the floor in perfect time with his caffeine buzz when the phone rang. The area code on the caller ID told him who must be on the other end, and he grabbed the receiver before the second ring. "Hello."

"Vic?" When he heard the voice, he headed for the back door.

"Hello, Val." He started to park himself on the porch but knew he couldn't sit through this phone call and charged down the steps into his yard.

"Well, you don't have to sound so enthused." Val's shrillness rang through the line like a siren.

"No," he pulled weeds out of his vegetable patch, "it's not that. It's just early." He glanced at his watch. Damn! Ten o'clock. Not early.

"Since when is ten early for you?" Val sounded irritated and didn't wait for a reply. "Anyway, have you talked to Mike recently?"

"He called, but I haven't connected with him yet." Vic yanked another weed.

"Well, you know his situation."

Vic took his handful of weeds to the compost heap. When it was apparent that she was waiting for him to speak, he asked, "What situation are you talking about?"

"Oh, Vic, sometimes you can be so dense." There it was, that judgmental voice Vic remembered. No lavender scent to diffuse her shrill words now. Dense? What the hell was she talking about? And she wondered what had gone wrong with their marriage? He sighed and waited for her to continue.

"Okay. I'll spell it out for you." She stretched out the last word with her usual flair for drama and paused before adding, "Did you get my letter?"

Vic was back at the vegetable patch searching for anything to distract him. "Yeah, I got it." The longer he stayed on the phone, the more weeds he saw. How long was she going to jerk him around before she said what she had to say?

"That should have clued you in."

Reaching between the zucchini and yellow squash, Vic flinched as the sharp leaves jabbed his bare hand. Shit! He knew his voice would sound harsh, but he couldn't stop himself. "You included everything from your pending divorce, to moving, to being concerned about Mike and his family. Now would you just say what you need to say?" He could picture her toe tapping while waiting to respond.

"You did read the letter. I'll give you that."

He imagined her plucked eyebrows arched high above her mascara-thick lashes. "Val!" He cleared his throat while walking to the porch to keep from cussing.

"His unit is being called up. God, I would have thought you already knew. Or at least heard. Don't you ever watch the news?"

Vic stopped. "Shit."

"Yeah, that's right. And there's more."

Vic heard her sniffle and felt the anger rush out of him. "Just take your time." He heard her blow her nose.

"Sorry."

"It's okay."

"I hope you'll help."

"Of course. Anything I can do for Tiffany and the girls."

"No, no. I mean that's fine, but he won't let me send the letter." She was sobbing now. He didn't have a clue what letter she was talking about.

"Do you need some time? Do you want to call me back later?"

More nose blowing. "No, no. I need you to talk to him. He's the last one to carry on your name. Don't you see?"

It was still a jigsaw puzzle, but he was getting an idea where she was going.

"I want to send a letter to his commanding officer asking that he not be sent overseas. It's still on the books. Since World War II. But Mike won't let me.

Says he can't do that. The other soldiers, you know, loyalty and all."

"Oh."

"You've got to talk to him. Convince him. I told him it's not fair for him to go to war and be killed, not fair for any of them to leave their loved ones here without them."

"I'll talk to him."

"Promise?"

"I promise I'll talk to him. Believe me. I promise."

"I just hate dealing with this over the phone. We need to talk in person. Come up with a game plan. Convince him together."

Vic let that sink in.

"Vic?"

"Yeah?"

"Thanks. I know he's grown up, but he's still my only little boy. I'm sure when we put our heads together we'll come up with some way to change his mind."

"I love him too." Vic didn't add, and I love him enough to listen to his side before I do anything.

"I've never doubted that," Val said, before they hung up without a goodbye.

Chapter 18

Friday–Saturday, Week Three

Sara was sitting at the bar smoking and counting her tips when Jane walked in. "Just get off work?" Sara asked, before taking a final drag and grinding the butt into the ashtray.

Jane slid onto the stool next to her. "Yeah, and next week the schedule changes start, so I'm not in the best mood. Plus, last night my neighbor died.

"Sorry to hear that."

Jane shrugged. "She was a nice person." She stood. "Join me at a back booth?"

"Okay, just let me cash in my coins." Sara walked to the register. Hearing about Jane's neighbor, she couldn't help but think of Fiona. How was she taking the news? Maybe she'd begin thinking about her own mortality and who she'd be leaving behind. Maybe Sara had laid the groundwork at the bookstore even though it didn't seem so.

When Jerry walked over, Jane pulled out her wallet and ordered a Heineken.

"Coke for me, please, Jerry." Sara feared she'd be floating on a carbonated stream before the night ended. Jerry handed them their drinks, and the two walked to the back of the bar.

Before Sara slid into the booth, she swapped her ashtray for a clean one from another table. Cigarettes were a fierce companion of tragedy, so surely Jane could put up with the smoke tonight.

Jane sat down with her beer. "I won't be able to do this after tonight because of my new schedule. Starting next week I go in early in the morning and get off mid-afternoon. No more late nights during the week for me." She gulped her Heineken. "But I don't want to discuss work."

"You don't come here too much, anyway, do you?" Sara nursed her Coke.

"No, but it's just one thing on top of another."

Boy, could Sara tell Jane about one thing on top of another, but she could see Jane was upset. "Well, having a neighbor die suddenly must be a bit of a shock."

Jane nodded. "It's not just that." She looked down. "My dad's cancer returned, and I don't really know how sick he is. I'm really worried about him." Before Sara could offer sympathy, Jane did a 180. "Then, there's my mom. We had an argument the other day, and she keeps calling me, but I'm not ready to talk to her." She tilted her head back and swigged her beer then set down the half-full bottle. "I'm so fed up with my mom and her so-called perfect daughter." She bit at a nail. "You know, Elizabeth. My mom's manipulating ways and Elizabeth's wedding plans are driving me over the edge."

They sat in silence for a few minutes. Someone played Janis Joplin on the jukebox and they sang along out of key until they looked at each other and smiled. Forced, Sara thought, but still an unspoken mutual attempt to lighten the moment. Sara said, "I guess we won't be awarded any singing contracts."

"I was just thinking it's a good thing Jerry doesn't have Karaoke." Jane guzzled the rest of her beer. "I'm going to get another drink. You want one?"

"I'm good."

Jane stood. "I might be a few. Have to visit the little girls' room, too."

Sara hummed along to "Kryptonite" until the song ended. When nothing played after that, someone shouted, "Hey, jukebox is dead."

Dead. Like Jane's neighbor. Sara wondered about her mother's role in that neighborhood, about the relationship between Jane and Fiona. Fee, as Jane called her. They must be closer than just neighbors. Was that because of the neighborhood? It was a hard concept to fathom. A neighborhood of people who were like family. Had Fiona replaced Sara with a family of neighbors? The idea hurt like a thousand stings from a hornets' nest. She wanted to shout, 'I'm here. Choose me,' but she knew where even a step in that direction had gotten her. After Jane came back, Sara asked, "So were you close to your neighbor?"

"Not really. I mean, I don't know that anyone was close to her." Jane studied her bottle and, without looking up, continued, "Well, there's Albert. He's just another neighbor, but they lived on the block before the rest of us and seemed to be friends. He's the one who found her and called 9-1-1."

"What about Fiona? She's lived there quite a while, hasn't she? Was she close to your neighbor?" Sara swallowed the remorse that engulfed her for using this tragedy to gain information. But could anyone ever understand the desperation that came from living a life filled with so many unknowns?

"She's lived there longer than I have, but it was hard to get close to Mrs. Peabody. She didn't open up much and never left her house. Fiona and I shopped for her once in a while." Jane took a drink. "Plus, Mrs. P tried to involve us in little projects from time to time."

"How did Fiona take it when she found out?"

"Actually, Fiona wasn't home last night when it happened, and by the time I left for work today, she'd already come and gone, so I don't know if Albert's told her yet. I thought we could find out if there's anyone we should contact, but maybe Fiona's done that already." Jane shrugged. "I don't want to talk about it anymore."

Then Jane brought up an old boyfriend, Greg, and started to talk about his e-mails and their past. Sara groaned silently as she listened to Jane's pretend love life, which is what it sounded like. But Sara couldn't think of a way to exit gracefully, so she lit a Marlboro.

". . . and I don't know what to do." Jane set the bottle down and waved away Sara's cigarette smoke.

Sara blew circles away from the booth. If she had to sit through 'Greg this, Greg that,' Jane would have to endure her smoking. Sara guessed that Jane didn't know that a habit like smoking *could* possess some merit. That lighting up had often taken her out of her life. Taken her to a far-off place. A place of escape. Still, she did want to have a handle on her life without needing an escape. But she couldn't say that to Jane. She was pretty sure Jane would think she was crazy.

Jane remained silent while Sara's smoke circles drifted into the hazy barroom, and Sara drew in the last drag. Jane took a drink and looked down at the table. "Greg really wants us to get together."

"What do *you* want?" Sara hoped indifference didn't flow from her words like the Coke that spilled from the glass she'd set down a little too hard. When she reached for a napkin, she knocked over what was left. "Shit."

Jane grabbed a handful of napkins from the dispenser and plopped them on the table. "Here. I'll go get you another Coke." Before Sara could say, 'No, thanks,' Jane was gone, leaving Sara alone with a pile of soppy napkins and a soaked Marlboro.

Jane returned with two shots and a Coke. Sara stared at the shots.

"Tequila." Jane shrugged. "It was last call, and I needed something strong."

Sara focused on her Coke, popping the can and pouring the soda into her glass. Before she took a sip, Jane had done one of the shots and began complaining about her mother again. The only words Sara heard were Mom, Elizabeth, wedding, and ugly dress. Sara didn't need this, but Jane had done the other shot and was quite buzzed. When she blew her nose and Sara saw the signs of an alcohol crash and burn, she spoke. "Let's go. I'll take you home." Jerry was looking at her and tapping his watch.

"No. S'awright. I can get home."

"No way. Is your Jeep parked out back?" Jane nodded. "Good. I'll let Jerry know, and we can get it tomorrow."

As Sara carried the bottles, cans, and glasses to the bar, Jane hollered, "Reeeshycle!"

"Freaking tree hugger," Sara mumbled but rinsed the cans and bottles and tossed them in a plastic bag.

By the time they reached Jane's house, Sara had to help find her keys and get her inside. She told Jane she'd come by tomorrow afternoon, and they'd get the Jeep. As she drove off, she glanced at Fiona's house and saw a light flicker off.

* * *

When Sara pulled into Jane's driveway the next day, she noticed a woman and two children entering the house across the street. From what Jane had told her, it must be the deceased neighbor's house. The boy wiped his forehead on his t-shirt's sleeve, raking it past the shaved Z on the side of his head. The girl, several inches taller, pulled up a mass of kinky curls with one hand while fanning the back of her neck with the other.

Sara glanced over at Fiona's place and thought she saw the blinds open and close. She shut off the engine and started for Jane's house. Jane came to the door in the same clothes she'd worn last night, except now the blouse was rumpled and partially unbuttoned, and her hair was stringy. "Hi again."

Jane ushered her inside. "Guess I look scary." She ran her fingers through her hair.

Sara threw her hands in the air. "Not saying a word."

"I can't believe I got so drunk last night." Jane gestured for Sara to sit. "Guess it was because I didn't eat anything on my lunch break. That'll teach me."

"So it didn't have anything to do with the two shots of tequila?" Sara cocked her head and raised her eyebrows then laughed.

Jane grabbed her temples and shook her head. "Don't remind me. Speaking of drinks, can I get you something? Less lethal than my two shots, of course." She laughed along with Sara.

"I'm good. Already had a cup of coffee at the Hut."

"What time is it anyway?"

"Around 2:00." Sara had driven around last night after taking Jane home, so she'd slept in this morning. Her mind had been reeling with how Fiona's neighbor's death might make Fiona think about her own life. "I figured you'd want your Jeep before too long."

"True, but do you mind if I get cleaned up first? I feel grungy. I'm good for a two-minute shower."

"Go ahead." Sara picked up a *Sierra* magazine lying on the coffee table and flipped through page after page of gray wolf, polar bear, greening, and global warming articles. She looked for another magazine and saw *Nature Conservancy*. Guessing Jane had no *People* magazine to browse, she mindlessly leafed through the pages.

In less than ten minutes, Jane, towel wrapped around her head, came down the hallway, zipping her jeans. "See, told you I'd be quick." She unwrapped the towel and grabbed a brush from her purse then ran it through her wet hair, and said, "I'm ready."

When they stepped outside, Fiona was on her porch talking to a woman. Fiona noticed them and motioned them over.

Sara told Jane, "That lady was going into the house across the street when I got here."

"Oh, Mrs. Peabody's house. You mind if we go over for a minute? She might be a relative."

"That's fine. That's the neighbor who died, right?"

Jane nodded and they walked across the lawn.

As they approached the porch, Fiona said, "Hi, Jane." A definite delay followed before she added, "Sara."

Sara thought this couldn't have worked out better. A chance to see Fiona away from the co-op. Maybe even to go into her house. See how she lived.

The rail-thin woman with red-rimmed eyes turned around. Fiona said, "This is Rebecca, Mrs. Peabody's daughter." Fiona grabbed Jane's arm. "This is Jane, she knew your mother, too." Then she seemed to remember Sara standing nearby. "Oh, and that's Sara. She doesn't belong here. I mean, she doesn't live here. She didn't know your mother."

Sara tried to smile as she shook the woman's hand, but she couldn't forget the words, 'she doesn't belong here.' They sliced into her heart like an axe splitting wood.

Fiona turned her back on Sara and spoke to Jane. "Rebecca was just telling me about the funeral. It's Monday, with the viewing before the service."

Rebecca looked like she was ready to burst into tears. Jane said, "I'm so sorry for your loss. Your mother was a kind woman."

Fiona chimed in, "Yes, she was," and patted Rebecca's arm.

Rebecca smiled faintly at her then broke down. Fiona asked if they wanted to come inside. The perfect hostess. Rebecca pointed across the street. "I have to keep an eye on the children."

Fiona said, "We can sit here." They walked to the porch glider, Sara trailing behind. It had room for only three, so Sara leaned against a splintered post.

Before Jane sat down, she looked at Sara. "You can sit here."

Sara waved it off, and as the other three sat on the glider, she slid down the post and sat on the top step.

Jane said, "Fiona, care if I grab a chair for Sara?"

Fiona looked at Sara. "You need a chair?"

"Don't bother." Sara could tell by Fiona's glare that she wasn't going to bother anyway.

Fiona twisted in her seat, turning her back to Sara. Maybe *this* is where Fiona thought Sara belonged. Sitting like a dog left to fend for itself. As if on cue, a dog barked from inside, and Fiona got up and let him out. His wagging tail thumped the guests as he ran from one to the other. When he started sniffing them and licking their hands, Fiona ordered, "Pet, sit!" He obeyed and now sat eye to eye with Sara. Fiona looked toward Pet and said, "Good dog."

Sara looked away and saw Rebecca dabbing her eyes as she said, "I'm sorry to drop this on you, but I really don't have anyone who would understand." Sara noticed how Fiona nodded at Rebecca's every word. "It's just that I feel so guilty."

Fiona patted her arm again. "I'm sure you did all you could for her."

Rebecca kept shaking her head. "No, I didn't. You don't understand."

When Rebecca buried her head in her hands, Fiona put her arm around her, and Sara couldn't believe how concerned Fiona seemed to be with this woman's loss. A woman she didn't even know. Where was Fiona's concern for her own daughter? Sara could tell Fiona a thing or two about how it felt to lose your mother, and wouldn't that get her attention. How could Sara have thought that any good could come from all this?

Then Rebecca reached in her pocket, pulled out another tissue, and blew her nose. "I'm sorry, but I just have to tell someone." She crumpled the tissue and crammed it in her pocket. "See, my mom and I had some disagreements, so I didn't come see her like I should've. But it was more than that." She paused. "I knew something that I couldn't tell her." She looked at Fiona then Jane. "I don't know what you know of my mom."

Jane said, "Not much, except that she never left the house." She shrugged. "And that she wasn't a gossip and didn't listen to any, either. Oh, and that she and Albert seemed close."

At that, Rebecca cringed. "Albert. Brings back bad memories, but maybe when I tell you the story, you'll understand." She smiled faintly. "Sorry I said that about Albert. It's not really him I'm upset with. And yeah, Mom would be tightlipped, that's true." Fiona smiled as Rebecca turned toward her. "I don't want to bother you. I'm probably keeping you," she added while they shook their heads.

"Oh, no, you go right ahead," Fiona said.

Sara had to look away.

"My parents," Rebecca continued, "were Baptist missionaries in Central America when I was young."

"Wow." Jane said while Fiona looked surprised. "I didn't know that."

"Well, they were, but then, my dad, he disappeared one day." Now their eyebrows rose in unison, and even Sara was curious. "He went to visit some church members who lived in a remote village in Nicaragua, and that was the last we saw of him." She sniffled. "You can only imagine what that was like, but I'll skip the sordid details. See, Mom never knew," her voice broke and it took a minute for her to recover, "what happened." She sighed. "Dad contacted me several years ago but made me promise not to tell her." Now Jane and Fiona looked as stunned as Sara felt.

Sara stared at Rebecca as she continued in a barely audible voice, "He'd left Mom for a woman he'd met while doing missionary work, and they lived together as husband and wife." She shook her head. "Still do." Rebecca shifted in the glider. "That brings me to Albert. When Mom moved us here, he lived in the same house with his ailing father and was on drugs or something. Mom focused all her attention on mending him while she left me to fend for myself. So I stopped trying and we drifted apart. But now I have to live with the guilt of not having ever told Mom the truth." She looked at her feet. "Believe me, that's the hardest thing to live with. Hiding something important from someone you love. And then they die and it's too late."

Chapter 19

Friday–Saturday, Week Three

Sara took Jane to her Jeep. "Hey, next time you need a taxi, don't call me!"

Jane laughed as she got in the Jeep.

On the drive home, Sara wondered if any of what Rebecca had said would help Fiona accept her truth. Sara could only hope so. If only Fiona could be as compassionate toward her as she had been toward Rebecca when Sara finally revealed her secret, then maybe, just maybe . . . Maybe Fiona could really be her mother again.

Her cell phone rang as soon as she got inside her apartment. Sprint had turned the phone back on as promised.

"Hello."

"Hello, Sara, it's Linda, Ma Linda. How are you, Honey?"

Sara struggled for her voice. Linda, Linda Jenkins. So, she had tracked Sara down. "Hi." She gulped. "I can't believe it's you. How'd you get my number?"

Several seconds elapsed before Ma Linda answered. "A mutual friend."

The answer took Sara aback for a moment. What mutual friend? Oh. Who else could it be except Mrs. Parker. No wonder Ma Linda was vague. "So how are you and the guys?"

"We're fine, but I'm still outnumbered. It's hard to have girl-power with just one girl." Linda laughed.

Sara smiled.

Linda went on to tell her how much they missed her and cared about her. Linda had asked what Sara had been doing for the last few years. Sara omitted the bad parts and didn't tell Linda that she had one more girl to add to their girl-power. Once Sara had Jamie back, she would tell Linda. She knew that Linda would insist on meeting Jamie, and if Sara told her now, she'd have to explain why Jamie was in foster care.

Sara fell onto the bed, still clutching the phone after sharing the promise to call soon. She remembered life had gotten better when she moved in with the Jenkins after getting expelled from school in Pacifica and kicked out of yet another foster home.

"Let me see how you look." Linda Jenkins spoke through Sara's closed bedroom door.

"I'm not ready yet." Sara slumped on her bed, not caring about wrinkling her prom dress. "Give me a minute."

"Okay." She heard Linda's footsteps then her voice from the hall. "Let me know if you want help with makeup or anything." The footsteps faded.

Prom. Sara had no desire to be the so-called typical teen looking forward to prom night. All she looked forward to was graduating. What a surprise that she'd actually be doing that. Prom was to please Linda and Jake, who'd been the best parents she'd had for a long time. She twirled a thick strand of hair around her finger. Better get it over with. She stood up and looked in the mirror Jake had installed on her door. She smoothed out the wrinkles, ran a comb through her curls then opened the door. "Linda, I'm done."

Linda came out of her bedroom so quickly Sara thought she must've been standing just inside the door. Linda had said she was thrilled to have a daughter after raising three rowdy boys. When Sara was placed with the Jenkins, the two older boys were long gone. She knew Chad better because he was still at home, attending City College.

"Oh, you look wonderful." Linda fluffed Sara's hair. Then she cupped Sara's chin. "Let's get some makeup on that pretty face."

Sara frowned. "If it's pretty, why does it need make-up?"

For a moment, Linda looked dumbfounded, but then she laughed. "It's just what we girls do for our men." She ushered Sara to the vanity in the master bathroom.

Sara didn't argue although there was plenty she could say about the whole 'we girls . . . our men' thing.

Linda guided Sara to her chair and, resting her hands on Sara's shoulders, bent down so both faces were reflected in the mirror. "This is so much fun." Linda planted a kiss on Sara's cheek and opened a drawer filled with makeup.

Oh great, Sara thought, her own live Barbie doll to dress up. Sara forced a smile and sat still while Linda went to work.

Sara rolled over on the bed and brushed her damp face with her arm. Why tears? Those were good memories even if she didn't know it at the time. And she did graduate from high school.

After Sara's high school graduation, the Jenkins took her to 7 Mile House Bar and Grill in Brisbane. Everyone was laughing except Ma Linda, who said, "Now that you've graduated, what do you want to do?"

Sara took a sip of her Virgin Mai Tai. "Not sure."

Chad, acting like a big brother, lightly punched her arm. "Why don't you follow in my footsteps?" He looked at his feet. "Oh, that's right, my feet are too big for you." He laughed then wrapped his arm around Sara.

Sara flashed him a crooked grin. She didn't say that *everybody's* footsteps were too big for her. That's why she didn't intend to follow anyone's.

Jake set down his Bloody Mary. "You know, Sara, if you decide to go to City College, you're welcome to stay with us. And no rent while you're a student." He took another sip, perhaps to disguise the lump Sara saw in his throat. "We consider you part of the family, you know."

Sara knew it wasn't a reasonable thought, but the first thing that came into her mind was, 'Where were you guys thirteen years ago?' Instead, she said, "I know. You've been like family to me, too." They smiled, but she knew they wanted to hear one thing she couldn't give them. Thank you. Damned if she'd thank anyone for the life she'd had, even if the three years with them weren't bad. But she did have a request, and maybe they'd think of that as gratitude. "I was wondering," she trailed rice around her plate with a fork, "if you'd mind," she couldn't look at them, "that is, if I . . ." She finally forged ahead. "Well, you know that Jones isn't really my last name." She shredded her napkin. "And I've always planned to change it when I turned eighteen." She looked around the table. "I wondered if you'd mind if I changed it to, uh, Jenkins?"

Huge grins broke out, and Jake lifted his glass. "Let's toast!"

Then Linda said, "To Sara. Sara Jenkins."

Sara paced in her living room after thinking about the Jenkins. She pulled a Marlboro from the pack and sat down. The chipped, heart-shaped candy dish on the coffee table was overflowing with butts. She really should buy an ashtray. She emptied the butts into the waste basket, tapping the dish against the side. It cracked in two. A jagged slash right down the center, half of the heart falling into the trash. No! She bent down and rescued the fallen piece. Clutching both pieces to her chest, she slumped down the wall, sobbing. Broken. Just like her life.

She held out the two pieces. Chips were missing. It couldn't just be patched and even if repaired would never be the same. Jamie had made this candy dish for her at a community program. Not long afterwards, Jamie was taken from her. Sara clung to the pieces and cried until she felt like a wrung-out rag. When the tears finally stopped, she set the two pieces on the counter, blew her nose, and lit the cigarette.

She couldn't go to work with red, puffy eyes. She tossed two teaspoons into the freezer. When Ma Linda's eyes looked bad, she put cold spoons on them, and it helped. Sara hoped it would work for her because she needed to make good tips tonight. The money was going straight into a jar then straight to pay her next cell phone bill. She absolutely would not lose touch with Jamie.

She was beginning to see how one decision could morph into a lifetime of unexpected consequences. Breaking the dish was almost worse than hearing Fiona say, 'She doesn't belong here.' Even though Fiona had clarified it afterwards, she hadn't retracted the words. As if she could say anything that would make the words stop echoing in Sara's head. One thing she knew for sure, she'd never speak to Jamie the way Fiona had spoken to her. Never. She leaned against the counter and flicked ashes into the sink. The longer she stayed here, the worse she felt. All her childhood illusions were being shattered a bit more every day. She took a final drag then turned on the faucet and held the butt under the stream, waving away the last remnant of smoke. She dropped the butt in the sink and stared at the broken dish as the water carried the disintegrating filter down the drain.

She stood until all the water had gurgled down the drain then reached into her back pocket, pulled out her wallet, and grabbed the key she kept there. She inserted the key into the roll-top desk she'd bought at Goodwill and lifted the top. Inside the desk was *The Story of Babar the Little Elephant*. The only thing she was told Fiona left for her before, *poof*, like dandelion fuzz being blown into the air, Fiona was gone. Sara flipped to the last page and saw the pressed orchid. 'My lil' Orchid,' she heard her mother say, or was it Leah? She couldn't be sure. She lay on the couch with the spoons covering her eyes and recalled someone prying the orchid out of her fingers at night before reading from this book. Sara had read to her own daughter from this very same book.

> "Hush, baby, Mommy's going to read you a story." Sara rocked in the chair next to Jamie's crib and began to read about the baby elephant. Jamie's sobs subsided, and her chubby fingers loosened their grip on the crib's rails. A thumb flew into her mouth, and her diapered bottom plopped onto the mattress. "Babar," Sara said, stroking Jamie's back as her eyelids grew heavy, and she slumped into a fetal position. Sara put the book down and crooned, "has a mother who loves him very much." Jamie's eyes closed, but Sara hummed a lullaby until she was sure Jamie was sound asleep. Sara rose and placed the book in a drawer. She knew she should sleep, too, but was restless and headed for the tiny kitchen. She reached into the refrigerator for the six-pack her friends had brought over then yanked a beer from its plastic ring and popped the top.

Screeching tires and grinding metal interrupted Sara's reverie. The spoons fell to the floor as she rushed to the front window to see two drivers staggering out of their cars. One was holding his head, blood dripping through his fingers. His car's passenger side was smashed into scrap metal. She didn't see any passengers in the car, but the other driver, whose car wasn't as badly damaged, was reaching into the backseat and pulling out a howling child, a little girl with huge, scared eyes. She wailed as the woman cuddled her. Sara stepped back as a police car screeched to the scene. The child's look haunted her.

Sara tried to ignore the noise outside. If only she had time to find St. John's. If only there was an AA meeting. If only she didn't have to work. The flashing lights were like a kaleidoscope dizzying her thoughts. Even so, she couldn't spend another minute in the apartment with tokens of her failures. The book, a sentinel for her unknown past. The jagged, broken pieces of the candy dish, a reminder of her mistakes. Still life without Jamie, that's what the lights flashed. Still life, still life, still life . . . The ambulance sped away and the lights disappeared . . . still, life without Jamie . . .

Chapter 20

Saturday, Week Three

Jane waved as Sara sped off. Meeting Mrs. Peabody's daughter and hearing her story made Jane decide to visit her dad. She hadn't talked to him in a couple of days and wondered how he was doing. Guilt engulfed her as she thought how grateful she was that it wasn't her dad in a funeral home today.

* * *

"Hey, Rusty!" Jane called to the barking dog. He jumped on the chain-link fence enclosing the backyard. She opened the gate and rubbed Rusty's head while he nuzzled her.

Marv came to the door. "Janey," he said, "what a wonderful surprise."

"Hi Dad." Jane turned to Rusty. "Hey, boy, let's go inside."

When they stepped into the living room, the first thing Jane said was, "You need some light in here, Pops." She opened the faded blinds, straightening the kinked slats.

Marv eased into his recliner while she walked to the couch. "How're you feeling?"

He shrugged. "So-so."

"So, today's not so good?"

Marv nodded.

"What did the doctor say?"

Marv pulled up the footrest. "Well," he pulled out his handkerchief and wiped his face before continuing, "seems he wants me to go under the knife." He stuffed the handkerchief back in his pocket. "But I need to think on it."

"What's to think about, Pops? Just do it."

"Never mind about me, now. What's new with you?"

Jane shook her head and sucked in her breath. "Nothing new with me." She certainly didn't want to tell him about Mrs. Peabody, and he wouldn't like knowing she had to be carted home last night because she was drunk. Jane shuffled through junk mail on her dad's coffee table but stopped when she saw a 'Jesus Saves!' pamphlet. "What's this?" She waved the tract. "Didn't you tell me religion was better off left inside churches?"

"Yeah, well, you know, people do change. You never know."

"Don't tell me you're going to church?"

"No, I didn't say that." Marv leaned forward.

"Then how'd this get here?" Jane dropped the pamphlet on the coffee table.

"You know how church folk are." He sat back again. "Came to my door, a young'un, that is. They always like to send their young out to grow the flock."

Jane frowned.

"Just couldn't shut the door in her little freckled face. Reminded me of . . ." Marv paused and coughed into his hand. When he continued, his voice was hoarse. "Kinda ignored the grownups with their plastered smiles standing behind her." Marv glanced away. "Anyways, I took it and thanked her then said goodbye. And, well, there it is."

Jane looked at him. Was he worried about dying and making a last ditch effort at some kind of salvation? She picked up a circular and rolled it up.

Marv shook his head. "Oh Janey, Hon-bun, have I turned you so much against religion that you don't believe in a god or the hereafter?"

"Don't know what I believe anymore, Dad. Not sure what I ever *did* believe in besides you, me, and Mom. Excuse me, *Mother*." She flung the circular onto the coffee table. "Our family, and that can be summed up like you said, 'Goodbye. And, well, there it is.'" She leaned back and folded her arms.

"Janey, it wasn't like your mother or I abandoned you." She looked away. Neither of her parents seemed to understand that having two homes and each parent part of the time wasn't the same as a family. "You know that Winnie and I both love you."

"Winifred, Dad, remember?"

Marv closed his eyes. "Let's don't go there today, Hon, okay? Your old man's all tuckered out." He opened his eyes. "But I am wondering how things are between you and your mother these days?"

Jane sat back and frowned.

"Well now, what's that for?"

"Nothing, Dad, nothing." Jane pushed loose strands of hair off her face. Her mother was the last person Jane wanted to think about. Her dad always had a way of twisting the conversation away from himself.

"Don't give me that, Janey. What's going on?" She looked at him and he added, "She's always tried to be a good mother, you know."

Jane glared at him.

"So you better get over whatever's going on with you two." He reached for the afghan draped over the recliner and shook it open over his legs.

"Yeah, Dad, but I can never be the daughter she wants me to be."

"What are you talking about, Janey?"

Jane folded her arms and shrugged.

"Believe me, the happiest day of her life was the day she held her baby girl for the first time. So don't try to give me any story about not being what she wants you to be." He looked up at the ceiling. "I know all about kids not being who their moms want them to be, and trust me, you got nothing to worry about."

"Whatever you say, Dad." She knew she couldn't say anything that would change his mind, and to continue would only fuel her frustration.

"No, Janey, I'm dead serious on that." They both seemed momentarily stunned at Marv's word choice. "Whatever's wrong between you two, you be the bigger person. You hear me?" He paused then added, "I'm tired, Janey. I don't have enough energy to argue."

"Guess I'll go, but I'm keeping my eye on you, Mr. Heffinger."

Marv smiled faintly.

"Promise you'll let me know if you need anything?"

"Sure, Hon-bun." He gave her a thumbs-up then pulled the afghan over his shoulders.

She kissed his cheek. "Love you, Pops."

I walk into the cabin, holding a bottle of J & B, which is tucked neatly in a brown paper bag and think that if the sack had a bow and card attached, it would be a gift. It is a gift. It's a gift for those who've taken themselves out of the flow of regular life. I drop ice cubes into a glass and pull the paper down around the bottle. I pour J & B to the top of the glass and sit at the worn kitchen table. Regular life, I muse as I swallow. What is regular life? I swirl the liquid and the ice cubes clink in the glass, but it's not an answer. I tell the glass how I've been exempting myself from regular life for years, but have I ever defined it, even for myself? Hell no! Let's see. Regular life. House in the suburbs. 2.3 kids. White picket fence, of course. Mini van. Piano and soccer for the beautiful fair-haired daughter. Baseball and guitar for the dark-haired son who would surely come after.

Another swig of my drink and the alcohol slowly penetrates my logic. I giggle. What about the .3 child? Where do they come up with these numbers? A fraction. Who has a fraction of a child? What is a fraction of a child? An arm? A leg? A heart? A heart. My clenched fist covers my chest, and the beats of my own heart seem to connect to my hand, which is connected to my arm, which is connected to my . . . I begin to picture my body parts sailing through space, attaching to each other and then, the heart, how my chest opens to receive my heart. My head swirls with the kaleidoscope my brain has created, and I don't want to think about what fraction my own life is, so I get more ice and refill my glass. Anyway, I tell my second drink, my second friend, that's not my idea of regular life. That's someone else's. I was part of a family once, and I could have had one of my own. I can see that the drink doesn't believe me by the way the ice just sits there. I had a mother. 'Course I'd like to forget about her. I had a dad. I drift over to the cast iron terrier and pet it as if it is made of flesh, blood, and bone like the one I had as a child. My dad left me this one. My brother brought the other one home. Yes, I had a brother. He gave me his cowboy hat, but I lost it. I lost my brother's hat, I tell my drink, and feel moisture on my cheeks as I stumble toward my bed. I lost my brother's hat . . . I lost my brother's . . . I lost my brother . . . I lost my . . .

Chapter 21

Sunday–Monday, Week Four

Sara awoke to a loud banging noise. When she realized someone was beating on her door, she hollered, "Just a minute," then sat up and flung her legs off the side of the bed. The light streaming through the broken slats in the blinds told her it was definitely day time. How late was it?

She'd been tempted to get drunk last night. In fact, she'd snuck a little from the tap. How many sober days had it been before this minor lapse? The beating persisted, and she stumbled toward the door. "I'm coming." When she opened the door, a scowling Fiona stood, fist raised to bang again.

"You're late." Fiona wagged her finger then folded her arms and tapped her foot.

"What time is it?" Sara squinted and shaded her eyes from the sunlight.

"Half-past the hour you should have been at work."

Sara tried to focus. "Sorry, I'll be right there." She slammed the door and heard Fiona say, "What the fuh," as Sara headed for the bathroom.

Fiona could just go to hell. Splashing water on her face, Sara tried to wake up. She brushed her teeth and ran a comb through her tangled hair. "Mirror, mirror, on the wall, who's *not* the fairest of them all?" Sara jerked off her nightshirt and cleaned up. She threw on a t-shirt and jeans then ran downstairs.

* * *

Sara wanted to slip quietly into the bookstore, but Fiona had already alerted Vic, who blocked the doorway. Sara hadn't forgotten that Vic wanted to talk to her anyway, and now she'd gone and made him mad. "Sara." Vic tilted his head and motioned toward the office. "We need to talk." Fiona stuck her head out of the doorway and said she'd cover the bookstore, glaring at Sara.

Vic stopped outside the office, pulled the current schedule from the bulletin board, and ushered Sara inside while flipping the Do Not Disturb sign. He motioned for her to sit. While he grabbed papers from the file cabinet, Sara shifted in her chair until he tapped the papers' edges on the desk. "So, looks like you were late for your shift today."

Sara twirled her hair and averted Vic's eyes by focusing on the twisted lock. "I know." She let go of the coiled strands and leaned on the desk, grabbing it with both hands. "What can I say, I'm sorry I was late, but really, Fiona didn't have to beat on my door." Bad enough Fiona left her, now she had to go out of her way to make trouble for her. That's what she wanted to tell Vic, and if she ever was tempted to spill her guts, it was now. Let him find out who Fiona really was.

"This is not about Fiona."

Sara sat back and folded her arms. "Sorry, Vic, really. It won't happen again, I promise." She could see she wasn't going to gain Vic's sympathy today.

"You're right, it won't." Vic flipped through the papers, faced them toward Sara, and spread them in the empty space in front of her. Sara glanced at the last two weeks' schedules. "See what I see?" Vic pointed to red lines on all the pages.

Sara squinted.

"Well, what do you have to say about it?" Vic stared at her and she wanted to run out the door or press a button that would make her invisible. When she didn't respond, Vic pointed to the papers, "As you can see here in black and white *and* red," he tapped the schedule, and his voice grew harsh, "you've been late or absent for too many shifts in your short time with us. Luckily, Fiona was here to help today." He leaned back in his chair and waited for her response.

Just as she was about to spill her guts, he said, in a softer voice, "Does all this have anything to do with the phone call to Jamie, was it?"

"No." Sara fidgeted, trying to find the right words. Where to begin? How much to tell? Had Fiona told him she had a daughter? Before she could figure it out, Vic broke the silence.

"Well," he began, once again sounding like a stern father. Clearly, if Sara'd had a chance to gain Vic's empathy, she'd lost it. "Whatever it is, I'm afraid I have to put you on notice." He kept the current schedule and stuffed the old ones in a desk drawer.

"What do you mean?" Sara's voice quivered like an unskilled archer's arrow sputtering through the air.

"I mean no more being late for shifts, and if you have to be absent, you need to be absolutely sure your shift is covered. And don't make it a habit." He stood. "If you can't follow these simple rules, we'll have to revisit your membership."

Sara's eyes widened. "You mean you'll kick me out of the apartment?"

"No, not the apartment." He looked directly at her. "We want people here who care about what they do. I know you have to work elsewhere to make a living, but the only way this kind of venture works is if everybody cooperates. I'm not sure I see that in your behavior."

She stood and balled her fists by her sides. "So . . . what? If I'm late again, or whatever, I get kicked out?"

"Kicked out's a harsh way of putting it, but you'd be out for six months at least before you'd get another chance to be reinstated."

Sara's balled fists were now perched on her hips, spreading her arms in a ready-for-flight formation.

Vic sat down. "You'd lose the use of the workshop rooms. Only members in good standing are allowed that privilege, member rules." Vic turned his attention to the computer.

His dismissal stunned her. What more could she say? She walked out the door. Fiona! She must've been behind this. Why else would Vic's attitude have changed so much? She tried to shake off the anger and anxiety, counting backwards as she crossed the hallway to return to the bookstore, wondering if she should call her sponsor. Wondering if her sponsor could say something to stop her from plummeting into the abyss. She bumped into Clem as she rounded the corner, knocking flyers out of his hands.

"Hey Sara."

"Sorry." She bent down to help him pick up the papers.

"No problem." They stood, and he straightened the flyers while she stared off into the distance. "Everything okay?"

"Yeah. And no. Oh, I don't know." How could she even begin to tell Clem her problems, but there he was just when she needed a friend.

"You know what I think?"

She was afraid to ask what he thought. Were her thoughts readable? God, she hoped not. She shook her head, hoping Clem wasn't going to invite her to church again. She wasn't up for that just now.

"I think we need a night out on the riverfront again." He smiled. "Yeah, that's what I think. Let's do it soon, okay."

She smiled, agreeing that was a good idea, but as she neared the bookstore, she remembered Fiona, sucked in a deep breath, and started counting.

* * *

"So, are you ready to work?" Fiona's forced smile made Sara want to spit.

"Yes, you can definitely leave now." Sara flipped her head so her face wasn't in Fiona's view. Sara had never been one to hide her emotions and could match Fiona any time when it came to angry words and flaring temper. But Sara was afraid of what she'd say, so she walked over to a shelf and, with trembling fingers, began straightening books.

"Well, then, have a good day," Fiona taunted as she left.

When Sara knew Fiona was well out of earshot, she couldn't hold in her anger any longer. "Sure, take your smug self to Vic where you can gloat together." She slammed a book down harder than she expected, and it slipped out of her sweaty palms. Just as she stooped to pick it up, two teenagers entered the bookstore and Sara forced a smile. By the time her shift was over, she'd worn out her fake cheerfulness.

* * *

The drunk at the bar whistled as Sara strode by carrying a pitcher of Bud Light, the special on Mondays, to a group of partiers at a back booth. "Whass up, Sweetie?" When he grabbed her ass, she swung around and started to slap him with her free hand, but Laurance jumped in between the two. He winked at Sara before turning to the drunk.

"I say, lad, don't you think you've reached your limit?"

"Wha? Mind yur own bizznezz, Bud." He started to grab Sara again.

Laurance slapped the drunk's hand down. "I say, there'll be no bum-grabbing tonight, lad." He looked at Jerry, who gave him the cut-off sign. "No more for you. We'll call you a cab."

Jerry picked up the phone behind the bar.

The drunk looked at Jerry with heavy-lidded eyes. "You're kickin' me out?"

"That's right." Jerry swept up the half-full whiskey glass with his free hand. "This one's on me." He dumped the contents into the sink then reached in his pocket and threw a few bills on the bar.

With a wobbling head, the drunk stood. "No cab." He pulled keys from his pocket.

Laurance snatched the key ring and removed the car keys. "These will be safe with Jerry." He laid those keys in Jerry's hand and returned the key ring to the drunk. "Pick them up tomorrow."

"You can't do tha . . ." The drunk reached over the bar to grab the car keys, but his foot slipped, and he slid to the floor.

By the time the man got back on his feet, the cab was on its way. Laurance helped the drunk to a chair, where he slumped and spewed cuss words that echoed throughout the bar.

Clasping his hands together, Laurance walked back to the bar and winked at Sara, who said, "Thank you," before taking drinks to a table behind him. She could hear what Laurance and Jerry were saying as she served her customers.

Jerry said, "Hey, fella, let me buy you a drink."

As Sara set the drinks on the table, Laurance answered, "I'll have Scotch neat, if you don't mind." She returned to the bar to find him perched on the stool vacated by the drunk.

Jerry nodded. "One Scotch neat, coming up." Jerry leaned over the bar and quietly added, "Sure's cheaper than a lawsuit'd be if that drunk caused a wreck after stumbling out of here." He set the drink in front of Laurance as Sara returned.

Captain caught her eye as she bent down behind the bar. "Ya awright, young lady?"

She flashed Captain a hesitant grin and checked out the woman with bright orange curls he was chatting up. She wore jeans and a paint-splotched shirt. Not exactly pick-me-up attire, but when the woman shot Sara a friendly smile, she returned it then answered Captain. "I'm fine." She hadn't said much more than hi to him since the day Jerry had introduced them, but he always offered a kind word.

When he beckoned her closer, she leaned in to hear him whisper, "You got a real knight there."

"And I see *you've* got company." She cocked her head in the redhead's direction as the woman plunked her empty mug on the bar.

The woman wiped her hand on her jeans. "Not anymore. Got to get back home." She reached over Captain to shake Sara's hand. "I'm Angie, and I'm a recovering renovator." She threw her head back and let out a belly howl.

Sara was speechless for a moment before muttering, "I'm Sara." Angie's heartwarming manner almost made Sara add, 'and I'm a recovering alcoholic,' but that wasn't something she advertised, and she stopped short of a public confession. This wasn't an AA meeting.

"Well, Sara, nice to meet you, but I've got to shake a leg cleaning up. I'm sprucing up the old homestead and boy, what a job! Work late into the night sometimes." She hopped off the stool and brushed Captain's cheek with a kiss. "See you both again when I come by for another break."

Sara nodded as Angie bustled out the door.

Captain grinned. "She's a catch, fer shure. If only I was twenty years younger, I'd reel her in." He raised his mug in the air while slapping some money on the counter. "Jer, this here should also cover mah tab from thu other day." He winked at Sara. "With a tip for th'young lady here, too."

Sara scooped up the bills and handed them to Jerry. He rang up Cap's total and handed the change to Sara. "Thanks Cap."

"Ah'll jes start a new tab when I git back from ans'rin' Mother Nature's call." Captain grinned and limped toward the restroom.

* * *

Jerry turned to Laurance after walking the drunk to the taxi. "Don't know how that one got away from me. Usually watch how the booze flows better than that." He wiped off the bar as Sara grabbed the pitchers of beer to deliver to the pool room.

She returned with a tray full of dirty glasses, and Laurance grabbed one before it rolled off the tray. "That's twice tonight you've saved my butt. Though that would have been one less glass to wash."

Laurance smiled.

Jerry put clean glasses on her tray and set a pitcher next to it. "Your order's up. Keep an eye on how much they drink, okay?"

* * *

After placing the last glass she'd washed in the drain, Sara wiped her hands and glanced around the room. All her customers had full or nearly full drinks, and she wanted a cigarette. She asked Jerry, "Care if I take a short break?"

"No, go ahead."

Sara stepped around the bar, and Laurance stopped shelling peanuts to pat the stool between him and Captain. She sat down and lit her cigarette, catching Captain's slight wink before he swiveled around and began chatting with another regular. Sara looked at Laurance more closely. He was tall and built. He had short black hair and the bluest eyes she'd ever seen. Handsome. Funny she didn't recall noticing that before. But she had to remember, also, soon to be married. "So, haven't seen you here since that night I was with Jane."

"No. Haven't had time to spare lately."

"Jane says the wedding plans are coming along."

"So I hear."

"You don't sound enthused?"

He raised his brows and shrugged.

"Second thoughts?" She took a drag.

Frowning, Laurance turned to her. "Have you ever had a decision to make, one that could change your whole life, and it seemed like everyone around you was planning your future except you?"

Sara forced a laugh. "How much time do you have?"

"Was that a funny question?" Laurance looked stung.

"Oh, no." She touched his arm. "It's just that, I. . ." She withdrew her hand and leaned on it. "I actually understand more than you know. Your words just struck me as ironic. One thing I can tell you for sure, don't let anyone talk you into anything so life changing as marriage if you don't want it."

Laurance stiffened. "I didn't mean to imply . . . It's all just getting so out of hand."

"That's what I mean. Take back the night, Laurance. Take back the night." She stubbed her cigarette in the ashtray and got up. She'd rather sit here and talk to Laurance, but there was no money to be made doing that. "Gotta get back to work." As she stood, she looked at him. "Don't be a stranger." When she walked around the bar, Captain tapped her arm and nodded with a grin spread across his weathered face like a bent train track rail.

Chapter 22

Tuesday, Week Four

"Coming. Coming," Winifred said as if whoever kept ringing her doorbell could hear her. It was too early for the women from her group. She laid down the knife she'd been using to slice peaches and kiwi and wiped her hands on a dish towel.

The front door's stained glass window revealed only a silhouette of the visitor. Winifred opened the door. "Mrs. Gentry, so good . . ."

Mrs. Gentry waved her hand and forced the door wide open, her air of superiority spinning around Winifred and stunning her like a sudden gust of wind. "No time for silly pleasantries, Winifred. I want you to speak to those women I see coming to your house every second Tuesday." She glanced at the circle of chairs then at her watch. "I assume they'll be here in half an hour. Isn't that right?"

Winifred closed the door and nodded. The group had met at her house for the last several months. Before that, the women alternated, but circumstances had changed for many of them, so Winifred took on the role of hostess.

"Winifred?" Mrs. Gentry snapped her fingers. "Those women. They come to the neighborhood and cars, cars, cars everywhere." She waved her hand. "I'm not telling you to stop having the meetings, whatever they are, but the neighborhood is not going to look like a used car lot. Tell them to carpool if they have to come here." Mrs. Gentry headed toward the door and almost ran into two women who arrived early.

"Oh, Myrtle, you're early," Winifred said.

"Sorry. We were out and about and thought we would time it better, but . . ." Myrtle shrugged.

Mrs. Gentry looked at them. "At least these two came together. Winifred, introduce me to your guests."

Winifred rolled her eyes and introduced Myrtle, who said, "This is my friend, Thelma."

"Nice to make your acquaintance, ladies." Mrs. Gentry turned to Winifred on her way out the door. "Winifred, don't forget what I told you." Winifred watched Mrs. Gentry strut down the driveway before shutting the door.

"What was that all about?" Myrtle, wide-eyed, asked as she reached in her purse, pulled out an address book, and fanned herself.

"Carpooling."

Winifred started to explain but then shook her head. "It's not important. She gestured toward the living room. "Have a seat. Would you like something to drink?"

Myrtle, still fanning herself, sat down, her stomach a mound and her buttocks spread on the chair like a fluffy pancake. "Oh, I'd die for some iced tea." She turned to Thelma, who nodded.

"I'll bring it right out."

* * *

Winifred returned to the kitchen and pulled out a tray for the drinks. She added cheese and crackers and carried the tray out to the two early birds. While

Winifred loved greeting guests and preparing food, she wasn't so fond of early arrivers. She loved being in control, though, so she forced herself to exhibit gracious manners to hide her irritation at the pair.

"Oh, Winifred, you're such a great hostess," Myrtle said, as she reached for a glass of tea and a cracker topped with cheese.

"Thank you so much. I haven't finished cutting up the fruit yet, but I'll bring you some in a minute."

Myrtle crinkled her nose. "No pastries today?"

Winifred wagged her finger. "Now, now, I thought we decided we were watching our waistlines."

Thelma chuckled. "Myrtle's watching hers, all right."

Myrtle brushed her off. "Well then, I'll just have to have another cracker with cheese."

Winifred shook her head and left.

* * *

Winifred continued cutting up the fruit. She couldn't believe it. Of all the women in the group, Myrtle was the last one who should be asking about pastries. Waistline? Could Myrtle still find hers? Oh, she shouldn't be catty. Those thoughts could lead to actions that would hurt the group. She didn't want anything to cause the group to disband. She loved the get-togethers. The group had begun as a book club but later became a card club, gardening club, recipe club, or any kind of club they needed it to be at the moment. The women didn't try to name it anymore.

The group had taken on a new dimension after Angie joined. Most weren't too sure of her at first. She was loud and opinionated, which Winifred thought went along with Angie's carrot-colored hair. But Angie also seemed to think that whatever she could do for someone else was as routine as brushing her teeth. She never stepped away from helping someone, that is, except her ex-husband, who she'd sooner see in chains tethered to his new Mrs. than anywhere near her.

Angie had joined the group a few months before she filed for divorce and told the women that her husband had cheated. "It'll make it easy to tap the dirty bastard's ass for every dime," she'd said and proceeded to do just that. Winifred had almost choked on her food. Angie had slapped her on the back and said, "Easy old girl. Not used to lexicon a la Angie?" She'd howled and her bright curls swung on her head. When Angie realized the other women weren't laughing, she said, "C'mon ladies. It's just us gals. No need for ostentatious behavior." She laughed again, and Winifred had noticed some of the other women smiling. Eventually, she accepted Angie's vulgarity, and now it was hard to imagine the group without her.

Another member, who worked at a bank, had told Winifred that Angie donated a thousand dollars to the Red Cross for Hurricane Katrina victims. Angie never said a word when the group discussed the disaster and even contributed to the group's donation.

Winifred had tried to adopt Angie's generous attitude when it came to Jane and bought things her daughter couldn't afford, but her gifts just seemed to irritate Jane. God knows, she'd tried with the girl, but Jane was just nothing like her and never seemed to want the same things Winifred wanted. She wanted

Jane to have what she'd never had and to become what she never could. Growing up, Winifred wanted to take ballet lessons at the prestigious Mrs. Peavy's School of Dance like many of her friends, and she finally got her parents to agree. But every time Winifred had tried to plié, she landed on her fanny. All the graceful would-be ballerinas laughed and teased her so much that she quit. Why couldn't Jane understand that sometimes she just wanted Jane to be that ballerina?

* * *

Winifred continued cutting fruit and cheese wedges in the kitchen, stopping from time to time to greet newly arriving guests. But after Myrtle answered the door to one of the women first, saying, when she saw Winifred's scowl, "I just wanted to help you," Winifred kept an ear to the doorbell and didn't allow a repeat performance. After serving everyone a beverage, she returned to the kitchen to get the food. While preparing to deliver it, she heard a rhythmic tapping on the door and saw Angie swaying on the side porch.

Winifred opened the door, and Angie sashayed in. "Win, Dear, I'm a little dusty. Had to sponge bathe at the kitchen sink. Bathroom's still torn up." Angie shook her head. "Been sanding in that damn room all morning. Didn't have time to wash and tame my unruly mop. That's why I came to the kitchen door." She laughed and pointed to the orange bandana covering her hair. "And why the rag on my head." The color was a shade darker than the curls that framed her face. Angie flared the skirt of her yellow shirtwaist dress and pranced around as if she'd stepped out of a book about nineteenth-century Irish immigrants. Angie stopped twirling when she saw the fruit. "Oh, fresh peaches." She grabbed a slice with her fingers, ignoring the toothpick holder in the center of the tray.

"I was just getting ready to take this out to the living room. Everyone else is here." As Winifred picked up the fruit tray, she and Angie heard a light tap on the kitchen door.

"I'll get it." Angie sucked the juice from her fingers and went to the door. Winifred stood in the doorway waiting to see who it was. Angie swung open the door.

There stood Jane. Winifred clutched the tray so tightly her fingers turned white as frost while Jane scanned Angie from head to toe.

"Oh. You're the off-shoot," Angie said. "I've seen pictures of you." She grabbed Jane's hand and led her into the kitchen.

"Pardon?" Jane looked from Angie to her mother.

Winifred's grip on the tray loosened, and she almost dropped it before managing to set it on the table. Winifred looked at each of them while her mouth formed a tentative smile.

The silence lasted several seconds before Angie piped up. "You're Win's daughter, right?"

Jane looked at Angie. "Win?" She wrinkled her brow and looked at Winifred, who began fussing with the fruit slices.

"Jane, this is Angie, one of the women in my group." Winifred stared at the floor.

"Nice to meet you." Jane held out her hand, but Angie threw her arms around Jane and hugged her.

Jane stood with her hands at her sides then stepped back from Angie's embrace and looked at her mother. "I forgot this was your meeting day until I pulled up and saw the cars. So I came to the side door in case you happened to be in the kitchen."

Winifred reached for Jane's arm but Jane pulled away. Winifred dropped her hand, bearing the sting of Jane's rejection.

Angie's eyes shifted between the two women. "Why don't I take the fruit out to the living room while you two talk?"

Winifred forced a smile and shook her head. "I can't ignore my guests."

Angie backed away from the table.

"I guess I should've called first," Jane said, as she headed toward the door.

"Can we talk later?" Winifred said.

"Okay." Jane sighed. "My neighbor died, and . . . Oh, never mind, I'll tell you later." She nodded at Angie as she walked to the door.

"That's fine."

As the door closed behind Jane, Angie said, "So glad I got to meet your daughter. She's great."

Winifred looked up at Angie and sighed. "She has her moments." She picked up the fruit tray. "But now I need to tend to my guests."

"Win, if you don't mind, can we sit in here today? I'd really hate to get dust on your furniture."

Winifred hesitated.

Angie gestured toward the breakfast nook. "There's enough room at the table."

"Oh, I . . ." Winifred started before Angie interrupted.

"C'mon, Win. It'll be cozy," Angie coaxed.

Winifred looked at the breakfast nook, trying to picture everyone seated around it. Before she could figure out how that would work, she remembered the dirty dishes in the sink. "Everyone's already comfortably seated, and anyway, I can get you an afghan to sit on."

Angie protested, "I'm way too cruddy."

"I insist. There's no other way. Too many women to fit in here." Winifred had made up her mind. She handed Angie the fruit tray. "Take this out to the living room while I get the afghan."

"Okay, but don't hold me responsible for any dust that might . . ." She grinned. "Or any dust mites that might . . ." Angie's laughter bounced between the two of them like a volley ball.

* * *

Winifred got Angie a bottle of Perrier from the refrigerator and filled a glass with crushed ice because she knew Angie liked her drinks extra cold. The ladies were carrying on several conversations until they finally settled down and discussed the possibility of a shopping excursion to Nashville. Myrtle asked about making it an overnight trip and including a night at the Grand Ol' Opry. Everyone added their own ideas about how to make it a fun trip until the voices swarmed like bees pollinating flowers.

Angie twisted off the bottle cap and poured the water into the glass. After a big sip, she stood and whistled. The chatter stopped and all eyes were on Angie.

"Forget about fun for a sec. I've got a project for us." Some of the ladies looked away or down. "Quit your moaning, gals. This is a worthy project." Slowly, she regained their full attention. "Fisher House Foundation needs our help." She looked at the ladies. "As you know, many of our brave soldiers coming back from Iraq and Afghanistan have serious medical needs, and their families need a place to stay while they're being treated. The Foundation builds houses near medical facilities for military families." The ladies listened as Angie detailed what help was needed, and they discussed fundraising options.

After the other women left, Angie said, "What do you want me to do with this afghan?"

"I'll take it."

"Let me help you clean up." Angie started gathering cups and saucers then got the tray. She set it on the counter and popped a kiwi slice into her mouth before grabbing a container for the remaining fruit.

When Winifred returned, she said, "Thanks for cleaning up the living room."

"Not sure how thankful you'll be if those dust mites start dancing." Angie laughed, grabbed her bag, and flung it over her shoulder. "Now you have time to pour yourself a glass of wine and relax." Angie headed toward the door. "I'd join you in that drink, but grit and grime await me. You take care now."

With that, Angie was out the door, and Winifred was alone. Winifred decided Angie was right. She reached into the liquor cabinet and pulled out a bottle of Chardonnay.

I wake and reach for the clock: 4:27. My head feels like it's bound with a tourniquet. I switch on a lamp and groan at the brightness. The tumbler is on the floor, and the ice has melted, leaving a dark stain on the wood. A tumor with tentacles reaching outward to spread its malignancy. I pick up the tumbler and head for the kitchen. Without rinsing it, I fill the glass with water and swallow most of it in one drink. My worn leather bag is on the table, and I sift through it for aspirin. One tablet left. Great, *I moan. I shake the bottle as if that will make more white pills appear. I look at it again. Nothing's changed. I dump the tablet into my hand then scoop it into my mouth. A second swig of water and the pill is gone. All that remains is another empty bottle. I toss it toward the trash can but miss, and the clattering causes my head to throb. Another hour and I'll need to get ready for work, but I know I won't fall asleep again. I think about the job and how I haven't called in sick all year. Just one day won't hurt. Someone else can take my tour groups. I need a day, just one day . . .*

I know my boss won't be at work until 6:30. All I have to do is wait two hours, then I can call her. I look at the half-empty bottle of J & B. I tighten the cap and put it in the cabinet. Later, friend, *I say, as I shut the cabinet door. I make coffee, good and strong, and wonder what to do for two hours. I walk toward the living area with my coffee and glance at the vase of eucalyptus leaves. The picture is propped against it—where I left it. I pick it up, set my mug on the table, and sit on the couch. How are you, big brother? I ask the picture, but it's like those children are gone. No more big brother, no more little sister. I wonder what he's doing now. For a moment, I think of the other picture, the one I left safely stashed among the clippings, the one I still can't look at and think, maybe someday I'll have the courage. I smooth out the picture and touch his red hat, the one I lost several years later. What do you look like now? I wonder if you're bald. I haven't let myself think about you for a long time. Then I set the picture on the table. I feel like I can't breathe. I drop to my side on the couch. What if you're dead?*

Chapter 23

Tuesday, Week Four

Sara splashed cold water on her face and looked in the mirror. Not pretty. She'd tossed and turned all night, determined not to be late for her shift at the co-op today. She felt like crap, but that was tough luck. Being late wasn't an option. She stuck a glass under the tap, filled it, and took a drink. All her hopes seemed to be shattering like the glass would if she flung it against the shower stall. Keep it together. She threw on her clothes and rushed out the door.

When she entered the Hut, Stan opened his mouth in feigned horror then laughed. "Not a good day for 'mirror, mirror.'"

Sara gave him the finger, hiding it from the few customers with her left hand. He hung his head, pretending to be offended.

"Looks like you could use a strong cup 'a java although not sure that'll help." He laughed again. "Seriously, I'm brewing a new pot right now. It'll be ready in a few. I mean the worst thing a strong cup of coffee could do is put hair on your chest."

She shot him a dirty look and ran her fingers through the matted curls she'd forgotten to comb.

"Couldn't be any worse than what the hair on your head looks like right now." He grinned so wide his teeth looked like piano keys.

"Double ha, ha." She wadded a napkin and threw it at him.

He spun away to keep from being hit, and when he turned back around, he pointed to a mug.

She saw that it was two minutes before 10:00. "No time now. I'll get some later." She slipped through the beaded entrance.

* * *

Sara was standing in front of the Handiwork House door when Vic came down the hallway, keys jangling in his hand. She smiled. Vic glanced at his watch, and his mouth stretched into a broad grin. "Good morning."

"Hi."

Vic unlocked the door then handed Sara a bank bag with fifty dollars for the register. "If you need more, just call." Then he was gone.

Sara was miffed that he hadn't complimented her for being on time. Playing by the rules didn't seem so great without an 'Atta girl.' Was she ever going to stop needing acceptance? Get over it. She sighed then unzipped the bag and counted the bills and coins, loading them into the cash drawer. She looked around at all the crafts for sale. How many more days would she be staying in this city? Maybe she should be asking herself how many more days she could stand to be pretending in this city. The longer she was Sara from San Francisco, the harder it was to be Orchid, long-lost daughter of . . . or should she be switching it to Fiona, long-lost mother of . . . Who was the lost person? She'd been the one to stay put. She'd never been lost, just like Jamie wasn't lost, wasn't going to be. She wouldn't let that happen. She was getting shaky. She needed a drink. Maybe she should get that coffee. She phoned the Hut. Before Stan could rattle off one of his famous greetings, she spoke. "Stan, it's Sara. Anyone there who could run a cup of coffee to me at Handiwork House?"

"I think so, hang on." She heard him yell, "Hey, Clem, you want to do Sara a favor?" In a few seconds, he was back on the line. "This is your lucky day. Clem just walked in, and he doesn't mind at all. And don't worry. I'll put some magic potion in it that will turn you back into Sexy Sara. You know, the one whose middle finger stays put."

"Ha, ha. You're so funny."

"Anything I can do to add beauty to the world."

"You mean like covering your head with a sack?" She laughed.

"Now, can you see *my* middle finger?"

"Ha, ha again." She started to hang up. "Oh, yeah, and thanks. I'll bring the money by later." When she hung up, she reached in her pocket for a comb and found none. A package of rubber bands sat in the drawer behind the counter. She grabbed a large one and pulled her hair back into a pony tail. Acceptable if nothing else.

Sara looked up when Clem walked in with her coffee.

"You're my hero." She winked then inhaled the aroma. Stan did brew the best she'd ever tasted. She set the cup on the counter and took a handful of sugar, sweetener, and cream packets from Clem.

"I didn't know how you liked it, so I brought everything."

"Thanks." She dumped sugar into her coffee. "I can always count on you."

Clem said, "At your service," and bowed. "Gotta go. I've got a class in ten." He left but poked his head back in. "Let's have that night out on the riverfront again soon."

"Sounds good." Sara stirred creamer into her coffee and drank half of it without a breather. She was starting to feel human again. Everything here seemed in order, so she grabbed a pencil and paper and hoisted herself onto a stool. Lately she'd been thinking about so many things she should say to Jamie, but words never came easy. Drawing was her strength, and sometimes after drawing, words came easier. She was missing Jamie so much and had to do something or she'd scream. Leaving couldn't be far behind the scream, and she still had hope that what had been lost and forgotten could be revived and reclaimed. She gripped the pencil between her fingers, sketched a little, erased what she'd drawn, and stared at the ceiling. Still, no words came.

When Myrtle barreled in with Thelma in tow, Sara flipped the paper over as if it were her life and each rubbed-out image a metaphor for mistakes she wanted to erase.

"Hello, hello, hello. Some cutie pie in the coffee shop said we'd find you here," Myrtle cooed while Thelma rolled her eyes to the sound of Myrtle's clinking bracelets.

"Hi there." Sara got off the stool and went around the counter. Before she could shake their hands, Myrtle gripped her in a bear hug, accidentally hitting Sara's back with her large tote bag.

"I just had to get your opinion on my new painting." Myrtle reached into the bag and pulled out a slightly curled watercolor of a tugboat on the river.

The drawing was good, but the colors looked more like acrylics because Myrtle hadn't blended her washes at the right times. Watercolor painting was tricky that way, but Sara wasn't going to hurt Myrtle's feelings. "Good job. I'm glad to see you're still painting." She looked at them both. "You didn't sign up for the next class, so I wondered if you'd given up."

"Oh, no, Dear." Myrtle looked at Thelma. "We've just had other commitments. We're busy working for our soldiers. We'll be back for another session."

Thelma picked up one of Fiona's mugs. "I want this."

"Oh, Dear, that is lovely. I think I'll buy one, too." Myrtle looked through Fiona's shelf of mugs and found one she liked before they said their goodbyes.

Sara closed the cash drawer as the ladies left. She looked at the blank paper sitting next to the drawer, turned it over, and scowled. She brushed the eraser shavings to the floor and wrote Jamie's name on the paper. She wanted to record what was going on in her life, so Jamie would have missing parts of her history filled in and wouldn't doubt her mother's love. With a scribbled slant next to Jamie's name, she wrote the words *I'm sorry* but then crossed them out. Those were the words *she* wanted to hear, but she was going to make damn sure not to give Jamie any more reasons to need an apology. She slammed the pencil on the counter and spun in circles on the stool until her knee hit the feather duster's handle, knocking it to the floor. She picked it up and twirled it in her hands. Maybe this was an omen telling her to get off her butt and do something. She hopped down.

Sara dusted some carved animals then moved them aside and brushed over the shelf. Yes, mind-numbing dirty work was just what the good ol' doc ordered. She replaced the carvings and came upon beaded jewelry draped over odd-shaped stands. She picked up a necklace with black beads, fastened it around her neck, and looked in the oval mirror on the shelf. She was the one who'd suggested they put a mirror there. Everyone except Fiona had told her it was a great idea. But one day Sara caught Fiona modeling a necklace and checking herself out in the very same mirror. Sara remembered Fiona's exact words. She'd swung around to face Sara, clutching the necklace. 'I'm going to buy it.' Her words clashed like cymbals. 'My money's in the office.' Then she'd hurried out the door, the chain still encircling her neck. She hadn't returned to pay while Sara was in the shop. Sara gazed once more at her reflection, stroked the necklace one last time, unclasped it, and draped it back on the stand.

Fiona's pottery was on the next shelf. Fine Art by Fiona is what her placard said. It sat in the center of the shelf. No one else had a placard, only business cards on small holders. Fine art my ass. Sara ran the duster over the shelf with enough force to knock the placard off its easel. She brushed the mugs, bowls, vases, and ashtrays but stopped when she got to an ashtray with San Francisco's seal rocks. She ran her finger over the nose of the seal on top of the rocks. She flipped the ashtray over to look at the price. It was way too expensive. All of Fiona's items were. Fiona must think she's some kind of celebrity, some sought-after artist. Sara put the ashtray back on the shelf. She wanted a cigarette, a drink, to be anywhere but here. She shoved the duster back under the counter and dialed Vic's extension.

"Hello."

"Vic? Can you cover me for a smoke break?"

"Sure. Give me five."

Sara grabbed her paper off the counter, tore it into tiny pieces, and dropped them into the waste basket.

* * *

Sara stood on the sidewalk flicking her ashes between puffs. A man pushing a grocery cart loaded with cans and overflowing sacks passed by. The frayed knees of his pants said *see my troubles.* His filthy shirt was a beacon: See what can happen? This could be you. What did people see when they looked at her? Were all her mistakes bright and visible like a tattoo?

She smashed her cigarette butt into a sand-filled coffee can. She could wonder all she wanted, but she still had to get back to work.

Vic closed his *Sports Illustrated* and rolled it into a cylinder when Sara walked in. She stepped behind the counter and stood next to him.

"You need me to relieve you for lunch?"

"No, I brought a sandwich. It's been a slow morning, so I'll just eat it in here. But I may need another smoke break."

"No problem." He held his hand to his ear like a phone.

She nodded and Vic tapped her arm lightly with the rolled magazine before leaving.

Sara paced around the shop picking up items and putting them down. No sense trying to sketch anymore today, much less trying to write. She was too restless to stay behind the counter. After moving several items around, she twisted a delicate teacup in her hands, eyeing the glazed Japanese symbol. She ran her finger over the careful brush strokes of the two characters and read *Peace* written in English below them. Another cup had a symbol with the word *Clarity* printed below it. A long drink from both is what she needed. Like that would do the trick. Who was she kidding?

A garden elf, smiling way too broadly, flashed into her line of vision, and she set down the teacup. "Well, hello, you ugly little man." She paced in front of the elf as if waiting for her comment to erase his smile. "What, no comment? I get it. You're the silent type. Hah! I've finally found someone who will listen." She curtsied and held out her hand then grabbed the elf and one of Fiona's famous coffee mugs and set them on a low shelf close to the counter. A small box served as a table to hold the mug near the elf's hand. She grabbed the tape dispenser, pulled a cigarette from her pocket, and taped the cigarette to the elf's mouth.

"Just what you need, little man, caffeine and nicotine. Twins of seduction."

* * *

Near the end of her shift, when she was straightening up the cash drawer, the elf was again in her line of vision. He still smiled behind the cigarette. "Pretty satisfied with yourself, aren't you?" Sara wanted Stan to see the elf like that, but he'd be tied up in the Hut until it closed, and Iris was on duty next. Sara didn't think Iris would appreciate the joke. "Well, little man, for now you're a closet smoker." Sara picked up the elf, mug, and box and set them inside the coat closet. "Stan will appreciate your new addictions."

* * *

Iris blew in with a huff. "Oh, my God, I hope I'm not late."

Sara glanced at the clock. "You're fine." Twenty minutes wasn't bad for Iris, but Sara wondered if Fiona had ever chewed Iris out for her tardy habits.

On her way out, she walked down the aisle that contained Fiona's items. Fiona's placard lay face down on the shelf, and Sara set it back on the easel, turned to leave then debated flicking it off again when the Seal Rock ashtray caught her attention. She had to have it. She reached in one back pocket then the other for her wallet, but both were empty. She must have forgotten it in her frenzy to be on time. Well, she needed an ashtray. She turned it over in her hands and fingered the seals. She hated to give Fiona the sale but had to admit Fiona had done a damn good job on this one. She held it to her chest and looked back at Iris who was dabbing her face with a frilly handkerchief and talking non-stop on the phone. Sara would just run upstairs and get the money. Besides, she still had to pay for her coffee. She clutched the ashtray and hurried toward the door. She felt like a thief. Why not get the money first and come back? No, someone would buy it in the meantime. That's what always happened. Any time she wanted something that was right there, right within her reach, the next moment it was gone. She'd get the money and come back.

After all, hadn't Fiona done the same thing with that necklace? But Sara could never strut proudly through life like Fiona did. No, she always felt like a fraud having to justify her existence. What was it her AA sponsor said? That her self-analysis always seemed to lead her to self-destruction. Okay, stop analyzing! As if she could. She scrambled down the hallway and out the door.

* * *

When Sara got to her apartment, she set the ashtray on the desk, thinking about how much she missed Jamie. Three generations of women all connected to this ashtray and the place it represented. And the link between all of them was broken but maybe not beyond repair. Sara grabbed her wallet and headed back downstairs.

Stan stood behind the counter with his arms folded as Vic snapped his cell phone shut. When Vic saw her, he motioned to her while Stan nodded. No sassy comments. Something must be wrong.

"What's up?" Sara asked.

"Need a big favor." Vic laid his phone on the counter, grabbed the pencil behind his ear, and wrote some directions on a napkin. "The supply truck I was expecting broke down, and I need the wood for some cabinets I'm making. If I want to stay on schedule, I have to go get the lumber. Stan's offered to help, but someone has to cover the Hut until closing. Any way you can do it? It'd sure save me the time of trying to rustle up someone. If you can't stay till closing, maybe you can find someone to relieve you?"

Sara shrugged. "Sure."

Vic smiled and patted her back. "Thanks. I owe you one."

* * *

Sara grabbed an apron and some clean mugs from the back, returned to the counter, and saw a well-dressed woman with an updo looking at her watercolor of Jamie. The woman's designer clothes and diamond tennis bracelet made her look more sophisticated than most people who came to the Hut, and Sara was a bit unnerved by her fixation on the picture. Just as Sara was about to take her order, the woman pointed to the painting.

"That location." She looked at Sara. "It's the carousel at Pier 39 in San Francisco, isn't it?"

Sara nodded. The woman returned her gaze to the picture, and Sara noticed her eyes watering.

The woman turned back to Sara. "I used to visit my daughter and her family there, and I took my granddaughter to the pier." She pulled out a tissue and dabbed her eyes. "She enjoyed riding the carousel more than anything." She stopped talking and blew her nose. "She got very ill not long after I returned home from my trip last year." She looked away. "I never saw her again."

"I'm so sorry." Sara was uncomfortable, but before she knew what to say next, the woman drew a deep breath and pulled up her shoulders.

"How much is it?"

Sara hadn't expected those words. "Uh, what do you mean?" That was dumb. But it bought her time. She'd never really considered selling the picture. She couldn't avoid thinking that this was the right reaction, wrong grandmother. Fiona hadn't been moved one iota by the painting and probably never would be. But sell it?

"The price." The woman stared at Sara. "It is for sale, isn't it?"

Sara started to say she wasn't sure, but a phone rang nearby. She discovered Vic's cell on the counter. She turned to the woman and said, "I'm sorry, I should answer that."

The woman opened her purse and pulled out a business card. "Here's my card. Please call me when you find out." She turned and left without ordering.

Sara wasn't really sure she should answer the phone, but it had been a timely distraction. She looked at the display. All it showed was a number, no name. It might be about the delivery truck. She opened the phone. "Hello."

"Who is this?"

Sara knew right away it was Fiona.

"This is Sara."

"Sara?" There was a lengthy pause. "Where's Vic? Why are you answering his phone?"

"Vic had to leave. The truck with his cabinet supplies broke down, and he had to go get them."

Sara listened to silence again for several seconds before breaking it. "Hello. You still there?"

"Of course I'm here. That doesn't explain why you're answering his phone."

"He asked me to take over for Stan in the Hut, so Stan could help him unload, but apparently, he forgot his phone. I answered in case the driver was trying to get a hold of him." Why did she feel she had to explain her every action to Fiona? She waited for a response but heard nothing and realized the connection had been broken.

Chapter 24

Tuesday, Week Four

Fiona slammed down the phone and fell back on her bed after hearing that Vic had left town. She reached over to stroke Pet. He wagged his tail and licked her hand. As she sat up, a wave of nausea overtook her, and she stumbled over Pet in her dash to the bathroom.

Her anger boiled as she thought of Vic leaving town without telling her. Shuffling back to the bedroom left her weak, and she struggled to punch in Stan's cell number. She was too irritated to listen to him rattle off some dumb spiel and didn't give him a chance to speak before she said, "Stan, it's Fiona."

"Well, it's the lovely Fiona. Hello, lovely Fiona."

"Stan, put Vic on." Her head was spinning, and she couldn't remember when she'd last felt so bad.

"Hi, Babe. What's going on? Why didn't you call my cell?"

He should've said, 'I was just going to call you,' not ask her what was going on. "Where is your cell?" She gave him a minute to discover his missing phone.

"Damn. I must've left it at the Hut."

"On the counter, to be exact, as I found out when I called." Another wave of nausea rolled over her. She cupped her mouth and swallowed. "You couldn't bother to tell me you were leaving town, but Sara knows? Thanks a lot." She was tempted to slam the phone down again but was too weak. Besides, she wanted to hear Vic wiggle out of this one.

"Whoa, Babe, slow down. The supply truck broke down, and I need those fittings and wood. The driver said he'd wait if I could get there right away. Stan offered to help me then Sara stopped by and agreed to cover for a few hours. Nothing I could do but haul ass out of there. I'd have called you once we got the supplies loaded."

Her head now throbbing, Fiona squinted and rubbed her temples. She knew his answer was reasonable but dammit she'd never admit it. "I felt like an idiot when she dropped that news on me."

"Sorry, Babe. I'll make it up to you when I get back. I promise."

"But I need you now. I'm sick."

"What's wrong?"

"I don't know, but I'm throwing up, and I feel like my head's stuck in a vise."

"Sounds like food poisoning. What'd you eat?"

"Well," She stopped when she heard honking cars on Vic's end.

"Listen Babe, I'm on the highway, and I've got to concentrate. Looks like a traffic jam up ahead, and I may have to take a detour. Call Jane. I'll see you in a bit. Love you."

"Luh . . ." Damn him. She hated when he hung up before she was done. Was he so sure of her love that he didn't need to hear her say it? She dropped the phone and lay back on the bed.

* * *

Jane closed the door and leaned against it. She was actually relieved that today was her mom's club meeting because she could put off dealing with *Mother* a while longer. Her mood was already as low as the bottom of a well since her boss had called and asked her to work nights for one more week. Just as she'd gotten used to the idea of working days, another delay. She dropped her shoulder bag on the couch and bent down to pet Cocoa. "C'mon Coke, let's see what Mommy has for you." At the sound of a popping lid, Cocoa meowed and rubbed against Jane's ankles. When she left the kitchen with a tall glass of iced tea, he was slurping tuna in loud, sloppy bites.

Jane headed to her spare room and booted up the computer. While it chirped to life, she heard the phone ring and decided to let the machine pick it up. Sipping tea, she heard Fiona's faint voice, "Jane, are you there? I'm sorry to bother you, but I'm feeling awful. Can you please come over when you get this message? I saw you pull up a few minutes ago, and I unlocked the back door. I'm nauseous and when I try to walk, my head spins." Jane heard a cough then a muffled gurgling sound before Fiona said, "Sorry." She cleared her throat before continuing. "I've been throwing up for an hour, and my doctor thinks I should come in. I'm afraid to drive, and Vic's out of town." Jane shut down the computer.

Two hours later, Fiona, who did have food poisoning, was heavily sedated and settled back in bed. Jane had to change clothes quickly and run out the door to get to work on time. She was two steps from her Jeep when Albert appeared. "Hi Albert," Jane said without stopping.

As she opened the door, Albert said, "H-h-hello," with his head hung so low his slumped body looked like a question mark.

"Albert, I'm sorry, but I really can't talk now. I'll be late for work." Jane climbed into the Jeep and rolled down the window. She knew he was still grieving. "Maybe we can talk tomorrow." Turning the corner of her block, she saw that Albert hadn't moved. His lonely stance made her vow to make time for him tomorrow.

By the time she pulled into the bank's parking lot, her guilt was replaced with concern for Fiona. Someone should check on Fee. She didn't know who else to call but Sara since Stan was with Vic.

"Hello."

Jane heard the cappuccino machine swooshing in the background. "Sara, it's Jane."

"Hey Jane, what's up?"

"I'm at work now, but I need a favor."

"Okay. Shoot."

"It's about Fiona. I didn't know who else to ask. Fiona got a call from Vic. They got a flat tire and discovered the spare one needed air too, so they don't know how late they'll get back in town."

"What do you mean?"

"When I got home, Fiona called. I had to take her to the doctor. Turned out to be food poisoning, and the meds knocked her out." Jane hesitated. "I think someone should check on her. Would you mind?"

"Not sure I should be the one."

Jane heard her inhale.

"Especially after she found out that I knew Vic left town before she did."

"She'll get over it. If there's one thing I know about Fiona, she's brutally honest. She speaks her mind and then she's over it."

Sara wanted to say, brutally honest? More like brutally dishonest.

Jane's message screen beeped, and she had to get off the phone. "Please, I can't leave work, and I'm concerned about her. The doc said she'd be out of it for several hours, so she should be fine for a while." Jane waited. "I'm not above begging, you know."

"Okay. But I'm only doing it because you asked."

"Thanks." Jane glanced at a flashing error message. "I've got to go. If you knock on her back door, she should hear you. If she doesn't, knock on the far corner window in back. That's her bedroom."

"Gotcha."

"Thanks again. Let me know how she is, okay?"

"Sure." Jane heard the click of Sara's phone before she could say goodbye. She wondered why Fiona and Sara didn't get along. But then, what did she really know about Sara? Sara hadn't said much about her life in California, and Jane hadn't asked. If she thought about it, how much did she know about anyone in her life? Meeting Angie at her mom's the other day had been an eye opener. Never would Jane have expected *Winifred* to have a friend like Angie. It was clear from even the short time she was there that the two were more than acquaintances and that Angie was more like Fiona than she was like her prim and proper mother. And Jane knew what Winnie thought about Fiona. Jane would never understand what made Winifred tick—never.

I don't move from the couch for a long time after the horrible thought that my brother could be dead. When I finally get up, it's 6:40. I call my boss and tell her I think I have the flu. She's very understanding, asks if I need anything. I say no and that I hate to miss work. It's not a total lie. That job is the best one I've ever had, or at least I like it more than any of the others.

I crawl into bed and pull the covers up to my chin. I want to fall into a deep sleep. I close my eyes. I try to clear my mind. I want to rest. I hum ohm, ohm, ohm.

* * *

I wake up sweating. In my dream my brother was dead. But he wasn't old. He was a boy. A boy in a red cowboy hat and black boots. He was laid out in a coffin, a boy-sized coffin. I shiver. I'm ready for my friend in the cabinet. All I have to do is walk to the kitchen, but as I reach for the cabinet door, my stomach churns. I lean into the sink and hurl last night's scotch. I turn on the faucet and lean into the stream. I swish the water in my mouth and spit. I clean up the sink with a towel and toss it in the trash.

I sit at the table and tap my chewed nails while I'm looking at the phone. It won't hurt to call information and see if they have a listing. Even if they don't, he might have moved to another city. That seems unlikely though. He was like a tree, once planted, there for life. Why did I say was? Is, is, *he* is *like a tree. Oh, shit. I pick up the phone and give the operator the city and name. I stand and circle the table as a recording spouts the number. I should write it down, just to have, just in case. I don't have to call, but I can if I want to. If I have an emergency. If I need, say, some medical information. If I want to know how his family is doing. If I want to see . . . But I don't know what I'll discover. Will I be accepted? Hated for leaving? Forgotten?*

I run to the bathroom, lift the lid, and throw up again. Forgotten. That's not something I'd ever considered. I flush then rinse my mouth, but the bitter taste runs deep, and bile churns in my gut.

I return to the kitchen, to the cabinet, to my J & B. I hold it by its slender neck and caress its smooth surface. I know this is it. Now or never. Do or die. Die. There it is again. I now know what I'll do. I twist the top and listen as the booze gurgles down the drain then toss the bottle in the trash. With a resolve I haven't felt in a very long time, I pick up the phone and dial information again.

Chapter 25

Tuesday, Week Four

Sara didn't have time to worry about Jane's request because just as she put her phone back in her pocket, a group of women approached the counter and ordered lattes. From then on, business was steady until Clem came by a couple of hours later and offered to close up. The worry didn't set in until she climbed the stairs to her apartment. What mood would Fiona be in? It wasn't until she closed the door and saw the ashtray that she realized she hadn't paid for it. Too late now. Handiwork House was closed. Well, she wouldn't use it until she paid for it, until it was hers.

She lit a Marlboro. The seal on the ashtray seemed to be barking at her, warning of a storm. Boy, was her imagination running wild. She was nervous and excited at the same time. Would she really be able to tell Fiona who she was now? Could it possibly happen today? She paced the rooms to the quickening beat of her heart. She took a deep drag on her Marlboro and spun on her heel toward the kitchen. Eat. That's what she should do. She stubbed out her half-smoked cigarette in the sink then laid it on the counter and looked in the fridge. Anything to get her mind off Fiona. But all she found was moldy cheese and stale bread. She slammed the door and picked up the half-smoked cigarette, relit it, and smoked it down to the filter then mashed it in the sink, turned on the faucet, and watched it disappear down the drain. She turned away from the sink. She knew Jane had no idea what emotions the request had unleashed, but a promise was a promise. Too many broken ones in her life already.

* * *

The Toyota's engine knocked then sputtered, echoing Sara's thoughts as she shut off the ignition. There was Fiona's red brick house with the white wicker glider on the front porch. Marigold-filled pots sat on top of the railing. Geraniums sprouted from window boxes while overflowing ferns hung in each corner. Had these flowers been there that awful day when she'd felt more like an ignored piece of furniture than a person? Surely they were, but all she could think of then was Fiona's hurtful words as she leaned against the splintered post. Now, she even noticed orange tiger lilies adorning the black iron fence. She looked at the windows. The house was dark. Maybe Fiona was sleeping. Maybe Sara should just leave.

Out of nowhere, came a slumped-over, scrawny man wearing a baseball cap. He didn't approach her car but walked back and forth nearby, stealing furtive glances in her direction. She opened the car door and eyed the stranger, who nodded and mumbled before scurrying away. She'd have to ask Jane about that odd little man. She walked down Fiona's driveway to the back gate that Jane assured her would be unlocked. She pulled the latch and stood on the brick walk while lighting a cigarette. Trying to summon courage, she puffed, paced, and glanced at the house then looked toward the garage window. A curtain hid its contents. She looked around the yard then noticed a shed in the corner. A chimney rose from one end. She walked across the yard to peek inside. A sliver of space separated the curtain panels, and even in the fading daylight, Sara could make out Fiona's pottery wheel. When she leaned in and pressed her nose to the window, she saw the edge of a kiln under the chimney. She sighed after the brief glimpse of Fiona's work space as she headed toward the back porch. There she saw a cushioned glider beneath hanging dream catchers. Wind chimes jingled and macramé planters swung with the warm breeze that blew through the trees behind the yard. Sara pictured herself sitting in the swing, closing her eyes, and rocking slowly. What would it be like to be a real part of Fiona's life and not be relegated to the floor and a post?

A creaking door hinge startled Sara. The man she'd seen earlier now stood inside the gate. Sara looked at him, wondering what the creepy man wanted. She tried to sound authoritative, but her voice cracked. Any courage she'd summoned earlier was gone, transformed into quivering lips. "Fiona is sick." Sara pointed to Jane's house. "Jane asked me to come by."

"O-o-oh." The man shuffled his feet.

"I'm Sara, Jane's friend. And you are?"

The man raised his head and stopped shuffling. "A-a-albert, a neighbor," he said, pointing down the block then lowering his eyes again.

Aha. This was the man the dead woman's daughter had mentioned. "Hi, Albert. Well, I need to check on Fiona." She turned back toward the house then glanced over her shoulder to see him ambling down the driveway.

Sara knocked tentatively. She knew Fiona wouldn't hear the tapping unless she was standing right on the other side of the door. She wanted to leave now. To tell Jane that she'd tried but couldn't wake Fiona. As much as she wanted to take that easier route, she knew she wouldn't. Besides, what if Fiona really did need her? Wouldn't she love to be Fiona's savior and have Fiona indebted to her? Sara began to dream of the two of them smiling, laughing, and maybe even walking together to a movie or something. She sighed, drew her shoulders up, and took a deep breath. Not the time for daydreaming. Time for action. One-hundred, ninety-nine, ninety-eight, oh hell. She banged on the door. Why did she agree to this? She was just turning to leave when a light came on in the kitchen, and the back door creaked as a blinking Fiona opened it slightly. Her dog trotted to the door, stood next to Fiona, and began barking, his tail wagging, like he remembered Sara. "Pet!" Fiona scolded and he stopped barking. Sara offered her hand to Pet, and he sniffed then licked it heartily. It felt good to be remembered even if it was by a dog.

Sara stared at Fiona, who looked as white as the tile floor. She pulled her terrycloth robe tightly around her and squinted. "What in the world?"

"Jane asked me to check on you."

"Check on me? You woke me up with your loud pounding. You may as well have been pounding my head instead of the door." She grabbed her head, and her robe fell open, showing a ratty nightshirt, unbuttoned almost to her naval. One breast was partially exposed. In that moment, Sara wondered if it had ever fed her. Sara tried not to stare, but the thought was making her head spin. One more minute, and she'd either be on the ground or out of sight. So much for opportunity. She'd been the only one doing the knocking today.

"Well? You've checked on me. Now, will you leave so I can go back to bed?" With Fiona's outburst, all Sara saw now was bloodshot eyes and a pallid, drawn face that reflected a woman no longer staying ahead of age.

It took Sara a few seconds to respond. "Yes, I'll leave, but Jane was worried." She stepped away from the door. "I'll tell her no need to."

"I just need rest, not visitors." Fiona pulled her robe around her and tied the belt. The nearly exposed breast was once again safely covered, and Sara, too, had recovered. Fiona's vulnerable moment disappeared like it had been tapped by a magician's wand. Not waiting for Sara's mumbled goodbye, Fiona shut the door, barricading herself from her daughter. Sara turned and rushed to her car.

After a few squeals and sputters, the car jolted to life. She drove a couple of blocks then pulled over and lit a Marlboro. She sat back and inhaled deeply. This is what Fiona is, right here, right now. A middle-aged childless woman who would never accept Sara. She could never again be the young mother Sara had always dreamed about. She flicked her ashes out the window, took one last puff then put the car in drive and pulled away.

* * *

Seconds after slamming the car door, Sara took the steps to her apartment two at a time. When she got inside, she kicked the door shut with her foot. She should call Jane. Breathe in, breathe out. Jane would want to know how Fiona was doing. She pulled her phone from her pocket. Ninety-nine, ninety-eight, ninety-seven.

The phone rang several times, but just as Sara was about to hang up, Jane said, "Hello," in a breathless voice. Sara heard tapping on a keyboard and regretted calling.

"It's Sara. You wanted me to let you know about Fiona, but you sound busy."

The tapping stopped. "Nothing's wrong, is it?"

"Well, nothing's right." Sara walked to her front window.

"My God, what is it? Is Fiona worse?"

Jane's voice rose and Sara realized her sincere concern showed how deep Jane and Fiona's friendship was. That triggered something in her. Was it jealousy? The wish that things were as they should've been? "Oh, don't worry about Fiona, she'll be just fine, believe me." Sara jerked the blind shut, circling the couch before plopping down.

"Then what's wrong?"

"Oh, she was just her usual bitchy self." As soon as Sara said it, she realized how petty she sounded. "I'm sorry, Jane, it's just that Fiona was less than pleased to see me." She paused. "You remember how she treated me at her house the other day? Well, compared to today, she was angelic." After she said it out loud, she realized how true it was and how bad it made her feel.

"I'm sorry. I don't know why she's like that with you." The line seemed to go dead, and Sara thought they'd been disconnected, but then Jane came back on the line. "Sorry, I had to put you on hold. I really can't stay on the phone."

Before Sara could say anything else, Jane continued. "Hey, what about meeting for a drink when I get off? That should be about 1:30. Will you still be up?"

"I think that's pretty likely." Sara stood and strode to the window, peeking outside as if expecting someone. "I doubt I'll be able to sleep for a while." She turned away. "In fact, I was thinking about heading to Jerry's to see if he could use me for a bit. Might as well make some money if I can't sleep."

"Okay, see you later then."

When Sara left the apartment, she craved a drink and thought about that AA meeting she'd never attended. She headed toward St. John's instead of Jerry's. Maybe there'd be a meeting tonight.

* * *

After catching the tail end of the AA meeting, Sara walked to Jerry's. The place was swamped, and Jerry was glad to put her to work. A group of middle-aged Harley riders had come to town on their cross-country trip. They were loud and rowdy but good tippers, and by the time Jane joined her, the bikers had moved on, and she was exhausted but in a better mood.

Sara poked the ice in her Coke with a straw while she listened to Jane complain about her job. Then Jane moved on to Greg. All Sara heard was e-mails, getting together, should she, shouldn't she . . . Sara twirled her straw, close to shouting how if Jane really wanted a problem to solve, she could give her one. When she looked up, there was Laurance, holding a tumbler, smiling and pointing to the booth. Saved again by her knight. Sara slid over. "Sure. Join us." He had no idea how thankful she was to see his smiling face.

"Jolly good. Can't think of anything better." He raised his glass.

Sara couldn't help but grin as she raised hers. Jane rolled her eyes but raised her mug to the unspoken toast.

Before Laurance got the glass to his lips, his phone rang. He pulled it from his pocket, and when he looked at the display, his smile disappeared. "Oh, bloody hell." He set his glass down. "Pardon me, ladies." He faced away from the booth as he answered it. "Hello." His free hand gestured as he explained. "You know I like a nightcap. As a matter of fact, I'm here with your sister and her friend." His back straightened as he listened. "When did this become a problem? I often go for a nightcap when I've been held up late with clients." Laurance drew his head back slightly. "I didn't know you felt that way. I didn't know that was your expectation."

Sara heard a noise from Laurance's phone then Laurance closed it, muttering something about reading minds.

"Trouble in Paradise?" Jane asked.

Before Laurance could react, Sara popped in. "Paradise? As in *Paradise Lost*? Does such a place exist to lose? I doubt it." She picked up her Coke, wishing more than ever it was mixed with Jack Daniel's.

"Spot on!" Laurance lifted his glass. "I don't know about you two, but I could go for a good American burger. Care to join me?"

"Won't you be in the doghouse if you don't get back to your bride-in-waiting?" Jane asked.

Laurance shrugged. "If I'm not mucking up wedding plans, I'm mucking up something else. Why change now?"

At the mention of food, Sara's stomach rumbled. "I'm game. I'm famished."

Laurance stood and looked over at Jane.

"I guess I'm in, too." Jane scooted out of the booth and the three headed out the door.

Chapter 26

Wednesday, Week Four

Marv got to the phone just in time to hear a sharp intake of breath before the line went dead. What was going on? His answering machine had several messages like that with *unknown caller* on the ID screen. Now this call seemed to confirm that somebody was on the other end. With the phone still in his hand, he walked to the recliner and slumped into it. He hadn't told anyone about the pain, and he'd kept the doctor's latest news from Janey. The treatments weren't working. The doc had said positive thinking could go a long way in healing and even in managing pain. He'd wanted to tell the doc, sure, easy for you to say. Find out you could die tomorrow while pain rips through your gut and see how easy it is to think positive thoughts. He closed his eyes.

Rusty's barking startled Marv from his nap. Before he could hush Rusty, someone knocked. He lifted himself up from the recliner and opened the door. A woman stood on the steps. Her eyes were closed and her head hung low. "Can I help you?" He asked. She opened her eyes and slowly raised her head.

"Hello, Marv." Tears trickled down her cheeks.

Marv searched her face for recognition. Seconds later, disbelief overwhelmed him. "My God, Glenny! Is it really you?" It took him a second to recover when she nodded, and he wrapped his arms around her. After they'd embraced, he led her inside. By now they both had wet faces, and he grabbed the tissue box.

"My God, where have you been all these years? Why didn't you call?" Marv stopped. "That was you on the phone, wasn't it?"

Glenda blew her nose and nodded at the same time. "I've been calling, but every time I did, I, well, I just, I couldn't say anything." She covered her face.

"I know. I know." He put his arms around his kid sister. "You're here. Nothing else matters right now."

"I thought you might still be here, but I wasn't sure till I dialed information for your number." When he finally let her go, she stepped back and looked around. "Quite a few changes since I was here last. Where's Winnie? She at work? And why are you home? Retired already?"

"Whoa. That's a lot of questions. Shouldn't I be the one asking them?" He noticed her flinch and motioned for them to sit. They both headed for the couch like they couldn't bear putting any more physical distance between them. As he sat down, Marv wondered how Glenda managed to show up when he most needed her. "First, Winnie. Well, we divorced years ago."

"What? I don't believe it." Her shock electrified the room.

Marv inhaled. "She's been remarried for a long time." He paused. "Came up in the world quite a bit. Lives in a highfalutin' neighborhood uptown."

Glenda lowered her head and whispered. "What about Jane?"

Marv stiffened. "She's all grown up. On her own now. Beautiful and all. The light of my life, that girl." But he wouldn't tell Glenda, that until just now, Jane was his only reason to go on. He wasn't going to smother the good news of her return with his cancer. And as happy as he was to see Glenda, her presence wasn't without problems. Problems he didn't want to think about right now.

Glenda said nothing, just wiped her eyes with a tissue and nodded. In a muffled voice, she said, "I'd like to, to see her."

Marv ignored his aches and lifted himself up. "We'll see." He hobbled toward the kitchen. How was he going to tell Glenda that he'd never even told Jane about her? He'd anticipated that battle for years. "Want some coffee?"

She nodded. "You can't put me off forever." She got up to help him. "I'm here now, and I, well, you know what that means."

Marv scooped coffee into the pot, added water, and turned it on to brew. "Yes, Glenny, I do." He sat on a stool. "We need to talk to Winnie first. We," he pointed at each of them, "owe her that much." So, the day he longed for and dreaded had arrived.

Glenda nodded. "I bet Winnie will be shocked to see me."

"I'm sure she will be." His words were sterner than any he'd uttered so far. "I mean, you took off and never let us know anything for all these long years. I didn't know if you were even still alive." His eyes blazed and for the first time since he answered the door, he felt anger. "How could you do that? How?" He clutched the counter's edge and waited for the coffee to stop brewing. He didn't want her to leave again for another thirty plus years. He didn't have that many left. He had to calm down. "We have to talk. Or maybe I should say you have to talk, and I'll listen. I want to know where you've been. What you've been up to." He poured coffee into the mugs and handed her one. "Then maybe I'll understand how you could just disappear. And then, we'll decide when and how to tell Winnie." He followed her back into the living room, but this time he sat in his recliner and waited.

* * *

". . . and so I ended up in Florida for the last couple of years. It was the only place in the states indigenous to the ghost orchid that I wanted so badly to see again." Glenda set down her empty mug.

Marv rubbed his eyes, smearing a tear or two. "Well, all I can say is that's some life. And here I sit, in the same spot I was when you left. My life must seem boring."

Glenda reached over to pat his knee. "Oh no, Marv, no. You're still the same big brother I remember. I'm so glad you're still here. You're my rock. It's why I, why I, you know." She slumped back on the couch and grabbed a tissue.

Marv pulled himself up from the recliner. "I think we could both use a bite to eat then we should just enjoy being together." He headed for the kitchen. "Now, how do you feel about some homemade vegetable soup?" He turned to her. "Janey made it."

Glenda smiled. "I'd love some."

"Jane brought me some sourdough and whole grain rolls from the bakery, too. They're both mighty scrumptious. You have a hankering for one over the other?"

"Whatever you're having is fine."

Marv looked at the bag of rolls. He had a decision to make, and it had nothing to do with food.

Glenda walked up behind him. "I'll help. Where are your pots?" He pointed to a cabinet and got Jane's soup from the fridge. He set it near the stove as Glenda shooed him out of her way. He grabbed the bag of rolls and laid them on the table then sat down. He was tuckered out anyway, but she couldn't know that. While he watched her take over in the kitchen, he wondered what was in store for all of them. He hoped that after a night's sleep, the answers would come. He felt that in some way he'd been preparing for this moment for years. Or was he just bracing himself against it? Now the day was here. Glenny was back. He didn't know what to do.

* * *

Winifred still clutched the phone and didn't move from the kitchen table after the call ended. Glenda. She couldn't believe it. After all these years, Winifred had put Marv's sister out of her mind. Yes, they'd been friends once, long ago. As much as you could be friends with someone who seemed determined to destroy herself. God knows, she'd been there for Glenda when she really needed to be. That was just it. She never thought she'd have to face this day. Until now, she hadn't really spent much time dwelling on all the reasons she and Marv divorced. But here it was right in front of her. They'd never agreed on how to explain

Glenda to Jane. She'd won out, and they'd said nothing. From then on, it was as if Glenda had never existed. Now Glenda was back, and Winifred could no longer ignore the inevitable. Inevitable. How she hated that word.

She looked at the phone still in her hand. If ever she needed a shopping spree, it was now. With Jane. Yes, a splendid idea. They hadn't talked since Jane had stopped by during her group's meeting. But how could she convince her daughter to come? Jane had nothing but disdain for spending time at the mall. Maybe for once Jane would do something just because Winifred wanted it. She knew how unlikely that was but had to try anyway. If only Jane could be more like Elizabeth, who'd never turn down an opportunity to shop. Elizabeth. That was how she'd convince Jane to come. Maybe they could shop for Elizabeth's shower gift. She stared at the phone as if for an answer. And she did want to ask Jane about Laurance. She'd overheard Elizabeth complaining to her father that Laurance had been out late with Jane and a friend. Winifred would find out what was going on. Elizabeth would be grateful for any information Winifred could glean about Laurance's late-night habits. And, she'd find out if Jane had talked to Glenda. Mary had assured Winifred that the three of them would talk first, but Winifred couldn't be sure Glenda would keep her word. She didn't know what kind of person Glenda had become, but she certainly remembered what kind of person Glenda had been. She shuddered. She couldn't press Jane's speed-dial number fast enough. Her call went straight to voicemail. Winifred hung up and dialed Jane's house, but this time it rang quite a while before the answering machine clicked on. Clearly, either Jane wasn't home, or she had turned off the ringer. Winifred thought for a moment about driving over there, but she knew how much Jane disliked unannounced visitors.

When the phone rang seconds later, she expected to hear Jane's voice, but surprisingly, it was Elizabeth. A half hour later, she was headed out the door to meet her stepdaughter. Winifred was pleased to be asked for help in buying the going-away dress. Why did that girl always seem to know what Winifred needed? That's the kind of relationship she wanted with Jane.

* * *

Winifred hoped Elizabeth hadn't thought she'd been too distracted while searching through tropical clothes for her honeymoon. A couple of times Elizabeth had called her name twice before Winifred heard her. The soon-to-be-bride seemed a bit down most of the time but had perked up at the jewelry counter when Winifred told her to pick out something nice. After looking at necklaces, bracelets, and earrings, Elizabeth settled on some diamond earrings she said were larger than the ones Laurance had gotten her for her birthday.

Over salads and bottled water at the food court, Winifred had tried to listen intently to Elizabeth's concerns about Laurance's recent behavior. She was pleased that Elizabeth confided in her and wished she had gotten information from Jane to share. From what Elizabeth said, Jane was entertaining her sister's fiancé at all hours of the night. Winifred hadn't raised Jane to act that way. Sometimes she wondered, just wondered.

Winifred dropped her shopping bags on the couch and looked at the Hummel figurines Elizabeth had gotten her over the years. She touched the delicate base of the Forget-Me-Not Hummel and ran her fingers over the little girl with the flower basket. What a lovely young woman Elizabeth was. Winifred would have to talk to Jane about her behavior, keeping Laurance out late when he should be home. And with a friend, no less. Remind her how much she was hurting Elizabeth going behind her back like that. This was what mothers did, wasn't it? Mothers taught their daughters, taught them and protected them. She'd have to convince Jane that everything she'd ever done had been for her own good. But who knew what their relationship would be like after she talked to Glenda? Could she convince Jane that her decisions had always been about protecting her? Winifred glanced out the window at her rose bushes. Yellow, red, pink, white. They were so bright and full of blooms. But fall was right around the corner, and sometimes that season reared its ugly head with a deep drop in temperature. Frost. She'd need to be sure she had something to cover them with, something to shield them from the harm the cold could bring.

Chapter 27

Friday, Week Four

At the sound of a blaring ringtone, Sara flung her feet off the couch and looked for the phone. She saw it mocking her from the kitchen counter. She jumped up, grabbed the phone, and flipped it open. "Hullow," she muttered, clearing her throat.

The caller seemed to pause before responding. "Hello. Is this Sara Jenkins?"

Sara grabbed a glass, turned on the tap, and swallowed a sip before answering, "Speaking."

"This is Mrs. Parker. "Is everything all right?"

Sara heard shuffling papers, and the rustling noise frazzled her nerves like fingernails scraping a chalkboard. She took another sip. "Yes." She couldn't admit she'd worked late at a bar last night.

"I've had trouble reaching you." Mrs. Parker sounded like Sara's high school math teacher when she'd failed to do her homework. Sara didn't want to alienate Mrs. Parker, who had understood her need to come to Indiana even if she didn't agree with it.

"I had some trouble with my phone." Sara wasn't going to tell her the trouble was a brief shut-off for nonpayment or that she turned it off when she worked at Jerry's. She pressed her aching temple till she entered the bathroom. An early morning phone call after the late night with Jane and Laurance was the last thing she needed.

"I expected you to stay in closer contact with me."

"I've been calling Jamie." She opened the medicine cabinet, struggled to twist off the bottle cap, swallowed a few aspirin, and whispered, "Or trying to." She shuffled back to the living room.

"What was that?"

Louder, Sara said, "I've been calling Jamie, but Mrs. Robison almost never lets me talk to her. She always has some excuse, like Jamie's taking a nap or getting ready for a party. But I keep trying."

"Sara." Mrs. Parker cleared her throat, and Sara held her breath. Only bad news could follow. "The Robisons want to adopt Jamie. They're pushing for it. They were contacted by a child advocate, who put them in touch with a family lawyer."

Sara felt her heart stop then start up again in warp speed. "Mrs. Parker, please, you can't let them. She's my daughter."

"I'm afraid your being so far away isn't helping. The Robisons pulled some strings and got a hearing date for two weeks from today."

"Please, you've got to stall them."

"I'm afraid there's nothing more I can do. You have to attend the hearing if you want any chance of getting Jamie back. I've seen the advocate's report, and it's pretty convincing. You're going to need a lot of help. You'll need advocates of your own." She paused. "You might even have a better shot if someone the courts approve offers to step in."

"What do you mean?" Was Mrs. Parker hinting at something that would help? Why wouldn't she just say it?

"I think you're smart enough to figure it out, Sara. Don't be so quick to write people out of your life. The fact that your mother left you doesn't make you unlovable. Speaking of your mother, how's that going?"

Sara couldn't explain the complexities of Fiona. She had to focus on Jamie. "I think it'll all be over one way or another very soon." She guessed it had to be, now. She was going to have to find the courage to follow through.

"No matter how that reunion is going, if you want Jamie in your life, you have to come home for the court date."

"But I'm not sure my car will make the trip back right now. And I don't have money for a plane ticket." Tears welled up and Sara grabbed a dishtowel to wipe her face.

"Sara . . ." Mrs. Parker's tone softened.

"She's my daughter. I love her. I just need a little more time. Please, don't let them do anything yet. Please, Mrs. Parker, please. I'm begging you." She was overtaken by a fear that was worse than her fear of monsters under the beds she'd slept in as a child.

"I know you love her, but here's something you have to think long and hard about. Is love the very reason you should let her go?" Sara heard a voice in the background, and Mrs. Parker's muffled response before her full attention returned to Sara.

"B-b-but, I can't," Sara said, her words sputtering like a falling firecracker. Just when she'd been convinced Mrs. Parker was on her side, Sara felt betrayed. "I'll never give her up—never, and you can take that to the bank." There. She'd made her stand. But who could ever be an advocate for her? No one ever had been.

"Well then, I suggest you take my earlier advice and find someone. I think you know you won't have to look far to find people who care about you. You just have to give up some of that pride that keeps you from reaching out. If you reach in the right direction, you just may find arms stretched to meet yours." Mrs. Parker paused. "I can't help you more than you can help yourself, Sara. But my last admonition is to reiterate your need to be in court on the date I told you."

Sara heard someone talking to Mrs. Parker and then papers shuffling again.

"Now I have to go." She heard Mrs. Parker's intake of breath. "Don't repeat the past." Then the phone went dead.

* * *

Sara would have to find a way back to San Francisco. She was beginning to understand what Mrs. Parker hadn't said. Linda Jenkins. But it was so hard. Asking for help wasn't something she was used to. She stood, patting her cheeks with the towel for a long time, thinking about all the years without her mother. And worse, she was starting to believe that those years could never be made up. That wasn't going to be Jamie's life. She wasn't going to repeat the past. Nothing could replace lost years. Nothing. Sara lit a cigarette and brushed back a new tear sliding down her puffy face.

* * *

It was nearly time for her shift at Jerry's. Going to work was about as appealing as slinging bleach in her eyes, but she had to think about the money. Friday nights were busy, so she could make good tips. She toyed with asking Clem for a loan, but she just couldn't. Besides, he didn't appear to have much himself. Of course, stiffing Vic on the last week's rent was an option. She hated the thought, but she'd pay him back later, leave a note in the apartment telling him that. And then there was the problem of Fiona. Okay. Okay. Breathe in, breathe out. One hundred, ninety-nine, ninety-eight.

* * *

Jerry had been staring at her off and on for a couple of hours. After taking care of each new group of customers, she was lighting up, and she knew he wanted to say something.

"Hey, Smokestack. I think cancer's ahead on this round." Jerry smiled.

She grunted. She wasn't in the mood for jokes and ground out the butt then went to check on her customers. When she got back to the bar and gave Jerry her order, Laurance was standing at the other end. Great. She liked mixing it up with him, but she wasn't feeling sociable tonight. She waved slightly and pulled a cigarette from the pack. He sat down next to her.

"Loan a chap a fag?"

"What?"

He pointed to her cigarette.

"Oh." She handed him the one in her hand. As he lit it, she realized she'd never seen him smoke before. "I didn't know you smoked." When he started coughing, she patted his back.

"I don't." He managed to squeak out between coughs. "But I've had a bit of a bad day." Sara walked around the bar to get him a glass of water. He took a drink. "Next time I'll just get pissed."

Sara raised her eyebrows, trying to imagine him mad.

"You know, as you Americans say, drunk." He pretended to chug a drink.

She nodded and turned her head, staring into space and puffing away.

Laurance looked around. "I say, plenty of action in here tonight."

"Sure is." Sara stubbed out her cigarette as a customer raised his mug. "Duty calls."

She stayed busy for another couple of hours. Each time she got back to the bar, Laurance was nursing a drink, but she couldn't stop to talk. Small talk was too hard right now anyway. Around 1:00, business came to a screeching halt as if everyone had to hurry home, or they'd turn into pumpkins.

"Hey, Jerry?"

"Yeah?"

"Mind if I take off?"

"Sure. I can handle things from here."

She gave him a thumbs-up and grabbed her cigarettes off the bar.

Laurance looked at her. "Care to get something to eat?"

Her first reaction was to say no thanks, but then she thought about the apartment and the walls that would entrap her, remind her that she wasn't where she needed to be. No, she didn't want to go back there now. If she could just hang on till daylight, maybe things wouldn't seem so bleak. But she didn't have an appetite. Food would be as difficult to swallow as Mrs. Parker's news had been. "I'd really like to just take a drive. Get away alone for a bit. You know."

"Sure." He looked at his watch. "I should go too. May I walk you out?"

Sara nodded.

When they got outside, Sara said, "See you," and got in her car.

He waved.

She turned the key and waited for the engine to turn over, to sputter. Nothing. She turned the key again, again, again. The car wasn't coming to life. She leaned her head on the steering wheel.

"Sara?"

She looked up to see Laurance's face at her window and rolled it down.

"Car trouble?"

"'Fraid so."

"Need a jump?"

She shook her head. "Battery's new, so it's probably the starter."

"My offer to get a bite still stands."

"I thought you needed to get going?"

He shrugged. "But I'm still hungry."

Guess she could sip a Coke. "Okay." She followed him to his Range Rover.

* * *

Laurance insisted Sara get a burger, and she was surprised at how fast she devoured it. It did taste good. When was the last time she'd eaten, anyway? She and Laurance sat in silence. Just two people caught up in their own worries keeping each other company. Eating. She left to use the restroom and to ask for the bill. Tips had been good tonight but nowhere near good enough to get her back to San Francisco in two weeks. So these few bucks wouldn't make a difference, and it was nice of Laurance to give her a ride. More importantly, he'd kept her from going back to her apartment. She certainly couldn't walk these dead streets all night like she had in San Francisco. There she had Union Square and the cable cars to Ghirardelli and the pier. A perfect city for insomniacs. Not so, River City.

When the server set the bill next to Sara's plate, Laurance reached for it, but Sara covered it with her hand. His hand landed on hers. It was warm. She looked up. His face blushed as he pulled it away. Her hand was shaking. She laughed quickly, hoarsely.

He smiled. "Please, allow me."

"In a word. No." She flipped the bill over and got out her cash. "Consider it payment for the ride." His smile was gone. He looked hurt, so she offered him her sweetest smile.

They got in the Range Rover. "I live above Addicted to the Arts co-op. Do you know where it is?"

He nodded but didn't speak. She didn't know what to say, so she kept quiet, too.

Laurance pulled into the parking lot right in front of the stairway to her apartment.

"Thanks." She had her hand on the door handle.

Laurance looked like he wanted to say something but didn't.

She hesitated before getting out.

"May I walk you to the door?"

She didn't say yes, but she didn't object.

On the landing, she pulled her keys from her pocket and promptly dropped them. She bent quickly and grabbed them. "Shit." She stuck her finger in her mouth.

"What's wrong? What happened?"

She pulled out her finger and looked at it. Blood pooled. "Key got my finger."

He looked at her hand then took her keys. "You need to hold it under running water."

She stuck her finger back in her mouth while he unlocked and opened the door. She flipped on the light, and Laurance walked to the sink. She was right behind him. He gently pulled her finger from her mouth and held it under the water. His hand was still warm, and he was standing so close. His musky scent stirred a familiar feeling in her, and she trembled.

After a minute or two, he pulled her finger from the water and looked at it then grabbed a dishtowel. He held her hand up to the light and examined her finger again. "Bleeding's stopped." He didn't let go of her hand. Slowly he drew it to him and kissed it. Sara didn't move. Now what? They stood together for several seconds. Sara knew she should pull her hand away but didn't. Instead, she traced his lips with her finger. When he didn't pull away either or take his eyes off of her, she stumbled backwards toward her bedroom, pulling him along and unbuttoning his shirt.

* * *

When Sara woke up a couple of hours later, Laurance was standing by the bed in his boxers. He pulled on his shirt and buttoned it. When he reached for his pants, she touched his arm. He brushed her cheek lightly before putting on his pants and shoes.

After Sara heard the front door close, she threw off the sheet that covered her naked body and walked to the window. She spread apart the blind's slats to watch Laurance walk to his Range Rover. For a few seconds, the street light illuminated his lowered head and hunched shoulders. Just as she started to close the blind, she saw Laurance turn and glance up at her window.

Chapter 28

Friday–Monday, Week Four

When Jane drove by Jerry's after work and saw Sara's Toyota in the nearly empty lot, she parked her Jeep alongside it. Monday was supposed to start her dayshift schedule for sure this time, and she wanted to celebrate. She hated the not knowing. Was she going to be working nights, days . . . A set schedule, regardless of the shift, was what she wanted. Actually, days might be a nice change—a way to get in sync with the rest of the world. A lightning bug landed on her shirt, and she brushed it into her palm then set it on a patch of grass. As she approached the bar, a couple stumbled out hand in hand. 'Yes, I'm already gone,' floated from the jukebox then faded as the door closed.

When she stepped inside Jerry's, she saw that the place was as dead as the parking lot had foretold. She squinted in the darkened room but didn't see Sara, so she walked up to the bar to wait. As she lifted herself onto a stool, the old man sitting nearby twisted his head to face her. "Yur a friend 'a Sara's, right?"

She nodded. "She here?"

"Nah." He reached for his mug and swallowed. "They lef' a while ago."

"They?"

"Don' know his name, but he's been here b'fore. Sounds like he hails fr'm the land 'a Her Majesty." He rolled his hand in downward circles and tipped his head then chuckled.

"Laurance," she mumbled.

"Wha's at?"

"Her car's out back?" She questioned as if he could explain why the car was here and Sara wasn't.

He shrugged. "Can't say 'bout that, but I didn' hear 'em make plans to go anywheres t'gether 'fore they lef'."

"Maybe he gave her a ride home." She spoke more to herself than to the old man.

"Sounds like you figgered it out fer yurself." He grinned. "I'm Cap'n, by the way. Why'nt ya set a spell an' have a beer? Last call'll be here soon 'nuf."

As if on cue, Jerry returned to the bar, flung a towel over his shoulder, and shouted, "Last call," to the few remaining patrons.

Captain looked at Jerry. "Me'n Sara's friend here," he glanced her way with a questioning look.

"Jane."

"Jane." Captain nodded. "Sara's friend, Jane 'n me'll have a beer." He pointed to himself. "On me." He turned to Jane.

"I'll have whatever you're having." She smiled. "Thanks."

* * *

Twenty minutes and more shared grievances than a barnyard of cows later, she was out the door just in front of Jerry flipping the Closed sign. Maybe Sara hadn't been available to chat with, but that old man, Captain, had been a good late-night companion. One beer hadn't given her a buzz, but it sure would help her sleep tonight. She needed her sleep because she'd agreed to go to what she assumed was a make-up lunch with her mom tomorrow. As she walked to her Jeep, a moth flew at her face, and she swatted it. When it fell to the ground, dead, she cringed, picked it up, and said, "Sorry little guy. I just reacted." She laid it gently back on the ground. Sorry. Whatever her mom's agenda was, it had better include an apology. Surely Winnie didn't expect her to apologize for not being Elizabeth. After all, Elizabeth was someone else's daughter, and as for Winnie saying she was her dad's daughter, well, what the hell, according to the last biology class she took, sperm plus egg is what equals baby.

* * *

Jane's alarm buzzed in her ear and jolted her awake at 11:00. Just enough time for a quick shower before her mom would arrive. Winnie thought meals should be at set times, and she'd allotted lunch for the usual noontime hour. That meant she'd be at Jane's at least twenty minutes before noon. Precision was not Jane's strong suit. Yet one more thing she apparently didn't inherit from her mom. She was blow-drying her hair when Winnie knocked on the front door.

Winnie's fist was raised mid knock, and Jane gave her mom a fist bump, leaving Winnie momentarily speechless. She recovered soon enough though and huffed her way past Jane. "Really, Jane." Her look clung to Jane like static electricity, and she stood rooted, waiting for the next charge, but instead, her mom said, "When is your landlord going to replace the broken doorbell?" Winnie then brushed some cat hair to a corner of the coffee table and set her purse down. "Haven't you complained about it?"

Jane rolled her eyes. Another typical day with Mom. "Doesn't really bother me." Now she'd get chewed out. Here it comes.

"I'll just wait here till you finish getting ready." She glanced at Jane's wet hair and looked at her watch. "But hurry or we'll be late."

"Oh, do they lock the doors at 12:01?" When Winnie failed to reprimand her sarcasm, Jane knew it was going be a long lunch. She ran her fingers through her damp hair. "Gotta finish drying my hair."

Winnie folded the afghan Jane left on the couch, set it aside, and sat up straight, legs crossed at the ankles, fingers thrumming on the armrest.

As Jane rounded the corner, she gritted her teeth. Winnie would just have to deal with Plain Jane if she was that impatient. Other than a dab of powder on her nose and a swipe of lip gloss, there'd be no fussing today.

Chapter 29

Friday–Monday, Week Four

Winifred was silent as they drove off. Jane had asked to follow in the Jeep, but Winifred insisted on driving. At least this way they'd have the ride home together after she talked to Jane. As Winifred turned into River View Country Club's parking lot, Jane's cell phone rang.

Jane looked at the display and said, "It's Dad."

"Must you talk to him now? Let him leave a message. It's time for lunch." Winifred hoped Jane hadn't caught the quiver in her voice.

"Look out, Mom!" Jane yelled in time for Winifred to swerve before sideswiping a parked car.

"Sorry." Winifred drove slowly around the parked cars to the first empty space, pulled in, and leaned over the steering wheel. Only then did Jane's use of *Mom* register. It hardly seemed worthwhile to mention it now. Why was *Mother* better than *Mom* anyway? Anyone could be a mother. Hadn't she been a good mom? She'd tried. When she sat up, she realized Jane's phone had stopped ringing. So, Jane had listened to her and would return Marv's call later. This was a good sign. But just as Winifred reached for her door handle, Jane's phone beeped.

"Dad must have left a message." Jane looked at her. "I'll meet you inside. I want to listen to it first."

Winifred released the door handle. "I'll wait." Her insides felt like mush. What would his message say? Would Jane's expression give her a clue?

Jane pressed the button on her phone. When she snapped the phone shut, she turned to Winifred. "Something's not right. He sounds strange." She looked at Winifred. "Give me a minute to call him back."

"It can wait till after lunch."

"No, it can't." Jane punched in a number. She snapped the phone shut. "Voicemail. I think we're going to have to cancel lunch. I need to check on him."

"I don't really see what . . ."

"Mom." Jane paused, and Winifred held her breath. "Dad has a serious problem."

Winifred's eyes widened. "What do you mean?" Her hands became clammy and a bead of sweat trickled down the side of her face.

"I guess you don't know."

"What don't I know?" Winifred clutched the door handle and braced her back against the seat.

Jane looked at her mother. "His cancer's returned."

Winifred gasped then covered her mouth, concerned but relieved at the same time, hoping Jane didn't catch the nuance of her reaction. "I didn't know. What's the prognosis? Is it treatable?"

"I don't know." Jane slumped and shook her head. "That's why I'm worried about him. He hasn't said much. Keeps putting things off." She straightened up and turned to Winfred. "Can you take me back to my place so I can get my Jeep?"

Winifred sighed. "I'll take you to Marv's. I should see him, too."

"Not sure that's such a hot idea. I don't think seeing you right now will be helpful."

"You're wrong. He does need to see me now." Winifred backed out of the parking space then sped away. This whole situation was out of her hands. Marv's diagnosis coinciding with Glenda's return felt like an out-of-control fire. Who knew what would survive the blaze.

Jane leaned back and looked out the window. "Whatever."

Winifred said, "I know you don't believe this, but I was a good wife to your dad for many years." Her voice quivered. "And I've always been a good mother to you even if you don't agree. I never left you. When things between your dad and me became unfixable, I took you with me. I never abandoned you."

Jane stared at her. "Neither did he." Her voice rose an octave, and Winifred knew she wouldn't like what followed. "Just because you walked out and forced me to leave didn't mean he didn't want me to stay."

"We both wanted you. Believe me, we had more than one," Winifred cleared her throat, "discussion about that."

Jane turned away, and Winifred could imagine Jane rolling her eyes. As she navigated the streets, she searched for the right words to tell Jane how much she loved her and always had, but she couldn't find them, and they drove on in silence.

Chapter 30

Friday–Monday, Week Four

When they pulled into Marv's driveway, Jane noticed a mud-splattered Cherokee. "Hmm, looks like Dad has company." Winnie jerked to a halt, and Jane flew forward. "What's wrong with you today?"

Winnie opened her mouth to speak, but nothing audible came out, and Jane thought she looked pale.

"You okay?" Jane was beginning to worry about her mom. Did she have bad news too?

As Jane was about to reach for her mom, Winnie turned to her and said, "I'm fine. Let's get this over with."

What the hell? Just when she thought she saw a real spark of humanity in her mom, she'd blown it. Jane got out and slammed the door. Obviously she'd been mistaken.

Before she climbed the first step to the trailer's porch, the door flung open, and her dad stood in the doorway with Rusty. At least her dad looked better than he had the last few times she'd seen him.

"Hon. You got my message. Didn't know I'd get a visit. I just expected a call back."

"I did call. Went to voicemail, and I got worried."

"Really? Must not've heard it." He looked beyond her to Winnie while Rusty barked. Something in Marv's look shifted for a moment, and Jane feared one of her parents' classic fights. Her mom's angry words. Her dad's silence. She knew her mom shouldn't have come. Her dad patted Rusty. "Quiet ol' boy." Then he turned back to them. "Hi, Winnie."

"Hello, Marv."

Jane tilted her head toward Winnie. "Mom and I were about to have lunch when you called." She looked at Winnie and raised her eyebrows. "I wanted to get the Jeep, but she insisted on bringing me here."

"That's okay, Hon." Marv stepped aside for them to enter. "We have some things to discuss anyway."

Jane was puzzled. She thought she'd been the one divulging secrets. What could they be holding back from her? The first thing that struck her when she stepped inside was how airy and neat the place was. The kitchen floor was clean, and there were no dirty dishes in the sink. At least her dad must have had some good days. Just as she turned to comment on how nice the place looked, she remembered the Cherokee. Maybe he had a girlfriend. Wow! That must be it.

She smiled as he closed the door and motioned for them to sit. "Can I get you some coffee or tea?" They both shook their heads, and he sat in his recliner. Rusty ran to Jane then to Winnie and, when he'd had enough attention, plopped down next to Marv.

Jane noticed Winnie wringing her hands. Did she really think Jane would be upset if her father had finally found someone who made him happy? She flicked her wrist toward Winnie. "I have to confess, I told Mom about your cancer. So if you thought you'd have to tiptoe around that one, you don't. We both want to know the latest. Don't we, Mom?"

Marv scratched Rusty's ear then looked at Winnie. "Fair enough. I will. But first things first."

Jane wondered what could be more important than her dad's health, but maybe to him the mystery person was. "Okay, so tell us about the owner of the Cherokee."

He leaned back, met Winnie's eyes for a moment then looked at Jane. He hollered, "Glenda, come on in here." Rusty ran down the hall and escorted a woman to the living room.

Jane smiled. She knew it! He had a girlfriend. She glanced at Winnie to see her reaction and was stunned at her blanched face. She wasn't smiling at all. How could she be anything but happy for Dad? After all, she had Eddie.

Stepping out of the shadows from the dark hallway, the woman forced a smile while Rusty dropped next to Marv's chair. Well, the woman wouldn't have to worry about Jane because she was happy for her dad. Just when she had it all figured out, the woman spoke. "Hi, Winnie."

Startled, Jane sat up and turned toward her mom. "Hi, *Winnie*? You two know each other?" She glanced from one to the other. The woman looked directly at her. With her mouth hanging open, Jane quizzed her dad. "What's going on? Am I the only one who's out of the loop?"

Marv sat up straight.

"Dad?"

"Jane, meet my kid sister, Glenda."

"Sister?" Jane shook her head. Glenda walked over and bent down to hug her, but Jane thrust her hand forward for a handshake instead. She turned again to her dad. "How come you never told me you had a sister?" She looked at Glenda. "I'm sorry, but it's true. All my life he never once mentioned you." Then she looked at her mom. "And you knew and never told me either?"

Glenda walked to the armchair in the far corner and stared at Jane. This newfound aunt seemed more interested in her than in either of her parents.

Her dad spoke before her mom had a chance. "It's a long story, Hon. And sometimes when you let too much time slip by without telling it, a story can get away from you, or . . ." He stopped midsentence.

"How can you not tell your daughter about your sister?" Jane stared at Glenda. "What in the world did you do that made you a pariah in this family?"

"Janey, Hon, calm down. There's lots to tell, and now's the time for telling."

"Marv." Winnie spoke no louder than a breath, and Jane saw how disturbed she seemed. None of this made sense.

Jane sat back and folded her arms. "Okay. I'm ready. Someone needs to start."

Finally, Glenda broke the silence. "I guess I could . . ."

"No, Glenda," Marv interrupted, "it has to be me." He glanced at his ex-wife. "Or Winnie."

A pale Winnie shook her head and waved him off. Jane couldn't believe how upset her mom looked. She almost felt sorry for her without knowing why.

"Janey, Hon, this is something your mom and me should've told you a long time ago." He stroked his clean-shaven chin. "Hard to know where to begin." He looked at Winnie. "Your mom and me, you know, we wanted you so badly, and we've always loved you. You know that, right?" He looked into Jane's eyes, and she nodded. "Of course you do." He nodded back at her. "Well, you see, my sister and me, we had a, well unusual childhood you could say."

Glenda chimed in, "Putting it mildly."

Marv glanced at his sister then turned back to Jane. "But you know some of how it was, the religious part and all. What I never told you was that I had a kid sister who got the worst end of the deal."

"And why was having a kid sister something you kept secret?" Jane wanted facts. The telling was taking too long.

Marv's face turned ashen, and for a moment, every crease appeared deeper, making him look like an old man about to die.

"Sorry, Dad, but I just don't understand. None of this is adding up. You're not the kind of person who could just write someone out of his life. I don't get it." She shook her head.

"You're right. I'm not the kind of person who would do that. And yet it happened. And as difficult as this truth is, it's time to tell it."

Jane heard Winnie gasp. Whatever it was that needed telling, Jane was the only one in the dark. Whatever shadows had hidden the truth, they'd all allowed them to exist for a very long time. More than ever, she felt like an outsider. Not only did she not know Aunt Glenda, but she didn't really know her parents either.

Marv took a deep breath and began to slowly tell Jane about his sister.

Jane let her dad talk. But when he came to the part where he said Glenda had gotten messed up then disappeared from their lives sometime after their mother died, she interrupted. "Okay, so let me understand this." She glanced at Glenda then Marv. "Your sister got fed up with your religious, controlling mother and got a little crazy wild. Then your mother died, and your sister was free. And that's when she runs off never to be seen for thirty-some years?" She shook her head. "Not adding up. I mean, Dad, I know you must care for each other. First thing I noticed today was how good you look." She swept her arm around the room. "And how much better your place looks than it did last time I was here." She folded her arms and looked at both parents. "So what aren't you telling me?"

Winnie dabbed her eyes, and Marv's face looked frozen. Neither seemed able to speak, and after a short pause, Glenda stood and squeezed in next to Jane on the couch, sitting between her and Winnie.

Glenda reached for Jane's hand. "Looks like I'm going to have to be the one to tell you this, after all."

Jane pulled her hand away then turned back to her parents. "Dad? Mom?" But neither of them said a word as if they both understood the inevitability of this moment.

Glenda spoke softly. "I'm not your aunt, Jane." She looked directly into Jane's eyes. "I'm your mother." Jane felt her blood drain.

"What?" She looked at her parents again for some denial. Some protestation against what she'd just heard. But none came. Their visible tears betrayed their lie. She stood and pushed the coffee table out of the way as she moved, putting distance between her and the mother she'd always had and the one she'd just discovered. "This can't be!" She glared at Glenda. "If you were my *real* mother, *why* did you leave me? *How* could you leave me?" Then she glared at Winnie. "And how could *you* lie to me all these years?" Then she looked at her dad. "And *you*, Dad? Not you, too."

Glenda stood and took a few steps toward Jane, but when she tried to touch her, Jane backed away. "No. Don't even."

"I love you, Jane. I've always loved you, but I just . . ."

"You just what, didn't want to be burdened by a baby?" Unblinking, she continued. "Did you even ever *look* at me? *Hold* me? *Feed* me? Or did you just say 'take her away' and split for greener pastures?"

"It wasn't like that." Glenda looked at her feet and whispered. "I wasn't in any shape to care for you. I kept you until Marv found me stoned out of my mind, with you screaming in your crib. I couldn't tell Marv when I'd last changed or fed you." She covered her face and shook her head. "I wish I could say that the memory has haunted me all these years, but I don't even remember it. I only remember the days after when I was sober enough that Marv and Winnie convinced me you'd be better off with them." She reached for a tissue and wiped her face. "And I agreed." She blew her nose and turned to Winnie. "But tell her, Winnie, tell her how many times I called." Winnie looked down and said nothing. Glenda raised her voice. "Tell her! I wanted to come back. I wanted my daughter back, but the papers were signed, and Winnie said it was best if I didn't return and confuse you." She slumped into the armchair. "And like a fool, I believed her, so I tried to move on with my life, but I never could, really." She pressed her fist to her chest. "You were with me every day, but the more time that passed, the harder it was to return. I didn't know how to."

Jane wasn't letting her off that easily. "So why now? Why do I matter enough now for you to disrupt my whole goddamn life? As if it's great to begin with. But this? Who I thought I was, is not who I really am. And if I'm not me, then who am I?" She shook her head, looking at all of them. "I've got to get out of here." She glared at Marv. "I need your truck." She thrust her hand out. "Keys."

Marv sat up and spoke in a cracked voice. "Hon, you're in no condition to drive."

"Never mind my condition, Dad, or should I say Uncle Marv?" The last words came out in a croak. "If you won't lend me your truck, I'll walk. I swear I will. I just can't be here right now."

Marv reached into his pocket and pulled out the keys. Rusty reared his head then tucked it under his paw. "Please be careful, Hon. I love you." He looked at Winnie and Glenda. "We all love you. Maybe that's always been the problem. We all loved you so much we each had our own idea of what was best for you, and now, because of our blindness, you feel lost in between us all."

"Yeah, Dad, I know you love me." She grabbed the keys then pulled her hand away, not letting his grasp linger. "But I can't really look at any of you right now. And don't call me. I'll call you when I'm ready." She slammed the door on her way out.

* * *

After leaving the trailer of co-conspirators, she went home, unplugged her landline, and turned off her cell. For the next two days, Jane felt like an alien in a sleepless, alternate universe. The only time she used a phone was to call in sick to work.

By the time Monday arrived, she hadn't seen anyone since Saturday, not even Fiona, who had no idea what had transpired. In between chugging cans of beer, Jane stayed busy tossing out moldy yogurt and cheese, scrubbing floors, rearranging kitchen cabinets. When she spilled sugar on the counter, she reached under the sink for a sponge and saw the Senseo. She slid to the floor. A gift from Mom. But who is Mom? Winnie? Glenda? Winnie? Glenda?

Jane drew up her knees and sat there until Cocoa brushed her legs. She rubbed his head and saw that she'd chewed her fingernails to the quick. When had she done that?

She wandered into the living room and peeked through the slats in the blinds. Inside, she felt protected. Outside was as dark as midnight during a new moon. A void with no visible path. The only beacon, Fiona's porch light. The only connection, the mail.

Clutching the door, she grabbed the mail from the box. No more Mrs. Peabody to 'Yoo hoo' from across the street. Even Albert was nowhere around. She closed the door and threw the mail on the coffee table before scuffling into the kitchen and grabbing her last can of beer. Damn. She didn't realize she'd drunk so much this weekend. Too bad no one offered beer delivery.

She popped the top, slurping the foam that spilled over the side then headed for her computer. She hadn't been online in days. Maybe now was a good time to read Greg's e-mails. She downed half of the can while waiting for the computer to boot up. When it stopped whirring and beeping, she clicked on Google mail. She had several e-mails from Greg but decided to skim through the others first.

After Jane read Greg's last e-mail, she guzzled the rest of her beer. He wanted to step up their relationship. All she could think of was high school when he'd pressured her for more and never understood why she stopped him every time. Now, she wondered if her reluctance had sprung from Winnie. *Good girls don't let boys peek up their skirts. Good girls cross their legs when they sit down.* She imagined Winnie had really wanted to say *Good girls don't get caught—like your mother did.* Spilling her guts to Greg may empty the venom, but it was the aftertaste she worried about. Still, it had to come out sooner or later. She sat down and clicked on *Compose Mail* and began typing.

> **G,**
>
> **I know I haven't written, but you won't believe what's going on here. Remember my mom, Winnie? Well, turns out she's not really my mother. That's right. She's my aunt. My dad has a sister, and she's my mother. They just bothered to tell me a couple of days ago. It's so screwed up, and now I just don't know who I am. I know you want to get together, but I can't even think of . . .**

She stopped typing when she heard a rapping at her window and got up to see what it was.

Chapter 31

Saturday, Week Four

Sara stepped back from the window and dropped the sheet then headed for the bathroom. Looking in the mirror, she cringed. Who was this person staring back at her? The sex had satisfied to the point of oblivious abandon. But reality had entered the room when Sara touched Laurance's arm. Why had she slept with him? Was falling for a great guy at the wrong time going to be her legacy? Is that what was happening? Was she falling for Laurance? And what about him? What was he feeling? Would she even see him again? Soon he'd be married, and she'd be gone.

She shivered and turned on the shower as hot as she could stand. The water streamed over every inch of her body, but although she scrubbed her skin raw, she couldn't scrub away the guilt or the tender feelings that had emerged.

She wrapped herself in a towel and went into the living room, fell onto the couch, and turned on the TV, flipping through the channels. She wanted a drink. No. Many drinks. Enough drinks that her brain could just float like some ship at sea. Nothing around. Miles and miles of nothing but gentle waves. She grabbed the phone to dial her sponsor but noticed the time and sucked in her breath. One hundred, ninety-nine . . .

It wasn't light yet, but she knew sleep would elude her. When she walked into the bedroom and saw the tangled sheets and clothes tossed near the bed, she pulled on a clean t-shirt and jeans then grabbed a pillow case and shoved everything inside. Sara slung the load on her back and lumbered down the street. The muggy air clung like a second layer of skin. After a few blocks, she stepped under the glow of All-Nite Laundromat's neon sign, promising a twenty-four-hour solution to all cleaning needs, satisfaction guaranteed. Sara stepped inside. Another late-nighter was propped in a corner chair, mouth open and snoring loud enough to compete with the machine. She listened to the washer hissing, spraying, and spinning the dirt away, wishing she could jump in there too.

* * *

By the time she got back to her apartment, the sun was peeking over the horizon. Sara dropped the pillowcase on the couch and mentally clicked off her Saturday chores. She had a shift at the Book Swap to cover then a stint at Jerry's. What if Jane showed up? Sara would have to keep her mouth shut and hope Laurance had done the same. She reached for her cigarettes. The pack was empty. Laurance. Would he stop by Jerry's tonight?

She shook the pillowcase over the couch, snatched the bed linens, and left the rest of the clothes in a rumpled heap. She tossed the sheets and pillow cases on the bed and went to the bathroom to get aspirin. She dumped two of them in her hand, but when she grabbed the water glass, it slipped, and fell to the floor, shattering. Shit. She went to the kitchen for a glass and turned on the tap. When she turned it off, she noticed water standing in the sink. What happened? She couldn't remember doing anything to clog the drain. Damn! Now she'd have to ask Vic to fix it, and he'd see her as a screw-up just when she'd impressed him with her punctuality.

She couldn't do anything about the drain, but she could at least clean up the broken glass. As she swept the pieces into the dust pan, she wondered if she'd missed a sliver that could injure her later.

Sara needed coffee, so she headed downstairs to the Hut. Since it was Saturday, Vic probably wasn't in the office yet, but she could leave him a message about the clogged drain. Clem and the guy who always wore blue flannel shirts had come in early for coffee, so she sat down with them. It turned out that Blue Shirt knew a lot about cars. After they had downed strong cups of coffee, and Sara had left a note for Vic, they decided to check on Sara's car. Blue Shirt's newer-model Ford Ranger was shiny and clean as if it had just been through a car wash, and the jets had sprayed away all the dirt. When the trio piled into the truck, Sara breathed in a whiff of the pine-scented air freshener hanging from the rear-view mirror. She was surrounded by cleanliness.

After hearing Sara's explanation of the problem and having no luck getting the car to even turn over, Blue Shirt said, "Could very well be the starter, but I'll need to slide under that bad boy to know for sure."

Sara kicked at a piece of loose asphalt in Jerry's parking lot. "Well, I can't do anything until I get some money together. Jerry probably won't mind if I leave it here."

Clem cleared his throat. "You're welcome to park it in my garage. I rarely use it for anything other than storage."

Blue Shirt offered to tow it for her.

Clem said, "Probably a better idea than leaving it here. You don't want someone to vandalize it."

When they got back in the truck, Sara squeezed in between the two men. She felt crushed by all these recent events. What would she do? She didn't tell them that even if she could find a way, by some miracle, to manage the car repairs, she'd have no money for the trip back home. While the men chatted and she nodded, all she could think about was downing a Jack and Coke. She really had to get out of this truck before she exploded. Just as she feared she'd jump over Clem to escape, they pulled up to his house. When Clem hopped out to open the garage door and clear some space, Sara almost fell out behind him. As he moved a few things around, Blue Shirt maneuvered the truck to back the car into the garage. Then, while he unhooked the car, Sara and Clem retrieved her Enya CDs, a towel, pens, sketch pad, and a few other items she'd left in the car. Sara grabbed a fast-food bag from the back seat and started filling it with trash that she'd thrown on the floorboards. She handed Clem some of her things as she emptied the car.

"No hurry on getting the car. You can leave it in my garage as long as you need to."

"Thanks." She knew he had no idea how long her need may be. Now she had another loose end to tie up or leave raveled. Clem. Her friend. What would she tell him and when?

* * *

They got back to the Hut just in time for Sara's shift at the Book Swap. She thanked Blue Shirt and said she'd call him. Clem headed for a workshop room to prepare for his classes. Stan told Sara that he'd relayed her message to Vic, and Vic said he'd fix her sink this afternoon. Sara got another cup of coffee, and Iris took over while Stan unlocked the Book Swap. Once alone, surrounded by books, Sara wanted to cry. But she couldn't.

* * *

Vic let himself into Sara's apartment and headed straight for the kitchen. He felt like an intruder since she wasn't home even though she knew he was coming. To say nothing of how aggravated he was to even have to be a plumber today. He'd wanted to talk to Sara about the drain, but when he stopped by the Book Swap, it was full of customers. Then he got busy, and now here he was.

He hated handyman chores, and if he'd been able to talk to her, she would have known that. He couldn't help grumbling to himself as he slid the bucket beneath the pipe then got on the floor and loosened the U-joint with his wrench. Filthy water dripped into the bucket. He twisted around to look at what was clogging the drain and was stunned to see loose tobacco and shreds of paper. What was she thinking? Struggling to contain his anger, he tapped the joint, releasing more wet wads then tightened the joint back and scooted out from under the sink, scraping his back on the cabinet. Cursing, he lifted himself up and turned on the tap. The water flowed down the drain. Now he had to get rid of the nasty water. He picked up the bucket and carried it into the bathroom then dumped the sludge into the commode. Even after two flushes, a grimy residue circled the bowl. He looked around for a brush and saw one propped against the shower stall. He didn't see any cleaning products, so he pumped a little hand soap into the bowl and scrubbed the inside as clean as possible. Vic heard the front door squeak as he walked back to the kitchen.

"Sara?"

"No, Vic." Fiona's voice was as sharp as paper slicing skin.

Vic walked into the living room with the empty bucket swinging at his side. Good thing she'd missed his toilet scrubbing. "Fiona, what are you doing just walking into Sara's apartment?" Times like this heightened their differences, and Fiona's nerve sometimes dismayed him.

"What?"

Vic saw by her arched eyebrows and pinched lips that any answer would be irrelevant.

She set her hands on her hips and continued. "When I asked Stan where you were, he said, in his most put-on sorrowful voice, that you were Victor the Vanquished today. He said you had the handyman blues and then sang several lines of a song he made up on the spot. I had to suffer through his little serenade before he'd tell me where you were and why."

"I know you didn't come to help, so why are you here?"

Instead of answering, she walked toward the cluttered couch. "God, look how she piles her laundry. Is that a pair of panties on top?" Fiona picked up a black lace thong with the tips of her fingers. "Look at this." She shook it at Vic. "Did she leave this here for your benefit?"

Vic hurried over to Fiona, grabbed the thong, tossed it back on the couch, and steered her toward the door while she looked around the room. "Go back downstairs. I'll see you when I get done."

Fiona shook off Vic's hand as if he hadn't spoken and headed toward the living room window.

"Fiona!" Vic gritted his teeth and clenched the bucket.

"Look, Vic." Fiona pointed to a battered desk by the window.

"Yeah, I see the desk. So what?"

In three quick steps, Fiona was at the desk and picked up an ashtray. She walked back to Vic and held it in front of him. "Look familiar?"

Vic set the bucket on the floor and took the ashtray. For God sakes, if Sara had an ashtray, why hadn't she used it? He looked at a barking seal perched on mounds that sloped into a tray painted like a foaming ocean. "One of yours?" He knew it must be the Seal Rocks by the Cliff House in San Francisco.

Fiona nodded.

"So she bought it. So what?" Vic knew Fiona would flush his attempt at diplomacy just like he'd flushed the water from the kitchen sink, but he'd try anyway. "You should be thrilled she liked it enough to buy it."

"You really are going to make me state the obvious, aren't you?" She glared at him. "It's one of the items that's unaccounted for. No, she didn't buy the goddamn thing." Fiona turned and headed for the bedroom.

"Where are you going?" In two long strides, Vic reached the doorway and blocked the entrance.

"I'm going to find out what else she's taken." She shoved his chest and he almost lost his balance. "Now get out of my way." She stormed past him. "Look at that." She pointed to the rumpled heap of sheets on the bed. Bet there's more stolen stuff under there."

"Fiona." Vic grabbed her shoulders rougher than he intended. He let go, shocked at his strong urge to let her have it. He wanted to throw up. He'd been bullied as a child and being pushed set off a trigger he could barely control. He'd never hit a woman before, but Fiona had no idea how much restraint it took right now to keep from slugging her. His fierce reaction scared him, and he held his breath for a moment. "You shouldn't even be here."

Fiona glared but stood her ground.

"Please. Leave. Now."

She crossed her arms in that defiant stance he knew so well. "What do you propose we do about Sara's stealing?"

He turned his head and looked at anything but her. "You need to go. Now. Let me get this damn sink taken care of, and we'll talk later." His calm words surprised him. He wanted to shout, 'Just get the hell out of here before I can't control my anger,' but he didn't.

"She's not going to get away with this," Fiona barked, with a shrill croak a ceramic seal could never utter.

Vic walked her to the door. This time she didn't object. He closed the door behind her and leaned against it. His hands shook, and he shuddered, relieved that Fiona was on the other side of the door. He returned the ashtray to the desk then collected the bucket, taking long, deep breaths on the way back to the kitchen.

Vic was checking the U-joint when he heard the door slam. He banged his head scooting out from under the sink. "Shit." He was ready to yell at Fiona, certain she was back to argue.

"Vic?" Sara said.

He was rubbing his head when she walked into the kitchen. "I thought you had a class after your shift?"

"So did I, but all four people were no-shows." Sara pinched the frayed edges of a dishtowel. "By the way, I just passed Fiona, and she looked really pissed. What's with her this time?"

Vic rubbed his head.

"What happened?" She asked.

"My head was under the sink when you came in, and you startled me. By the way, cigarette butts are what clogged your drain." He gave her a look cold enough to freeze the water he'd removed.

She clenched her teeth and seemed to deflate with his words. "I'm so sorry. Don't know what I was thinking. It won't happen again. I promise."

He wanted to chastise her but her hangdog expression let him know she was taking care of that herself.

Vic wondered if he should mention the ashtray, but just as he was about to speak, his phone rang. When he pulled it out, he saw it was Mike and looked at Sara. "I have to take this." He dropped the wrench in the bucket and flipped open the phone. "Mike, just a sec." He nodded goodbye to Sara, picked up the bucket, and left.

Once outside, he resumed talking. "I'm so glad you called. I've been trying to reach you since your messages, but you didn't return my calls." Damn. Don't make him feel guilty. That won't help anything. "Well, we're talking now, so that's good." He stopped, hoping Mike would speak, but Mike just mumbled. Vic figured he'd have to be the one to bring up the letter Val had mentioned. He set down the bucket and sat on a step. "Your mom told me about your unit being called up to Iraq." He listened as Mike began to talk.

Mike wasn't thrilled about the letter Val wanted to write to his commander requesting noncombat duty. Loyalty to his unit was more important than being the only surviving male heir. After Mike finished talking, Vic said, "Son, you know I'll support you any way I can. It's your decision. Personally, I hate the thought of you in Iraq, but it's your choice, so I'll try to explain to your mom how you feel." When Vic snapped the phone shut, he remained sitting. God, how he wanted to dissuade Mike from going to this goddamn war, but he had to let Mike be the man he wanted to be. No matter how much it hurt him or Val. Vic had long ago joined the ranks of parents who knew the job was tough as hell.

Chapter 32

Saturday–Monday, Week Four

Sara was relieved that Vic left in a hurry. Cigarette butts. Un-freaking-believable! When had she put them down the drain? What must he think of her? How could she show her face again? And imagine Fiona's reaction when she discovered Vic removing butts. God, she really should run away from this mess. Now. Sara shoved aside her laundry and dropped down on the couch. What she really wanted to do was get out of the apartment. How had she ever thought she'd have a chance for a new start with Fiona? She'd been living some kind of fantasy with a fairy tale ending. Now this apartment brought back nothing but the memory of sleeping with Laurance. Funny how connecting with someone here had only increased the loss that smacked her in the face every time she closed the door. Sara picked up a towel to fold but then dropped it on the couch. Connection? Or one-night-stand? And any place she lived should be a place to recuperate and renew, but every time she came to this home, she wanted to leave again. Her stomach growled, and she remembered she hadn't eaten. She decided to walk to Mickey D's for a cheap burger.

As she crossed the parking lot, she heard someone shout her name and turned to see Clem. "Hey," she said, stopping while he caught up.

"Where're you off to?"

"To get a burger and then to work." She didn't really want company but felt obligated to say, "Care to join me?"

"Sure."

"Just going to Mickey D's."

"Okay by me."

While they walked, Clem's words sounded like a distant hum until she heard her name. She turned to him. "Sorry, guess I zoned out. What'd I miss?"

Clem said, "That'd be a complete understatement. I kind of thought you weren't paying attention, but when you agreed to marry me, I knew you were in la la land." He laughed.

Sara sighed. "You're right. I'm not really here. Afraid I'm not good company at the moment. I won't be offended if you want to leave. It's not you. I promise."

"I know." Clem smiled. "You're worried about your car, but like I said, it can stay put."

"It's not that. Well, it is that, but it's so much more."

"Well, if there's anything else I can do . . ."

"Thanks, but it's just stuff I've got to work out."

"Okay, I'll just bet everything will seem better on a full stomach."

* * *

By the time they'd finished eating and returned to the co-op, Clem had timidly invited Sara to go to his niece's birthday party tomorrow in Nashville. Clem said his sister's house was about three hours away and that they could spend the night and return Monday afternoon, quickly adding that his sister had plenty of room. It was a welcomed invitation, especially since she was free the next two days and the distraction from her problems would be a relief.

* * *

When Sara returned home on Monday from Nashville, she stood on the landing, thinking about Clem's family. On Sunday, she'd watched children sing Happy Birthday to a lucky five-year-old. How much better off Clem's niece was than Jamie. That little girl was surrounded by family and friends who loved and adored her. She had everything a child could ask for, a catered party with a clown and a magician. Sara had never known any children who had such parties. And then there was the child's bedroom. It was bigger than Sara's apartment. And the toys! Just like Clem, his sister had been very gracious and hadn't minded making up an extra bedroom. In fact, everyone had been friendly.

As Sara unlocked the door to her apartment, the first thing she saw was the pile of laundry heaped on the chair, where she'd thrown it so she could sleep on the couch Saturday night. The unfolded clothes reminded Sara of everything left undone, and she began to crave that drink she'd avoided Saturday. She dropped her overnight bag on the floor and immediately started folding clothes until she gave up and tossed the remaining pile into a dresser drawer. When she turned around and saw the unmade bed, she snapped the sheets and tucked in the corners then threw the blanket on top. She walked out of the bedroom, grabbed her keys, and headed out the door. A walk on the riverfront was better than staying put and longing for Mr. Jack.

She walked to the river's edge, glanced at the sparkly water then lit up her last Marlboro and watched smoke circles fade into the atmosphere. God, a drink was the best companion for a smoke. She tossed the butt into the river, and the tide carried it away. She wished the rolling waves would carry her away, too. She stepped back on the path just as a bicyclist zoomed past, almost knocking her down. Life was doing a good enough job of that. Clogging the drain had pissed off Vic, and she didn't want to run into him at the co-op. Where else could she go now but to Jerry's? Just because she wanted a drink didn't mean she'd order one. She would slink into a back booth, sip a Coke, and watch those around her, imagining their lives.

* * *

When Sara got to the bar, she never made it to a back booth. Captain was there, and he patted the stool next to him. "Keep an ol' man comp'ny for a li'l while."

She smiled half-heartedly. Damn. She didn't want company now, but she sure could use a cigarette. She sat down, watching the ash on his cigarette lengthen and droop. "Can I bum a smoke, Cap?"

"'Course." Captain slid his pack of Camels to her. "Hep yurself."

Sara pulled out a cigarette then handed the pack to Captain as he flicked his lighter. She leaned toward the flame. They sat in silence puffing and tapping ashes into the ashtray.

Jerry returned to the bar from the poolroom just as Sara had almost finished her first Camel. "Didn't expect to see you tonight." He unloaded empty mugs from a tray. "Nothing better to do, Smokestack?" He laughed. "Should I round up some extra ashtrays?"

"No need. Had to bum this one from Cap." She sucked in the last drag and stubbed out the cigarette. "Just got back in town and thought I'd see what was going on here." She tilted her head toward Captain. "Cap asked me to keep him company, so here I am."

Jerry leaned on the bar. "Can I get you a Coke?"

Sara looked at the bottles of liquor lined up against the mirror. The mirror multiplied the number of bottles, making her feel like Alice in her own horrific Wonderland.

Jerry reached into the cooler and pulled out a Coke.

Sara knew he hadn't seen her drink anything stronger than soda. He didn't know she used to throw back more Jack than a sailor on leave, and tonight screamed Jack Daniel's. Starting with Jack, she counted backwards but never got to the Coca Cola number. She stopped counting at beer and raised her hand when he lifted the can. "Bud Light." Whatever kind of a night this was, it wasn't a Coke night. What the hell. One beer wouldn't kill her. She had controlled those few sips before. She could do it again.

Jerry raised his brows but put the can back and turned to get her a beer.

Sara looked at Captain's cigarettes. "Mind if I have another?"

Captain nodded and handed her the Camels.

She pulled out a cigarette. "I'll bring you a pack tomorrow 'cause I'm pretty sure two won't be enough."

"S'my treat. Call it yur tip fer keepin' an ol' man from bein' lonely." Captain grinned, swigged the last of his beer, and held up the empty mug for a refill.

"Guess if yur gonna be a real customer this ev'nin', I'll hafta join ya."

"I'm just having one beer." She could do it. She had it under control. Anyway, her sponsor wasn't here to dissuade her with catch phrases and woeful looks. When Jerry set the mug on the bar, Sara pulled out a few bills, but Captain rested his hand on hers. "Jerry, put this here beer on muh tab."

"Thanks," Sara said and stuffed the bills in her pocket. A customer dropped money in the jukebox, and music filled the bar. *Freedom's just another word for nothing left . . .* Sara decided what-the-hell. Least she'd get a drink out of listening to an old man's stories.

Captain tipped his head and gulped from the fresh mug Jerry set down. He wiped the foam off his mouth with the back of his hand. "I knew him, ya know."

She looked around. "Who?"

Captain pointed at the jukebox. "Kristofferson." He took another swig.

"That who's singing?"

"Yep."

"Sure is a gritty version of Janis Joplin's song."

He shook his head. "T'ain't her song." He looked at Sara and pointed at the jukebox again. "He wrote it."

Sara cocked her head. "Really? How'd you know him?"

"Workin' in the Gulf. Was a chopper pilot on an oil rig same time as me."

"You were a pilot?"

Captain cleared his throat. "Nah. I skippered a tugboat in N'awlins when oil wells was spoutin' lotsa that black gold."

Sara's eyebrows arched. "So, how'd you meet him?"

"We all met up one way er other." He smiled at Sara. "Lotsa good bars in N'awlins, ya know."

Sara finished her Bud as the song ended.

Captain signaled to Jerry for another round.

"Thanks." Sara ignored the twisting in her gut. It was just beer. Two wouldn't hurt. Jerry set mugs in front of them. Sara lifted hers. "To the captain of the tugboat." Glass clinked against glass. "And knower of people." Sara threw back her head and gulped. Thanks to Cap's generosity, the edge was gone. The past was becoming a distant, dull ache. Forget about the blue six-month chip, and throw the orange, green, and red ones she'd earned into the trashcan. This Bud definitely satisfied more than a rainbow of chips right now, even if that fact made her want to crumple into a heap and bawl.

Captain sipped his suds. "You look kinda sad."

Sara glanced at Jerry mixing drinks. Sad? That's an understatement. But she'd always hidden her sorrow. At least that's what she thought. There were her paintings, though, and all the comments others made about her use of gray. She took another sip. She hadn't sketched anything in at least a week, much less painted. Her lifeline was slipping away.

Captain scratched his head. "I guess ever'body's got a sad story." He tapped her arm. "You think that's true? You think ever'body's got a sad story?"

Sara looked at Captain's glazed eyes. "I guess." She thought of Clem's niece having so much fun without a care in the world and the guests who seemed to have it all. She hadn't seen a sad face at that party. Were each of them hiding some private pain, or was Captain wrong?

"Yeah, I guess too." He took a sip of his beer. "I could tell ya mine." He said the last part so quietly Sara barely heard him.

"What?"

"My story." He stroked his gray stubble.

She thought of what he'd already divulged and figured the story could only get better. Besides, the buzz was craving more alcohol to return her to a level of oblivious abandon. Today's one-day-at-a-time battle was already lost. "Okay, I'll bite. What's your story?" She swigged half the mug, and Captain signaled Jerry again.

"Sure you wanna hear an ol' man's tale?" Captain pointed to his lighter, and she slid it to him. He lit his cigarette with an unsteady hand and took a drag. Embers flickered, and a few sparks dropped on the bar. He swept the invisible ashes to the floor.

"Why not." Sara wondered what in his life made him a daily drinker. If he was an alcoholic, he seemed to be a functioning one. Lucky him. Unlucky her. Abstinence had already left her in the dust. Sobriety's wagon train would have to pick her back up tomorrow.

Captain picked up the mug Jerry set in front of him then gestured with his free hand. "See, I got this here bum leg."

Sara nodded and blew a smoke circle.

"Well, I was trainin' as a boxer, see. 'Course that was a long time ago. Not anytime recent." Captain coughed for several seconds.

"Need some water?" Sara asked.

Captain shook his head as he reached for his mug. "I'm okay. This here's all I need." He lifted it at the same time Sara lifted hers, and they both chugged.

He set the mug down and wiped the froth from his mouth. "So when I wudn't trainin' I was ridin' my Hawg. All goshdurn day sometimes."

She cocked her head and blew smoke at the ceiling. "Was that before or after your tugboating days?"

"Oh, b'fore 'em. Waay b'fore 'em." He tapped his knee. "Didn't get in the way 'a my tugboatin'. Hell, half 'a the crew was busted up in some way er other."

Captain stubbed out his cigarette. "What was I sayin'? Oh, yeah, so one day I'm out on the highway." He flung his arm. "Out there. And I hit some kinda slick spot. I dunno. Never did figger it out. And durned if I didn't bust up this knee." He patted his left knee.

Sara shook her head. "That is sad."

He nodded. "That was the end 'a boxin' for me." He coughed again then cleared his throat. "Only two things I ever loved, boxin' and my Hawg. And that was the end of 'em both." Captain looked down the bar. "Hey, Jer, get this here young lady and me another beer."

"Thanks, Cap." She should turn it down. Her life was full of shouldas these days. Why not one more.

"Yur a good list'ner." He got up, leaning on the bar. "Be right back."

Sara watched him limp to the restroom while his cane remained on the floor beneath the bar. Jerry set two more beers on the bar. "Thanks." She nodded toward Captain's stool. "Hey, Jerry, what about Cap?"

"What about him?" Jerry wiped his hands on a towel.

"Is it true?"

"What's that?"

"That he was a boxer and busted up his knee on his Harley."

"Oh, yeah. All true." He pulled the tap to fill a mug.

"Was he any good?" She sipped her beer.

Jerry served a man at the other end of the bar and rang it up before he answered. "Yeah. I used to go watch his matches all the time. Never seen nothing like it. He could'a been a contender." Jerry snickered as he mimicked the late Marlon Brando then shuffled to the ringing phone.

Sara was impressed. She was halfway finished with her beer when Captain limped back and sat down. He chugged the one Jerry had just brought and waved for another round.

Sara didn't even pretend to protest and prodded Captain further. "So, what'd you do then?"

Jerry set the mugs down and looked at Sara. "You doing all right?"

"I'm fine." What must Jerry think? Oh, fuck it. She turned to Captain. "Well?"

"Oh, too much ta tell in one night." He lifted his mug to his lips and slurped. His rheumy eyes were shot through with red lines. "So how 'bout you?" He patted her shoulder. "Ya look like ya could use a good shoulder."

Sara looked at her mug. How many did this make? She couldn't remember. Her mind was becoming as hazy as the smoky bar.

Captain tugged at Sara's sleeve. "Y'okay?"

"Wha?"

"I said, are ya aw'right?" He looked as concerned as someone who'd been drinking all evening could. "Maybe you've had enough, huh?"

"No way!" Sara guzzled her beer and waved at Jerry. "This round's on me." She slapped the bar.

"S'not necessary." Captain slurred, but when Sara nodded, he said, "Okay, but jes' one. And I tole you mine, now you hafta tell me yurs." He hunched over the bar and looked at Sara with hound dog eyes she couldn't resist.

"My story, huh?" Fifty-two, fifty-one, fifty. Bingo! Beer numbers're up. "How about a shot."

Captain leaned sideways and looked at her. "Ya shur?"

"Jerry, two shots of Jack." Sara pulled out some bills and dropped them on the bar.

Jerry hesitated. "Did I hear you right?"

Sara nodded and pushed the bills toward him.

When Jerry set the shots on the bar, he said, "I think you two should take a break after this."

"Shur thing, Chief." Captain picked up his shot glass and clinked Sara's. "Here's ta us!"

They downed the shots and slapped the glasses on the bar.

"So, out with it." Captain grinned.

Sara saw Cap's gold tooth glint again like a pot of gold at the end of a rainbow. She looked at the empty shot glasses. A cloud had just wiped out her rainbow.

Jerry scooped up the empty glasses, set down a bowl of peanuts, and left.

Sara shoved the bowl aside. "Would'ja like me to begin when my mother abandoned me?"

"Ahh." He stretched his bum leg.

"Yeah, that's right. What kinda mother leaves her two-year-old child with friends and never returns?" She tapped his arm. "Huh? What kind? That's what I wanna know!" She pounded her fist on the bar loud enough for Jerry to glance their way. She picked up her hand and mouthed, sorry. Now that the well had been uncapped, she seemed unable to stop the gusher or drown the inner voice that shouted hypocrite, hypocrite. "Then years of foster homes with a last name they had to invent." She grabbed the last cigarette, and Captain crumpled the empty pack, reaching in his pocket for another one and opening it. "But I fixed that." His brow lifted. "Yep, shur did. Changed my name when I got outta their goddamn system!" They both lit up and Sara drew in a deep drag. "But you know the wors' thing of all?" Captain shook his head. "She seems as happy as can be. S'if I never existed."

"You've met 'er?" Captain scratched his head.

"Yeah. I've met 'er all right. But she doesn't know who I am." Then she mumbled to herself, "and neither do I." Through her drunken stupor, Captain's face looked like a distorted reflection in a house of mirrors. "Yeah, that's right, I haven't outed myself to her yet." Sara jabbed her cigarette into the ashtray.

"Whatcha waitin' fer?"

Sara drew her shoulders up. "You know? I have no idea anymore. Maybe the waitin' should be over. She works at the co-op down the street, so I joined it, too." She spun the ashtray thinking the yarn she was spinning might sound a bit sinister. She wasn't Fiona's stalker. She was her daughter. "I thought, ya know, she'd see me, and the light would flick on. But no light flicked on. We both stood in the dark." She lit another cigarette and steadied herself on the bar. "And we're still in the dark. Been in the dark so long, don't know how to find the light." She looked at Captain and saw two of him. "I jus' know we don't get along, and every day, the telling gets harder to do." She shook her head. "S'not at all like I expected. Not at all." She slumped over the bar. "Oh, Cap, I'm no better. Not really. I've done so many bad things."

Captain gently patted her shoulder. "It'll be aw right."

She sat up. "There's more. Ya ever hear how history repeats itself?" He nodded. "Well, I've got a daughter." Her eyes filled with tears. "And if I don't get back home real soon, she'll be lost to me forever. So, ya see, I really do have to end the charade. That's right." She pounded her fist on the bar again, and this time everyone sitting at bar looked at her. She mumbled sorry and hung her head.

"Sara," Captain spoke softly, "if there's one thing I've learned in life, it's that ya can't move for'ard if yur stuck in the past." She wiped her eyes. "Ya gotta fix the past 'fore ya ken move for'ard." Captain patted Sara's back and handed her a napkin. "'Kay?"

Sara blew her nose and nodded.

Captain motioned to Jerry, who walked over. "Hey, Chief, ken I settle up with ya tomorra?"

"Sure, Cap."

"Thanks, Chief." Captain slid off the stool then turned to Sara. "Remember what I tole ya, gal. 'S gonna be awright." He squeezed her shoulder gently.

He picked up the cane Sara'd never seen him use, grabbing the bar to steady himself before hobbling off to the restroom.

Sara saw two Captains limping away. And tonight both of their canes boomed like bass drums.

"You want some coffee?" Jerry asked.

She shook her head. "Walkin' home." Tonight she'd face Fiona. If she wasn't at the co-op, Sara'd walk to her goddamn house. Tonight. Yes, tonight. "Tell Cap bye."

* * *

Sara snickered, "Whoops!" as she stepped on a crack while stumbling on the sidewalk. "Sorry, Motherrr . . . guess I broke your back!" Giggling, she almost fell but hugged a lamppost before she went down. "Oooh, Sara's had a lil' too much ta drink." She straightened when a police car slowed. "Uh oh, better getchurself home before you get hauled aww . . ." A belch split the one-syllable word in two, and when she spit out the f, she added ". . . uck yewww! Tastes gross." She straightened up, breathed in the evening's damp air, and zigzagged on in determination.

When Sara approached the co-op, she saw a group of smokers huddling near the Hut's entrance and heard someone say, "Yeah, looks like Fiona really has it in for Sara." No one seemed to notice her, so she slipped into the alley and hid around the corner, listening. She started to sober up. Monday night. Must be a meeting. Did she forget? No, she'd been out of town. She started for the front when she heard her name again, but before she stepped out of the shadows, someone said, "Better get back inside for the verdict. Because no matter how we vote, you can bet Fiona's already made up her mind." Sara slumped against the wall. Tears began to flow, but then she stopped crying and stumbled down the alley toward the parking lot. When she got to the corner, she saw Clem propping the back door open with a large rock then walking toward his car. She started to call out but hesitated long enough to change her mind. She snuck around the corner while his back was to the building and slipped inside. She'd find out what the damn meeting was all about. Then she'd fix Fiona for good. She reached to open the ladies' room door, but Iris came out just before Sara grabbed the handle. Thank God it was Iris. She waddled down the hallway, never looking behind her when the door swung shut to reveal Sara. She tiptoed quickly to a little alcove where the three workshop rooms converged. She could hide there until everyone returned to the Hut and the meeting resumed. She'd wait till she heard Clem come back in before heading to the beaded entrance where she'd be invisible until, well, until she couldn't stand it anymore.

Chapter 33

Monday, Week Five

Postscript

After Clem shut the back door, Sara listened for other members. When she thought everyone was back in the Hut, she walked quietly down the hallway and stopped before she reached the beaded entrance. Sara remained hidden until she heard Fiona say, 'We didn't have these problems until Sara arrived. What do we really know about her anyway? I'll tell you what, nothing. I say we take a vote on removing her from our ranks.' As soon as Sara heard those words, she pushed her way into the room and stopped in front of Fiona.

"What's this all about, Fiona?"

Fiona's eyes widened and she flinched. "Seems you already know."

"What I *know*," Sara leaned her face in close to Fiona's and almost fell into her. Jack had given her courage, for sure, but had stolen her steadiness. And her thoughts were becoming as unsteady as her legs. Could she spit out the words she'd come here to say? "What I *know*," Sara repeated, as a splash of her saliva hit Fiona's cheek, "is a lot more than *you* know." She stepped back and looked around the room. "And if you don't want everyone here to know what I know, you better end this stupid meeting right now." It took all of Sara's focus to keep her speech coherent.

Fiona swiped her hand across her cheek then rubbed it across her jeans.

Sara said, "Because believe me, I won't hold anything back."

One by one, except for Vic, the members shuffled out. Clem was last out the door, and as it shut behind him, he mouthed, *you okay*? Through her haze, Sara managed a nod before she turned to Fiona, put her hands on her hips, and said, "Sure you want Vic to hear this?"

"What could you possibly say that I wouldn't want him to hear?"

Sara squinted and the slivers of her eyes became swords. "Okay. Don't say I didn't warn you because, you see, I know all about you."

"What the hell are you talking about?"

Sara covered her ears. "Shut up, shut up, shut up!" She slashed the air with her finger and yelled, "Shut your mouth and listen."

Vic stepped in between them, creating a barrier. "Sara. There's no need . . ."

Sara cut him off. "There's no need for what? There's no need to expose your precious Fiona for the fraud that she is?" She ignored Vic's puzzled stare and turned to Fiona, shaking her finger in Fiona's face. "Did you ever tell him about what you left behind in San Francisco? Did you?" She looked at Vic. "Go ahead, ask her. Ask her what she left in San Francisco." Then she turned back to Fiona. "And I dare you to tell him the truth."

Vic looked at Fiona. "Babe?"

Sara folded her arms but didn't take her eyes off Fiona. "Go ahead, *Babe*. Tell him." She leaned in toward

Fiona. "And while you're 'fessing up, *Babe*, tell him how you walked away and never looked back."

Fiona's face went pale.

Sara looked at Vic. "*Babe*. God, you hit it out of irony park with that one."

As Sara lashed out at Vic, Fiona regained her color. "I don't know who you think you are to talk to me like this, but you can just take your sorry ass out of here," she pointed at the door, "and never set foot in here again."

Sara leaned into Fiona again, only inches from her face. "Oh, really? So you think denial is still possible?" She pointed at Vic. "What does he really know about your life in San Francisco?"

Fiona backed up and screamed. "I said get out. You're drunk. You smell like a brewery. We don't need your kind here. Get out!"

"My kind? What kind would that be?"

Fiona looked at Vic. "She needs to leave." She pointed at the door. "Now." But he didn't move.

Sara stepped in front of Fiona's pointed finger. "Since you won't answer the question, and you're very good at throwing accusations, let me help you out." Sara leaned toward Fiona and braced herself on a chair. "Tonight was a great example, and your rant just a postscript. Well, here's my postscript." She paused for a moment. "Your little Orchid has bloomed and is now a full-grown blossom standing right in front of you." She glared at Fiona whose eyes had widened and whose color had drained. "Hello, Mother."

Fiona slid into a chair.

Vic broke his silence. "Mother?" He didn't blink. "Fiona, is this true?"

Sara thought Vic looked like someone who'd been stunned by a taser, but he wasn't her main concern right now, and she turned back to face Fiona.

"What do you have to say for yourself?" She gestured toward Vic. "I'm sure your significant other would like to be significantly informed." She looked at Vic. "Isn't that right, Vic? I'm sure you're dying to know all about me. When I was born." She turned to Fiona. "That's an answer I've wanted my whole fucking life!" She stumbled as she stepped backwards. "Oh yeah, and who's my daddy? That's another piece of the puzzle."

Fiona sat crumpled like a ragdoll and said in a whisper, "You're her?"

Sara began laughing hysterically. She was some kind of fiery sum of every awful thing that had ever happened to her. Every moment of fear, confusion, loneliness, anger, and she was hurling it all directly at Fiona.

"Oh, yes, *Mommy*. It's me. The little girl you abandoned all those years ago. What do you have to say for yourself, *Mommy*?" Sara felt Jack rise to her throat and swallowed it back down.

Fiona dropped her head into her hands as Vic dropped into a chair next to her. "Fiona?"

She mumbled something about a headache and rubbed her temples.

Sara said, "Oh, no you don't. You're not playing the feel-sorry-for-me card now." When Sara spit the words out, Vic pushed back his chair, stood, and looked at Fiona.

"I can't handle this right now." Vic shoved his chair toward the table.

"Vic, please, please . . ." Fiona pleaded.

He shook his head. "Goddamn. How could you?" Vic stormed toward the Hut door, pushing chairs out of his way. He slammed the door as he left, shattering the stained glass in the transom then sending the pieces flying to the floor.

When Fiona cringed at the sound of clinking glass shards, Sara leaned over the table and glared at her. "Okay, now it's just you and me. What do you have to say?"

"Why are you doing this to me? Why didn't you tell me who you were when we first met? We were alone then." Fiona sat up straight. "Yes. We were alone that first time when you came to see Vic at the office. And now you want to point out *my* failings? What kind of person skulks around hiding a secret like that for over a month?" Now she glared at Sara.

"Oh, no you don't. You're not twisting things to find fault with anything I did." Sara shook her head over and over. "No freaking way. I was just a child when you deserted me. How could you do that? How?"

"There's so much you don't know."

Sara wasn't about to let her off the hook. "Oh, I know plenty." Fiona would get no sympathy and no more chance for redemption. In this moment, Sara blamed her for every sordid, wrongful thing that had ever happened, and she could think only how best to punish Fiona. Sara pointed to the painting of Jamie on the carousel. "You see that picture? That's your granddaughter." Sara walked over to the painting and lifted it off the hooks then carried it to where Fiona sat and set it down in front of her. "Take a good look at another person you've abandoned." Sara saw Fiona's shoulders hunch forward and thought she saw a tear form. "That's right. Your very own flesh and blood, and what was your response the first time you saw this picture? Do you remember, or do I need to remind you?"

Fiona just stared.

"You couldn't have answered it better. Nothing. That was your reaction. You ignored her picture just like you ignored me."

Fiona pulled a tissue from her bag and pinched her nose with it. "That's not fair. I didn't know who you were, so how could I know she was my," her voice cracked, "my granddaughter?"

"Like it would've made a difference? You were no more interested in the child in my painting than you were in me as a child."

"That's not true. There's so much you don't know . . . you'll never understand."

"You got that right!"

Fiona looked down at the picture. "She's beautiful."

"Of course she's beautiful." Sara touched Jamie's hair in the picture and pulled the painting toward her and away from Fiona.

"Where is she?" Fiona dabbed at her eyes.

"That's none of your business. But just know that I haven't abandoned my daughter."

All this purging had cleared Sara's thoughts. Now things were making sense. She knew who her real family was and who she could count on. Ma and Pa Jenkins would get her back home and be the advocates she needed. She knew that fact without any doubt and would no longer be too proud to ask for help. Sara held the painting at her side and headed for the beaded exit.

"Wait." Fiona sounded desperate, which made Sara stop. She turned around and Fiona said, "I did go back to San Francisco and try to find you, but no one there could help me. I just didn't know what else to do." She shook her head. "There was no internet then, and even if there was, it may not have helped." Fiona wadded her tissue. "Is that how you found me?"

So Fiona did go back to San Francisco. Really? Couldn't have tried very hard. Now she could stew in her guilt. She deserved it. Sara started to say it was none of her goddamn business, but she wanted Fiona to know how lousy her life had been. "I ran into your old friend, Jon, on Fisherman's Wharf. Still making jewelry, no less. One thing that hasn't changed." Sara laughed at the irony. "I'm sure you remember Jon and Leah. The people you dumped me on when you left. The ones you couldn't find, I guess?" She sneered at Fiona. "Yeah, they didn't stay together too long, and I ended up in the welfare system tossed from one foster home to another. A great life, *Mommy*. Thanks a whole hell of a lot. But don't worry. I won't burden you again."

Sara turned away and hurried down the hall before Fiona could respond. She went out the back door but stopped before climbing the stairway to her apartment. She couldn't go back there. Not right now. Hearing a car door slam in the parking lot, she turned to see Clem walking toward her.

"Are you okay?"

"I don't know." She pointed to the apartment with her free hand. "I just can't go up there right now."

"You need a ride someplace? Or you could come to my house. I've got lots of room."

Sara appreciated Clem's offer, but she couldn't sit in his house either. Surely he wondered what was going on, but she didn't want to tell him more than the basic facts. Where could she go? Jane. If Laurance had told Jane anything, Sara would've heard about it by now. Besides, once Jane knew the truth about Fiona, Fiona may just have to find a new friend, or should she say *daughter* to act as Sara's surrogate. That would be Sara's ultimate revenge.

Clem waited patiently for her answer.

"Can you take me to my friend Jane's house? It's not far from here."

Clem nodded.

"One more favor?"

"Sure."

"Could you run this painting upstairs?" Sara stared at a crack in the concrete and the children's jingle, 'step on a crack, break your mother's back' popped into her head again. "I can't face that apartment right now." Sara looked up in time to see Clem nodding and handed him her keys.

While she waited for Clem, she toed a rock on the sidewalk then jumped directly onto the crack. She thought about asking Clem to stop so she could buy a six-pack. Once she started telling Jane her story, she figured they'd both need the beer. Sobriety would have one more delay.

* * *

After a quick stop at a liquor store, Sara set the six-pack on the floorboard and told Clem who she was, but little more, and he was polite enough not to pry.

He shook his head. "Fiona's daughter. I'll be." When Clem parked in front of Jane's, he turned to Sara. "I'm sorry about how everything has turned out." He glanced at the six-pack. "I'll pray for you."

"You've been a good friend." She squeezed his arm gently. "Thanks for that."

Clem blushed. "How will you get back home?"

"If home is where the heart is, it's too far away for you to drive me to, believe me." Sara sighed. "I don't know. I can't go back to the apartment tonight. But don't worry. I'll figure it all out."

"Okay. But call if you get stranded. I'll come, even in the middle of the night."

Sara gave him a quick peck on the cheek then grabbed the beer and hurried to Jane's front door. She knocked several times but no one answered even though she could see light coming through the blinds. She walked around to the driveway, noticing that Clem was still parked out front. Jane's Jeep was blocked in by an old truck. She hadn't thought about

Jane having company. Greg? Maybe she should leave. She looked down the side of the house and noticed light in one of the windows. She hurried to it, swatting mosquitoes with her free hand as she walked, then tapped the window when she saw Jane at the computer. Jane glanced at the window then got up and walked to it. Sara lifted the six-pack. Jane squinted then nodded and pointed to the front of the house. As Sara headed to the front door, she waved to Clem, and he drove off.

Jane opened the door and said, "Hey, what's with the six-pack?" and ushered her inside.

Sara handed her the beer. "I'll explain." She looked around. "That is, if you don't have company."

"Only if you count Cocoa." Jane frowned. "Oh, you mean the truck? Long story."

"Then be prepared for a long night."

They sat down, and Jane pulled out two cans from the six-pack.

* * *

Fiona sat for what seemed like ages after Sara left. She wasn't sure her legs would hold her if she stood. Her eyes were drawn to the blank space on the wall where Sara's painting no longer hung. Sara. Her daughter. My God. She leaned over the table and held her throbbing head. She'd locked away the memory of her daughter long ago and was stunned by the shock of its resurfacing. And Vic. He said he couldn't handle this. What would she do if Vic turned away? She had no one else. She lifted herself up, still leaning on the table. She had to get out of here.

She stepped around the broken glass and closed the door behind her. She knew where she had to go. Vic's house. She had to talk to him, reason with him. Only then could she even begin to think about Sara. Orchid. Sara was her little Orchid. She trudged to the parking lot, swung her VW bus onto the street then drove in a trance to Vic's. His house was dark, and Vic didn't come to the door. Where could he have gone? Now she was really worried. She reached into her purse and pulled out his spare key then let herself in. She'd wait for him, no matter how long it took.

* * *

When Vic stormed out of the Hut, he heard the glass shatter. He knew Stan would be pissed, but at that moment, he really didn't care. Fiona had lied to him. No, that wasn't true. She had withheld the single most important truth of her past. That was worse. Who was she? How could he have loved her so much for so long and not known something so important? How? He got into his Bronco and drove off. He knew he'd have to board up the transom but didn't want to be anywhere near Fiona right now. He saw the sign for Jerry's Place and pulled up to the curb. When he got inside, he saw that old man, Captain, he'd talked to a while back. Captain looked toward the door and smiled at Vic, raising his mug. Vic walked over to join him. He could use some broad shoulders tonight.

Chapter 34

Tuesday, Week Five

When Jane awoke the next morning, she peeked in her spare room where Sara was sprawled on the air mattress, still out from last night. What revelations she'd brought with that six-pack! Today, Jane actually felt better. Not great, but, how'd that saying go? Misery loves company. And Fiona. Wow! You think you know someone then you find out you don't know anything.

Jane called work again. One more day without her wouldn't kill them. She gathered the empty cans and dropped them in her recycling bin before brewing a pot of tea. Sorting through her unopened mail, she found a letter from her landlord. After reading it, she flung it onto the coffee table. He was planning to sell the house, and this letter was her ninety-day notice to vacate. She should've expected it after the remodeling. If only she could come up with a down payment.

Sara shuffled out of the spare room and croaked, "Hi," then fell onto the couch next to Jane.

"Hey." Jane thought Sara looked like hell. "Want some tea?"

"Any coffee?"

"I've got instant."

"Instant's fine." Sara slowly stood. "Lead the way."

Jane held out her hand. "I'll get it. How do you like it?"

Sara plopped back down. "Strong and black today." She grabbed her head. "I can't believe I screwed up so bad last night. Now I've got to start my sobriety all over again. I'm such a fuck-up."

Jane stood in the doorway. "Don't beat yourself up. Truthfully, I can't believe you didn't explode sooner. I mean, Fiona is your *mother*, my God, what next?" The microwave beeped, and seconds later Jane set a steaming mug in front of Sara then sat in the recliner. "So, look at us." Jane shook her head. "Who knew?"

Sara clutched her mug and blew the steam. "Yeah, well, my story wasn't a shock to me, just to everyone else."

"I never could've imagined Fee having a daughter. I'm still trying to wrap my mind around that."

Sara nodded. "What about you? Your news was pretty mind-blowing, too."

"I have to confess I was in a deep funk, but after hearing your story, mine doesn't sting as much. I'll still have to deal with the unholy trio, but somehow I feel less alone. Except," Jane pointed to the stack on the coffee table, "I got rotten news this morning when I finally opened my mail. My landlord plans to sell this house."

"Man." Sara shook her head. "That sucks."

"Yeah, I've got ninety days to figure out what I'm going to do. But what are you going to do?"

Sara set down her mug. "I plan to call my last foster family. They never wanted to lose touch and even asked me to stay after I 'aged out' of the system, but I was too proud then. I really believe they'll send me a plane ticket in time for Jamie's court date. I just hate that it took me so long to see who really matters and who really cares. I mean, they're usually the same, you know?" Jane nodded and Sara continued. "I spent too many years fantasizing about the mother I believed was out there," she swept the air with her hand, "sad and missing me, and just waiting for me to show up and make our lives whole again."

Sara's words hit Jane square in the heart. Had her mother been out there missing her? Hard to imagine since she'd always known where to find her.

* * *

Several mugs later, Sara called the Jenkins. Jane was slathering peanut butter on thick slices of multi-grain bread when Sara joined her.

"So, how'd it go?" Jane asked.

"Couldn't have been more perfect. They kept telling me how glad they were that I'd called, and, of course, they would help me. They even bought my plane ticket online while we were on the phone. Looks like I'll be leaving for San Francisco day after tomorrow."

"Great. I guess. I hate to see you go although I know you have to."

Sara leaned against the counter. "I just hope I can get out of here without seeing Fiona again. Then there's Vic, and well, all the others. I can't face them." She grabbed the slab of bread Jane handed her, joined her at the kitchen table, and took a bite. "Then there's my car at Clem's house. I'll be back at some point long enough to get it repaired and pick it up."

"Make sure you let me know when you're coming back. In fact, you can stay with me no matter where I end up."

"Thanks."

"Speaking of cars," Jane stood and tossed her napkin in the trash, "I've got to return Dad's truck. Sure could use your help. Don't really want to talk to them yet, and if you're with me, they won't press. Would you mind following in the Jeep?"

"Not at all. I've got plenty of time between now and the day after tomorrow. One favor, though, can I stay here till I leave?"

"Sure. We can get your stuff after we drop off the truck."

"I just hope Fiona doesn't pop in while I'm here."

"Don't worry, if she does, I'll chase her away."

* * *

When they got to Marv's trailer, the Cherokee was gone. Jane was relieved she wouldn't have to see Glenda, but she cringed at facing her dad. Sara stayed in the Jeep while Jane trudged to the front door. She knocked and knocked and knocked, but all she heard was Rusty barking, so she opened the door with the spare key. Rusty greeted her with sloppy kisses. "Dad? You there?" She headed to the bedroom, hoping he wasn't feeling bad. It was empty. She scribbled a quick note then laid the truck key on top. She wondered where her dad and Glenda were but was glad she didn't have to talk to them. She glanced at the chair where Glenda had sat, remembering the moment she'd learned that the woman sitting there was her mother. She closed her eyes and shook her head, still stunned by what she'd learned. Before locking the door, she gave the room a last glance. Would this place ever again feel like the home it had once been?

* * *

As soon as Jane stepped out of the trailer, Glenda's Cherokee pulled in behind her Jeep. Great! Jane headed for the Jeep, but Glenda looked frantic and hurried toward the trailer, so Jane stopped. The last thing she wanted to do was to talk to Glenda.

Glenda approached Jane and said, "I know you're mad at all of us, but you need to know that Marv's in the hospital."

"What? When? What's going on?"

"He's stabilized now, but early this morning I thought I'd lost him. I had to call an ambulance."

"Stabilized?"

"He's in intensive care, but his vitals are stable. It was touch and go for a bit, and I tried to call you. Winnie's there now. I just came back to get his insurance card." Please, Jane, go see him." She started to go up the steps but turned her head. "No matter how you feel now, we're going to have to sort through everything eventually. When you're ready, I'll be here." Glenda turned and went inside the trailer.

Jane had to go see her dad. No matter how deceptive they had all been, they were her family. Her only family. And after all, who knows what her life would have been like with Glenda for a mother if she couldn't even care for her own self back then. Secrets. They're poison. Poison kills. Maybe it was time to siphon it all out. Jane got into the Jeep.

"So, is that your mother?" Sara asked.

"Yeah, that's her."

Sara tugged at her seatbelt. "How'd it go?"

"Well, her final words to me were, 'When you're ready, I'll be here,' but I'll have to deal with her later." Jane pulled the Jeep up as far as she could then backed out alongside Glenda's Cherokee, barely missing the fir trees where she and her dad had played hide and seek so long ago. Had she been hiding from them?

Jane stopped the Jeep at the end of the driveway and turned to Sara. "Yeah, I really will have to talk to them at some point."

"You should." Sara reached in her pocket and clutched her Marlboros. "If Fiona had come looking for me years ago and not given up so easily, who knows where we'd be today. At least your mother showed up and stuck around to face you. Even if it was years later than it should've been."

Jane backed onto the road, put the Jeep in drive, and headed toward her house. "You're probably right, but I have a bigger concern right now. Glenda was there to pick up Dad's insurance card. He's in the hospital. Intensive care. I've got to go see him."

"Sorry to hear that." Sara looked out the window. "Let me call Clem. If he's home, you can drop me off there. That way you don't have to worry about me." She punched in Clem's number, and he told her to come on over.

* * *

Jane stood by her dad's bed side as the machines beeped and whooshed. She looked at his ashen face. His eyes were closed. Nobody could say how aware he was as he drifted in and out of consciousness. She held his hand. "Dad, you know I love you. You've got to get better. You just have to. We'll work things out." She felt a slight squeeze of her hand. She couldn't have imagined it.

A nurse came in as Jane was brushing back a tear. "Dear, his sister would like to come in for a few minutes."

Jane kissed Marv's cheek. "I'll be back, Dad."

* * *

Jane walked into the waiting room and saw Winnie sitting on a couch. She ambled over to the chair next to her and sat down. Jane looked down but glanced up to see Winnie looking at her.

"How is he?" Winnie asked.

She shrugged. "Don't know. He doesn't look good. But he did squeeze my hand. I know he did."

Just as Winnie opened her mouth to speak, Elizabeth pushed open the door and hurried to Winnie's side. Elizabeth looked from one woman to the other. "Sorry about Mr. Heffinger. Hope he's doing okay."

Winnie said, "Thanks, Dear. I certainly didn't expect you to come all the way down here."

"Well, after we talked on the phone, and you sounded so upset, I had to come."

"That was nice of you." Winnie patted Elizabeth's hand. "Your father said he'd try to stop by after work."

Elizabeth nodded. "I can't stay, but there's something else I need to tell both of you." She looked at Jane and reached for a tissue. "The wedding has been postponed." A tear fell and she dabbed her eyes.

"Oh, Elizabeth, I'm so sorry. Will you be okay?" Winnie asked.

Elizabeth grabbed another tissue and shrugged. "I can't talk about it right now. But I thought you both needed to know." She stood and looked at Jane and said, "I hope your father recovers," then turned to Winnie. "Call me later."

Winnie patted her hand again. "Yes, I'll call you tonight."

After Elizabeth left, Jane stared at Winnie. "Unbelievable."

"What?"

"You can't even see how selfish she is, can you?"

"Jane. She must be devastated about the wedding, yet she still took time to come here and be supportive."

"*That's* what you call being supportive?" Jane stood. "Oh, forget it. I don't want to think about anything but Dad right now." She crossed her arms. "I need some tea. You want anything?"

Winnie shook her head as Glenda stepped into the room.

Chapter 35

Monday–Friday, Week Five

Monday (after the meeting at ATTA)
Fiona

Fiona walked through Vic's house, stopping at his bedroom, where they'd spent many nights entwined in his king-sized bed. The place where she'd often whispered in his ear but never confessed her most important secret. Would he ever again give her the chance to lie next to him? She hurried down the hallway to the kitchen. Dishes were piled high in the sink. She stacked them, plugged the drain, squirted detergent, and turned on the hot tap as if she were an automaton. After finishing the dishes, she reached under the cabinet for a dust rag and the can of Lemon Pledge.

Once Fiona had finished her flurry of mindless activity, she slumped in a chair. Her brief repose reminded her that Pet was probably whining to be fed and let outside, and she stood to leave. She locked Vic's front door. Where was he anyway? Vic wasn't in the habit of staying out late, but she'd never seen him so angry. He might have assumed she'd be here waiting. Had he driven by, seen her VW, and left?

Fiona drove down deserted streets, overhead lights illuminating the interior of her VW in intermittent flashes. She moved from shadow to light, light to shadow, San Francisco to River City, River City to San Francisco as she turned from this street to that, driving on autopilot until she pulled onto her street. Marv's truck was in Jane's driveway, but the house was dark. Just as well that Jane had company. How could she tell her about Sara? How could life have taken this turn? If Sara, Orchid—she didn't know what to call her—had only let her explain. Could she ever find the right words to make her daughter understand? Fiona pressed her fingers to her temples and sat in the bus until Pet's barking compelled her to get out.

Monday (after the meeting at ATTA)
Vic

As Vic unlocked his front door, the smell of Lemon Pledge screamed of Fiona's presence. Magazines and newspapers were left open on the coffee table, and a *Sports Illustrated* had fallen onto the hardwood floor. He picked it up and tossed it on the pile then walked into the kitchen. No dirty dishes. Things Fiona had a hard time managing at her own house, she'd taken care of here. Vic slammed his keys onto the kitchen table. Did she think a little domestic offering would get them back on track?

He stripped down to his boxers and went to bed. Tomorrow he'd have to get to the co-op early, clean up the broken glass, and explain to Stan why a plank was covering the transom.

Tuesday
Vic

Vic got to the co-op an hour before Stan usually arrived and swept up the colored bits of glass. He dumped them in a trash bag and set it aside. Vic couldn't bear pitching them in the dumpster just yet. He brewed a pot of coffee and sat at the counter with the newspaper. The news on the pages of the *Daily Ledger* made about as much sense as Sara's words had last night.

The Hut door jerked open and Vic watched Stan stare at the board where his stained glass had been.

"What the fuck happened?"

"Sit down. I'll pour you some coffee."

"There's a goddamn sign that says: Do Not Slam Door. What imbecile couldn't remember to close the door carefully?"

Vic scooted out a stool and patted the seat.

Stan sunk down and Vic handed him a cup of coffee.

"It was me. I was so pissed when I left last night that I slammed the door."

"You?" Stan stared at him.

"Yeah."

Stan drummed his fingers on the table. "And?" Stan had never looked so angry as he gulped down coffee then slammed the half-empty cup on the counter.

"You deserve an answer, but this is going to be a shocker."

"It better be that God himself made you slam that door."

Vic folded the paper and laid it aside. "Sara told us that Fiona is her mother." Even as he said it, the reality hadn't sunk in. "And Fiona didn't deny it." That was the hardest reality for Vic.

Stan's jaw dropped. "Seriously? And you didn't know?"

"Yes on both counts."

"You're shittin' me." Stan shook his head. "Vic, my man, I wouldn't want to be you right now." Stan grabbed his coffee, finished it off, and stood. "Don't think you're getting off the hook for that window, though. I'll make another one, but you're paying for my time and supplies."

"Of course." Vic grabbed his newspaper and cup and escaped to the office.

Tuesday
Fiona

Other than letting Pet out a couple of times, Fiona spent the day sleeping and trying to get rid of her headache. She'd been scheduled for a shift at the co-op at 2:00, but when she woke up, the clock said 4:00. Vic hadn't called. Maybe he'd assumed she wouldn't be in. Maybe he had it covered. Maybe he just didn't care. She poured herself a cup of coffee then sat on the couch, sipping and looking outside. Marv's truck was gone. She should ask Jane how he was doing. Maybe tomorrow. Maybe then she'd have a better handle on things. Maybe she could get Vic to listen to her tomorrow. Maybe, maybe, maybe. Nothing seemed certain.

Wednesday
Vic

Vic hurried from the parking lot to the office door. The humid air stuck like glue on his skin and the coolness inside was a welcome relief. He wanted to avoid everyone like he'd done yesterday.

Vic had brought coffee from home today, avoiding the Hut. Stan said he wasn't mad, but when he'd called Vic yesterday, wondering if anyone had seen Fiona since she hadn't shown up for her shift in the bookstore, Vic heard the anger in Stan's voice and things banging around in the background. Iris had come to the rescue. She'd just finished a class and offered to cover for Fiona. Vic was relieved he didn't have to call her.

Vic noticed the flashing light on the answering machine and pressed play. "Vic, it's Sara. I've vacated the apartment, and I left the key on the kitchen counter. Sorry about the other night. I never meant for you to find out that way. I really do appreciate all you've done. I guess that's it. Take care."

Boy, when he thought back to first meeting Sara, he couldn't have imagined how things would turn out. He knew he should check out the apartment, make sure the faucets weren't dripping, the commode wasn't running, and that the air conditioning was set at a reasonable temperature. Sara surely wouldn't have damaged anything, but after the other night, he wasn't making any assumptions.

He locked the office door and walked outside once again into the blistering day. The humid air pulled at his lungs like a magnet.

Vic had just turned on the tap in the apartment to be sure the water was draining when he heard the apartment door creak open.

"Vic?"

Fiona's voice ripped through him. His back was to the door, but he felt her walk up behind him. He shut off the tap and turned to face her. "Fiona."

"Would you let me explain?"

He edged past her and stood several feet away.

"I . . ."

Vic held up his hand. "For Christ's sake we've known each other since high school, and you didn't trust me enough to tell me you had a daughter? I don't have any idea what you were thinking, but I'll tell you what I'm thinking. I'm thinking I don't know you one goddamn bit." Vic turned and punched the wall, leaving a hole in the drywall.

"I know." She said it so softly Vic barely heard her. "But please don't write us off. Give it some time. Like you said, we've known each other most of our lives."

He didn't say anything. Didn't want to look at her. How could he tell her that if she could walk away from her own child so easily, he'd never really known her? When he finally turned, he saw her bent over the desk Sara had left behind. Surely she wasn't crying. That would be out of character. When she turned around, she was clutching something to her chest.

"No matter what you think of me, would you do something for me?"

"No promises."

"Just keep Pet for me. I have to go." She looked down then back at him. "I have to go to San Francisco."

Thursday
Fiona

Vic had agreed to let Fiona drop off Pet tonight since her flight was so early Friday morning. Truth was, she hoped Vic would talk to her tonight because the trip to California couldn't wait. She had no idea what memories would jump out to haunt her from the streets of San Francisco. All she knew was that's where it all began and that's where she had to settle it. No matter what it took, she'd find her daughter this time.

When Fiona pulled up in front of Vic's, there was a car in the driveway that she didn't recognize. She saw a woman with a suitcase standing at Vic's door. The woman turned to look at her. Val! She didn't look any different than she had several years ago at Mike's wedding. Well, maybe a little thinner if Fiona had to be truthful. Fiona watched as Vic opened the door and the two of them talked for a minute before he grabbed Val's suitcase and they went inside. Fiona hooked Pet to his leash, and he barked all the way to the door where Vic stood. Fiona nuzzled Pet before handing Vic the leash. Without either of them speaking, she went back to the VW for Pet's food. When she returned to the house, the door was open and Vic and Pet were inside. Val's suitcase sat on the living room floor next to Pet's leash. Fiona saw her dog up on his haunches next to Val, who was scratching his ears. Pet ignored Fiona, and she shoved his food at Vic, said she'd be in touch then hurried down the steps. So much for second chances.

As Fiona pulled into her driveway, she saw that lights were on at Jane's house. Fiona had one more dreaded task to complete. She needed someone to keep an eye on things while she was gone. She got out of the VW bus, walked to Jane's, and knocked on the door.

Jane cracked the door open. "Fiona." In that instant, Fiona knew Sara must have told her. The current that ran between them was like two north ends of a magnet. But Fiona couldn't tell Jane her side of things now. She had to reserve all of her mental energy for whatever lay ahead.

"Hi, Jane. Listen, I have to leave town for a while. Vic has Pet, but would you mind picking up my mail and keeping an eye on the house?"

"Sure."

Fiona guessed monosyllables were about all she'd get right now. Then she remembered Marv. "By the way, how's your dad?"

"Fine."

Fiona forced a slight smile and nodded. "That's good. Okay then, I'm flying out in the morning. Thanks again." Jane shut the door before Fiona had turned to leave.

Friday
Fiona

Fiona finally gave up trying to sleep and went into the bathroom. The mirror exposed every line in her face. They seemed etched from an engraver's stylus, and the bags under her eyes were puffier than balloons. She looked away quickly.

* * *

Fiona fidgeted in the terminal's seat while waiting for her boarding call. Some of the other passengers read books or newspapers. One mother scolded her child for running off. Fiona looked at her watch then glanced at the airline counter. Finally, her flight was called and she hurried to get in line.

Fiona fastened her seat belt and looked out the plane's window. She reached in her bag and grabbed the book she'd taken from Sara's desk. Babar. She traced the name with her finger then opened the book. A fragile flower from long ago fell into her lap.

Acknowledgements

We are grateful for support and help from Larry and Tammy Neisen. We also want to thank the following people, who read an earlier version of our novel and offered feedback: Penny Borden, Amy Carlisle, Kim DuPlissey, Jonelle Garrett, Kim Gates, Mandy Lehman, and Carol Stumpf. Along with the readers, there were friends and family members who offered input and moral support as well. We appreciate everyone's contribution.

Robin also gratefully acknowledges the editors at *Zygote in My Coffee,* where the poem, "Sex and Margaritas," was first published.

About the Author

B. W. Wrighthard is the pseudonym for Robin Wright and Maryanne Burkhard, two friends who met in a creative writing class in college.

Robin Wright has lived in Evansville, Indiana all her life and currently resides with her husband in a home two cats graciously share with them.

Maryanne Burkhard has lived in Evansville, Indiana since 1990. Before moving to Indiana, she lived in New York, California, Colorado, Louisiana, Florida, and for a short stint, Egaila, Kuwait. Although she's been a guardian to dogs and many cats throughout the years, she is currently a servant to only one member of royalty, her cat, Smokey.

CPSIA information can be obtained at www.ICGtesting.com
Printed in the USA
LVOW06s1542300713

345404LV00003B/235/P